"IT'S ALL A MATTER OF TIMING."

Garth circled around her. "In wrestling, Katie girl, timing is everything." Lightning fast, he made his move and she found herself on her back.

Turning quickly onto her stomach, she tried to crawl away, only to be tightly pinioned beneath Garth's weight. His legs were positioned firmly on either side of hers. His bare chest crushed her to the mat.

"Let me up!" she commanded.

"What'll you give me?" Garth ground his hips against her bottom, and she felt the throbbing strength of the hard, wanting male above her.

"A thump on the head if you don't!"

Garth laughed throatily. "I've been promised a lot of things by a lot of women in similarly uncompromising circumstances, Katie, but no one has ever promised me pleasures of the kind that you do."

ABOUT THE AUTHOR

When Francine Christopher entered a national
competition for aspiring writers she had no idea her
lifelong dream of being published by Harlequin
was about to come true. *Hold on to Forever* is
Francine's first Superromance as well as her first
novel, and she was able to research all of Katie
O'Connell's wrestling moves right in the privacy of
her California home. For, like her heroine, Francine
is married to a romantic hero who knows how to
expertly enfold her in a "cradle of love."

Francine Christopher

HOLD ON TO FOREVER

Harlequin Books

TORONTO • NEW YORK • LONDON
AMSTERDAM • PARIS • SYDNEY • HAMBURG
STOCKHOLM • ATHENS • TOKYO • MILAN

Published December 1985

First printing October 1985
Second printing January 1986

ISBN 0-373-70191-8

Printed in Canada

To Marc
and to Mom and Dad

CHAPTER ONE

"THIS'D BETTER BE GOOD, BRIAN!" Katie O'Connell pointed a warning finger at her twin brother before crossing the slate entryway of his condo to receive a warm bear hug.

"I knew your curiosity would get the better of you." One look at Katie's face, and his self-satisfied grin became a hearty chuckle.

Katie's laugh was a softer, more bubbling sound than her brother's. A love of laughter and a voracious curiosity were only two of the many traits they had in common. As fraternal twins they could have looked a lot less alike than they did. Instead, except for the difference in their sex, they were remarkably alike. Katie was five foot three and weighed 110 on a fat day. Built like the gymnast she was: compact, firmly muscled, deceptively slight.

Her brother was only three inches taller and some forty-five pounds heavier, a fact that might have given Brian cause for dismay had it not been for his supreme self-confidence, another characteristic he shared with his sister. They were both possessed of a quick wit, an even quicker intelligence, a natural independence and a head of dark-auburn hair.

"I mean it, brother dear! When you haul me out of bed at four-thirty in the morning, the reason better be absolutely fantastic!'' Her words were softened by the teasing, affectionate tone she and Brian always used when addressing each other. Like most twins, they shared a deep sense of connection. Sometimes it took only a look for each of them to understand instantly and perfectly what the other was thinking or needing.

"I think you mentioned something about receiving a wild telephone call that was going to change your life...but only with my help?''

"Uh, why don't we go into the kitchen, and I'll fix us breakfast while we talk," Brian suggested smoothly. He put a thickly muscled arm around Katie's shoulders and led her into his kitchen, whistling. It was the whistling that tipped her off.

"One of your schemes, huh?" Katie's curiosity mingled with mounting anxiety. The only time Brian ever whistled was in contemplation of an action he couldn't resist but which was unfortunately either forbidden, dangerous or both. Invariably the plan required his sibling's generally reluctant participation.

"Not exactly. What about cheese omelets with mushrooms, tomatoes and avocados, and a side order of bacon and French toast?''

"Brian, when you *start* the ante on the bribe with all of my favorite breakfast foods I begin to believe I should say 'no' immediately, on principle!'' Anxiety changed to dismay; she felt intuitively that there was bound to be trouble. At the same time, she felt oddly excited.

"You *always* say no on principle. Principle is the guiding light of your life. This is the chance of a lifetime. You've got to help me. Besides," he said slyly, "you still owe me one for snaring Ray Mathews as your date for the senior prom at Ohio State."

"No way. I paid that back by setting you up with Tish Spiller last year," she said with equanimity, effectively meeting his opening salvo in the bargaining game that always preceded his requests for favors.

"No, Tish Spiller was payment for Desiree Minton our sophomore year in college."

Katie felt her lower lip twitch slightly. "Desiree Minton?" she asked innocently. "I can't quite place the name...."

"Surely you remember Desiree? You had a beautiful friend that year with long blond hair, Tina Turner legs, and very accommodating ideas about sex? I begged for a blind date and what did I get when I picked up my date? I got Mildred, from your English Lit class. The one who barked instead of talked and was damn near two hundred pounds of pure beef on the hoof!"

"She was just as nice as Desiree," Katie said hotly.

"Which was pretty much *all* she had to recommend her!" snorted her brother.

A small frown furrowed Katie's brow. Sexual escapades were the one thing she did *not* have in common with Brian. In fact, his affairs had been a source of unending consternation for her since the night he'd come into her room with a stupid grin on his fifteen-year-old face proclaiming he was now "a man." She loved her brother, but heartily disapproved of his casual attitude toward sex. Over the years, she'd observed a seemingly endless parade of girls, then women, eagerly submit themselves to Brian's carefree ritual of pursuit, capture and abandonment. The experience had made her vow never to emulate Brian in her relationships with men and never to be like the women in his life. Females were notches on his bedpost, toys to be played with for a while, then tossed aside.

Katie wanted more than that. She wanted to *be* more than that to the man with whom she finally shared her body. Viewing intimacy as the fullest expression of love, she was unwilling to separate the two. No matter how naive and idealistic such a belief labeled her, she felt sex should be reserved for a commitment deeper than "temporary mutual satisfaction." As a result, she was something of an anomaly among women her age. She was twenty-eight years old, intelligent, well-educated and thoroughly modern in most of her opinions.

She was also a virgin.

Brian found her "condition," as he liked to call it, amusing. But though he teased her unmercifully, Katie knew he wasn't in any hurry to see her lower her standards for a man who would never be her husband.

"You still owe me, so you might as well agree to pay up on this one!" charged Brian triumphantly.

Katie nodded her head affirmatively, acknowledging a debt still owed. "Okay, send me to my doom. Let's hear about the phone call," she said gloomily, tucking into her omelet and French toast with gusto, nonetheless.

"Cheer up! I'm about to tell you something that will change our lives forever."

TWENTY-FIVE MINUTES LATER Katie knew she'd been had. Her niggling sense of excitement had vanished and the look on her face was one of undiluted consternation.

"I don't care what I promised. There is absolutely no way the Granby school board will ever allow me to take your place as their wrestling coach. Read my lips, Brian...N-O, *no*." How could he hope to get away with his plan? Or more accurately, how could he hope she would help him?

"Forget the fact that you owe me for a minute," he said placatingly, trying a new tactic. "Think of the money."

"This is the first mention I've heard of money," responded Katie suspiciously. "Exactly how much are we talking about?"

"If I split the bonus I'll get if we win, and you count the $10,000 extra you'll make in salary by agreeing to do it, and what you already have stashed away in United Bank, you should have enough for the down payment on that house you want out near The Broadmoor."

Katie chewed her bacon pensively. Brian was right; she'd been dreaming of owning a house out by The Broadmoor since she was a child. Big, sprawling, surrounded by huge lawns and gardens, the houses just south of town were remnants of another age. They'd been built around the luxurious 1920's era resort by descendants of the wealthy who'd flocked to Colorado Springs in the late 1800's when the city was still known as Little London. There was one house in particular she had her eye on. It was Victorian in style, had gingerbread trim and was in desperate need of renovation. She coveted it to a nearly sinful degree.

With a sigh, Katie quit arguing with herself. She'd made her decision. Number one, her uncompromising loyalty to her twin dictated that she should do whatever she could to help him take advantage of the career opportunity of a lifetime. Number two, she just had to have that house. The only thing left to do was negotiate a few perks by refusing to give in immediately.

"What will mom and dad say?" she asked fiercely.

"You can borrow my Blazer for the duration," countered Brian.

"It's a lot colder in those tiny mountain towns than here at the foot of Pike's Peak. It's already September. Winter is almost here," she angled.

"You can have all my credit cards to complete your wardrobe with whatever you need." He began to sweat; Katie was showing no mercy. "I have a $1,000 limit at each store, and I paid off my accounts last month."

"What about my own job?" Wasson, where she taught, was one of the best public high schools in Colorado Springs, and Katie had worked hard to achieve her position as head coach of the girls' gymnastics team and assistant chairman of the math department.

"After bringing home the state trophy last year, Buck Anderson will be only too happy to do anything it takes to keep you at Wasson permanently. You'll only need a year's sabbatical."

Katie's expression remained skeptical. "What happens if after giving your plan my best shot, I still can't convince them to accept me in your place?" she asked, playing her trump card with a flourish.

"I'll give you the entire bonus if the U.S. wins," said Brian persuasively. "What I really want out of this is the experience, contacts and opportunity to make a name for myself in international wrestling circles." He paused. "Besides, you and I both know that when you really set your mind to something, you can convince anyone to do anything."

Katie didn't respond immediately, and Brian spoke again. "*All right*, I'll help you with the hard stuff on your house. But that's absolutely my last concession."

"Bring on the lions, the Christian is ready to be devoured," said Katie resignedly. "I still don't think the idea will work, but I'll give it a try. I don't want your bonus money, either. The extra salary the school board is offering is fair enough compensation," she added generously.

Brian gave her a hug, pulled her from her chair and swung her around off the ground. "Katie, you will never regret it. This is going to be fantastic! Thanks, pal."

THREE DAYS LATER Katie was waiting outside the Granby High School principal's office at the end of a long, empty hallway that smelled strongly of fresh wax. She felt a trepidation she hadn't felt since the seventh grade. Back then, Sister Mary Simon had decided to "take the O'Connell twins in hand." She and Brian had spent the better part of a year outside the nun's office, waiting for the axe to fall, which it did with painful regularity. Katie kicked at the shiny green linoleum floor with the toe of her new boot, careful not to scuff the dove-gray Italian leather.

The argument inside the principal's office raged on. Yesterday, her announcement that she'd come to honor Brian O'Connell's contract as Granby's new wrestling coach and math teacher had met with stunned disbelief. The small-town school board had listened in shell-shocked silence, then asked her to come back the next day after they discussed the matter.

Katie had been standing outside the principal's office listening to round two of the "discussion" for over three hours. In spite of the thin air at this high altitude, the school-board members were proving tiresomely long-winded. It didn't sound like they were very close to reaching a decision, so she fretted impatiently.

Lunchtime had come and gone. A huge tray of thick sandwiches and several pots of delicious-smelling coffee had been delivered to the men in the room from the school cafeteria. Why hadn't she thought to swipe a sandwich off the tray as it was whisked efficiently past her by the principal's secretary? She probably wouldn't eat until dinner time now.

"Here, eat these before you drop from starvation."

Gentle hands wrapped Katie's fingers around two cookies so rich looking they could only be homemade. She turned in surprise to greet the friendliest eyes and the warmest smile she'd seen since leaving Colorado Springs several days before.

"Thanks. I'm..."

"Katie O'Connell." The woman finished her sentence for her, and a touch of wry humor in her voice mingled with the open warmth of her smile. "Your fame has preceded you."

"Sure you don't mean infamy?" asked Katie, arching her reddish-gold brows upward. She took a bite of one cookie. "Oatmeal raisin cookies. Perfect. With chocolate chips no less. I only know a handful of people who make them this way, and that's counting my mother and me. Thanks."

The woman laughed. "You're welcome. I usually keep some munchies in my desk in case I don't make it home for lunch. Help yourself anytime. I've been peeking at you from my room all morning." She pointed toward a classroom down the hall. "When they kept you standing out here past lunch without sharing something from that huge tray of sandwiches I saw being sailed down the corridor, I decided you needed a friend. I'm Liz Adams."

"Thanks, Liz. I could use a friend. And the cookies are a lifesaver. I'm not sure how much longer I'll be out here."

"A while yet, I would think. Execution is a relatively simple matter; it's either death or not. But deciding on a suitable torture, well, that's entirely different. It could take days!" Liz's brown eyes twinkled gleefully.

Katie laughed outright. "Of course, how logical." She liked Liz more every minute. Kindness and intelligence were stamped all over her face, and her sense of humor seemed to mesh with Katie's.

Liz turned to go. "Let me know the final verdict."

"I will. Thanks." Feeling considerably encouraged, Katie returned her attention to the meeting in progress. She heard loud snippets of the debate from one or another of the school-board members when their voices raised to a particularly aggressive pitch.

"Twenty-five thousand dollars to resurrect the wrestling program here at Granby High School, and this is what you come up with? A girl!"

Katie grimaced. The athletic world was full of chauvinists. In her five years as a girls' gymnastics coach she'd become used to hearing similar comments, but they never failed to infuriate her.

"We hired her brother, but—"

"Then where the hell is he? Get *him* up here, and dump *her*!"

She flinched. Whoever was speaking had a voice that could flay a strip off a person a mile wide. The speaker was furiously angry, and she was the cause. A flurry of more tentative but no less angry, voices continued the "discussion."

"Brian O'Connell…accepted another job…."

"Lawsuit too expensive…if we lose?"

"Bad publicity?"

"Who else…this late date? We already called…"

"Six weeks…wrestling season."

"But we need a math teacher *tomorrow*!"

Katie smiled. The board members should keep their voices down. She was learning all their weak points.

"Money…best coach available. I can't believe you couldn't do any better…hell…! Keeping my eye on her…better perform!"

The Voice again. She wondered who he was. None of the men she'd met yesterday fit her image of how she thought the owner of the Voice should look. She grinned naughtily. Of course, none of them said very much yesterday. They just turned a nice chartreuse shade of green.

"Miss O'Connell, they are ready for you." The principal's secretary held the door open just wide enough for Katie to squeeze through, giving her a grimly disapproving look over the top of rimless spectacles. They were so old-fashioned Katie couldn't bring herself to think of them as glasses.

She squared her shoulders, pushed open the door another few inches and sailed into the principal's office, ready for battle. She had only two weapons at her disposal. The first was a clear understanding of the psychology of winning, employed by numerous coaches she and Brian had observed in their years of competitive athletics. Her strongest weapon was a very firm determination to best the group of grim-faced men sitting around the principal's desk like Supreme Court judges.

"Miss O'Connell, the members of the school board have some reservations about hiring you in your brother's place," said the stony-faced principal.

"I'm sorry to hear that, Mr. Penrose." Katie kept her tone cordial in spite of the growing dislike she felt for the school board. These men had impressed her on the first meeting as small minded, patronizing and disgustingly chauvinistic. "Perhaps if I tell you a bit more about myself?" There was total silence. "Perhaps if I explain my experience and qualifications?" Now the response was hostile silence. "Is there anything *at all* I can say?"

"By damn, you sure can't!" a florid faced man said, jumping from his seat in his agitation. "My boy wrestles on that team, and there ain't no damn way we're gonna let some fancy-faced liberated female take over! We might not be as sophisticated—" he sneered "—as people down in the Springs, but up here women know their place, and it sure as hell ain't coaching the wrestling team!"

"Thank you, Mr. Jenkins, I was wondering which of you gentlemen would offer me a chair." Katie ignored the man's comments, then quickly pulled his chair over and sat down. Two points for the visiting team, she thought.

"Watch your mouth, Jenkins! We all want to resolve this...problem, not make it worse." The giant perched incongruously on the corner of the principal's desk spoke softly, but in a tone that brooked no disobedience. He was definitely the owner of the Voice. He looked like Conan the Barbarian. The Voice, she thought. Katie knew he wasn't a member of the school board, but no one had bothered to introduce him. So far she hadn't been able to figure out just *who* he was. Nor had she been able to think of a way to ask discreetly.

"I'm going to be frank with you, Miss O'Connell." Mr. Willis, the school-board president, as well as the president of the local bank, fixed her with a level stare and leaned forward in his chair. "Your arrival came as quite a shock to us yesterday."

"I can understand your surprise," murmured Katie. She bit the inside of her lower lip hard to keep from laughing. The poor man had nearly had a coronary when she introduced herself.

"But not our dismay." The president's double chins quivered indignantly. "We received a large donation from an ex-student conditioned expressly upon our use of that money to hire the best wrestling coach we could find. As a result, we were able to offer your brother an additional $10,000 in salary, as well as considerably increase the budget for our wrestling program. We expect your brother to honor his contract with us."

His stubborn stare dared her to argue, but Katie's common sense told her that challenging him would be a useless exercise. She'd met his type before. She knew direct confrontation was not the most effective way to change his mind. It was time for a lateral maneuver, the kind her brother called "unfair blind-siding" because she used the tactic against him so successfully.

"That's certainly a reasonable expectation," agreed Katie, softening her speech to a low, persuasive timbre. "But you know from my brother's telegram that he's accepted the position as assistant coach to the U.S. Pan-American Wrestling Team." She bent gracefully to retrieve the crumpled yellow ball of paper she spied on the floor, smoothed out the wrinkled sheet in front of the principal, then sat back down. "This makes it very clear to all of you that he has absolutely no intention of coaching in Granby this year."

Katie trained a steely gaze on each of the men before her. "I'm ready, willing and able to take his place. You may have six weeks before wrestling season begins, but you need to find a math teacher by the time school starts tomorrow. Under the circumstances, hiring me seems like the most logical thing for the board to do.'' Not one of them could meet her eyes except for the broad giant who had earlier quelled Jenkins. He met her gaze with a look she couldn't decipher and then, even more inexplicably, he winked.

It happened so fast, she almost couldn't believe she'd seen it. For a minute, she was tempted to wink back. He was certainly handsome in a street-tough sort of way. He was a little...bigger than she liked her men to be, but he did have the sort of body she found irresistible. Strong, muscular, he definitely looked like the athletes she preferred. He also had a pair of the silveriest gray eyes she could ever remember seeing, with the soft, thick lashes she would have killed for in the days before her mother finally consented to let her use mascara.

Then with a jolt she remembered the context of the present situation and suddenly couldn't control a rising anger at the plaid-shirted man she'd privately nicknamed Conan. He sat there flirting cavalierly to her face, while behind her back he'd tried to convince his cronies they shouldn't let her coach their wrestling team. His attitude was insulting. He could just take his red-plaid shirt and black turtleneck and stuff them.

Not that they weren't admirably filled already, one perverse inner devil's voice insisted. And his jeans were pulled awfully taut across his...With an embarrassed flush, Katie raised her eyes to find she'd been caught giving him the sort of frank perusal she'd often found demeaning as a female recipient of unwelcome male attention. She wasn't at all mollified when his mouth widened in a slow, lazy smile that seemed to acknowledge his recognition of her admiration, while inviting her to look him over for as long as she liked.

"I still say we should sue her brother and *make* him honor his contract!"

Katie winced at Mr. Jenkins's thundering growl and belligerent attitude. Protectiveness of her brother made her own temper flare briefly, but she managed to answer the man in a calm, understanding manner. "I can appreciate your frustration, Mr. Jenkins. You were expecting my brother, and I've been sprung on you without warning, instead."

She paused for a moment, then shrewdly brought the argument to an area where she knew, from earlier remarks, the board was vulnerable. "Do any of you really want a long, drawn-out legal battle with no guarantee of winning?"

Her attention focused first on Mr. Willis, then on the principal. She wanted to address her arguments to Conan since she suspected he was the one most opposed to hiring her, but without a formal introduction or some indication that he served in an official capacity she didn't dare.

"Well...well, of course not," blustered Mr. Willis. "But we may not have a choice."

"Who would you get to teach math and coach wrestling in the meantime?" She challenged Mr. Penrose.

"Well, ah, it could be difficult, but..."

"Can Granby afford the financial drain or the unfavorable publicity such a suit would undoubtedly generate?" she pushed.

"No, but..."

"We aren't entirely convinced the publicity would be unfavorable to our position, Miss O'Connell." The Voice was now pleasant, but Katie perceived the man's steely will from his clipped enunciation. He liked to get his own way.

"Can't you see the headlines when the national press gets wind of this story? 'Selfish Mountain Town Battles U.S. Pan-Am Team For Coach, Gold Medals Hang In Balance,'" said Katie dramatically. She conjured up a sympathetic expression, looking deliberately at each one of the board members. They lowered their heads and looked worried.

Her eyes met Conan's. His amused expression disgruntled her, and she quickly looked away. She hadn't laid it on *that* thick, had she? She snuck another peek at him. He rolled his eyes heavenward.

"You can't possibly want that kind of publicity," she continued, undaunted. "The rest of the country never quite forgave Colorado for refusing to host the 1976 Olympics. Making things difficult for my brother would just seem like more of the same provincialism they accused our state of then." Katie could see confusion and uncertainty replacing the formerly rigid expressions on the faces of the principal and the president.

"Isn't the bottom line really your need for a math teacher and the best wrestling coach you can find?" She shot up from her seat and looked the harried school-board president straight in the eye from a distance of four inches. The action was guaranteed to cause discomfort in all but the most intrepid souls, or those privy to her intent. Mr. Willis obviously wasn't, since he looked away first.

"Yes," he said resignedly.

"Then in spite of your reservations, hiring me seems to be the best solution all around. If you'll just give me a chance, I know I can do the job for you." Katie spoke confidently.

"Miss O'Connell, even acknowledging the truth of all you've said so far, there's still the matter of your..." Mr. Penrose's voice trailed off as Katie gave him her best forthright glare.

"Of my..." she prompted silkily. She knew exactly what was at the heart of the board's unwillingness to hire her in Brian's place.

"Of your qualifications." Mr. Penrose reached clumsily for a handkerchief to mop his reddened face, perspiring in spite of the cool autumn breeze blowing in through the open window behind him.

"My qualifications are apparently not the issue here. If they were, we wouldn't be having this discussion. I have a master's degree in education, a bachelor's degree in mathematics, five years of coaching experience and I probably know more about wrestling than anyone else in this room."

"You're a gymnastics coach. What can you possibly know about wrestling?" Conan challenged her, his tone mildly mocking. Katie glared at him.

She hated to admit it after his last remark, but this man's voice was as attractive as his muscular build. Husky, deep and masculine, it possessed a range and power an opera singer would be proud to claim. Or a drill sergeant, thought Katie. She remembered how harsh and commanding he had sounded earlier with Jenkins, and hastened to answer.

"My brother's wrestling achievements are a state legend. Our whole household revolved around wrestling. I went to all of Brian's meets when we were growing up and quite a few of his practices. I was probably the first person he ever pinned. He used to practice all his moves on me. Technically, I know everything he knows, even though I never competed in the sport."

She paused to take a breath. "The issue here is not my qualifications. It's my *sex*!"

Katie said the word loudly, with emphasis, and was satisfied by the result. The men all seemed to draw back uncomfortably, not quite sure how to respond to her impassioned speech. All except Conan. Upon hearing the word "sex," he leaned forward with interest, a gleam in his eye.

"Now look here, Miss O'Connell, there's more to being a wrestling coach than you apparently realize." Of course he was the only one bold enough to respond. "We may be somewhat isolated by our mountain location, but up here we take our sports seriously."

Conan continued to sit comfortably on the principal's desk, one long leg swinging lazily from the knee. Katie tried not to stare at him, to fix her eyes on some neutral point just past his head. His face and body were an alluring distraction. She tried to give his words her full attention but failed miserably. Why couldn't he keep those strong legs still for just one minute? She couldn't help thinking of the song about where the knee bone is connected, and where all the rest of the bones and muscles went after that. A tingle of excitement brought a rush of color to her fair, Irish skin.

"In the small-school Division A league we're known for our winning teams. We usually rank first in our league in football, basketball, baseball, hockey and soccer. That's just the boys. With the donation from...our ex-student, we expected your brother to build a wrestling program with an equally impressive record." He looked disapprovingly at Katie, as though she was somehow responsible for Brian's decision to repudiate his contract.

"Sounds like the kind of challenge I enjoy," she assured him. "Last year I coached fifty girls to the state gymnastics championship. I think that experience will help me *perform* for you," she said pointedly. She'd rather undergo open-heart surgery without benefit of anesthesia than admit this man's words had caused her a moment of horrified recoil.

What kind of a mess had Brian gotten her into? She had no doubt that her experience and knowledge were adequate to coach a small high-school wrestling team on an acceptably competent level. Coaching them to a winning season and bringing home the state trophy called for a degree of skill she couldn't swear she possessed.

"Your enthusiasm is charming, Miss O'Connell." Conan's deep voice was layered heavily with amusement. "But we need a *man* who can guide the boys with a strong hand. The last thing we need is a pint-sized female who's never coached wrestling. You're unequipped to deal with the pranks, rebellions and just plain orneriness of strong-willed teenage boys."

That did it.

"No," said Katie softly, shaking her head in the negative. "The last thing you need is a sex discrimination suit." She paused for several tense seconds to let her threat sink in, wishing she had a name besides Conan to pin on this plaid-shirted giant.

"As for my ability to deal with the pranks, rebellions and orneriness of teenage boys, let me remind you that I grew up with a twin brother. The subspecies holds no mysteries, or terrors, for me after having survived an adolescence with him! Moreover, five years coaching teenage girls, who are not always little bundles of sweet delight, makes me well-equipped to deal with their male counterparts."

Katie's adversary picked up a sheet of paper from the desk and held it out to her. "This is the job description approved by the Colorado State Teacher's Union. Are you sure you can meet every single qualification?" He looked at Katie with a stern intensity she knew was intended to intimidate her. Instead she sensed the queer excitement of near victory.

"Absolutely," she said with conviction, waving away the paper he offered with one hand and reaching into her briefcase with the other. "I brought my own copy. My brother served on the committee that wrote the revised version just last year. You do have the revised version, don't you?" asked Katie sweetly.

She began to tick of the qualifications aloud, trying to ignore the magnetic pull of his silvery eyes. "I am a member in good standing of the teacher's union." *The man's hair is the most amazing color. No one has pitch-black hair, do they? Isn't hair supposed to have a lot of similar colors and highlights?*

"I have never advocated the overthrow of the U.S. government by force or violence." *He must have spent the entire summer in the sun to get that deep tan.* Even so, it didn't do much to camouflage the chiselled planes of his face. His features were a little too strongly defined really to be called handsome. There were too many hard angles and sharp corners. He looked like a professional boxer or a soldier of fortune, she mused whimsically.

"Don't stop there, Miss O'Connell. Things are just getting interesting."

Katie felt a heat she told herself was anger suffusing her face, and gritted her teeth to keep from retorting sharply. She hadn't blushed in a long time. Despite the propensity of her fair skin for doing so, she'd learned to control the telltale rise of color that could give away her emotions. The number of times Conan had easily drawn a blush forth this afternoon was a hot needle of sheer aggravation pricking her pride, but she couldn't help such an automatic reaction. For a minute, she'd thought he was reading her mind.

"I have never been convicted of a crime involving moral turpitude," she continued in a tight voice, "and I have at least a bachelor's degree from an accredited college or university in the subject I wish to teach. Finally, I've passed the state coaching examination, which authorizes me to coach any sport for which I am hired in the State of Colorado, provided I can pass a sport specific exam administered by the state in any sport I wish to coach if my principal requests."

Katie looked up and smiled triumphantly at the imposing figure regarding her intently. "I passed the wrestling exam two days ago. Here are my results. I think they'll pretty well lay to rest any doubts you may have about my qualifications."

"Hmm...598 out of a possible 600. Not bad." Conan paused. "What did you miss?" he asked innocently.

Not bad? Indeed!

With a deep sigh the school-board president stood and counted the grudging nods of the other board members. He turned a tentative face toward Conan who shrugged his shoulders, grimaced and gave him a thumbs up gesture. "It seems you and your brother have us over a barrel, Miss O'Connell. None of us can conceive of a truly feminine woman *wanting* to coach the wrestling team, but...you're hired," he said regretfully. "Just don't make the mistake of thinking you've found a home here. The job is only for one year."

A victorious thrill shot through Katie's entire body, making it difficult to maintain a calm outward demeanor. She'd done it; she had the job!

"Thank you," she said simply. She didn't trust herself to say more. The remark about femininity had been a low blow, but she wasn't going to let herself dwell on it. Nor would she give Mr. Penrose the satisfaction of seeing he'd struck a raw nerve.

The principal thrust a large key ring with twelve keys on it into Katie's hands. "I am not happy about this, Miss O'Connell. Not happy at all. Let me warn you, it won't be all your way."

"I never expected it to be, Mr. Penrose."

The principal smiled in a way that made Katie think of some hungry, malevolent cat toying with a troublesomely evasive mouse it was intent on devouring. "Because this is such an unusual situation, the board has appointed an official liaison to help smooth over the rough spots we anticipate during the next few weeks.''

Katie began to have a sick feeling in the pit of her stomach. The principal kept glancing over at Conan.

"Miss O'Connell, I'd like you to meet Garth D'Anno, the ex-student who donated $25,000 to our wrestling program. I'm sure that under his watchful eye you'll earn each and every cent of the $10,000 salary bonus!"

CHAPTER TWO

"MISS O'CONNELL...or may I call you Katie? I can't say I'm entirely pleased by the way things have turned out, but I'm always glad to meet a pretty woman. Welcome to Granby." Garth's gracious words acknowledged he'd lost the skirmish over hiring her. The hard glint in his eyes promised anything but friendly cooperation between them over the next few weeks. Without moving from his spot on the desk, he held out a hand as big as both of Katie's two put together.

"The pleasure is all mine, Mr. D'Anno," said Katie, ignoring the outstretched hand and remaining in her seat. She recognized a declaration of war. Get up and walk across the room to shake *his* hand? To do so would be tantamount to a public acknowledgment of his right to *make* her do so. It was far too early in the game to permit the balance of power to tip so solidly in his direction. He might be due a few considerations as the wrestling team's benefactor, but the perimeters of their respective areas of authority had yet to be defined.

"As for what you should call me, let me put it this way. My friends call me Katie, my team calls me Coach, but you, Mr. D'Anno, may call me Ms O'Connell."

"We don't like none of that liberated *Ms* bull—"
Jenkins was stopped by a stern warning look from
Garth "—baloney. Our unmarried lady teachers go by
Miss! So will you," he muttered darkly.

Katie pretended she hadn't heard. She needed to
mend some bridges with these men, not engage in
further argument over which courtesy title she preferred. Weighed against what she hoped to accomplish in Granby, the issue just wasn't that important.
It would be a long year if she couldn't win the board
over and make them feel their decision to hire her had
been a good one. Letting the men win an inconse-
quential point seemed like a step in the right direction.

"How about a late lunch and something to drink,
Miss O'Connell?" Garth D'Anno suggested. "It's
been a long couple of hours. The sandwiches are
starting to wear off, and *you* must be starved."

"No thank you, Mr. D'Anno. I have a lot of work
to do to get ready for school tomorrow." How dare he
ask her out in front of all those beady-eyed school-
board members just waiting for her to make a mistake! Did he really think she'd agree to something as
compromising as "lunch and drinks," while every
member on the board listened with his tongue hanging out?

"That was not a request for a date, Miss O'Connell," Garth said crisply, in a manner reminiscent of
the way he'd brought Jenkins to heel. "Frankly, it was
not a *request* at all. There are a number of points the
board has asked me to go over with you. Ours will be
a working lunch."

How dare he *not* ask her out! What was she thinking? She wouldn't go out with him anyway, knowing
he was on their side. But oh, how her female soul
needed him to want her to!

"Let's go," he said in a commanding tone of voice.

Rebellion fomented inside Katie. She could be asked
almost anything, but told next to nothing. When she
noticed the board members casting approving glances
at each other, as if to congratulate themselves on the
way Garth had shown her who was boss, she had an
almost irresistible impulse to slap his tan, handsome
face. Instead, she acquiesced graciously, rationalizing
that she was lulling the enemy into a false sense of security.

"Very well, Mr. D'Anno. Since you put it that way,
I would be delighted to have a late lunch with you."
Katie rose gracefully from her seat and scribbled a
bold signature at the bottom of the contract resting on
the principal's desk. Her hand shook slightly as she
did so.

She told herself that her trembling script had nothing to do with the proximity of her wrist to Garth's
jean clad thigh, or with the clean, warm scent assail-
ing her nostrils when he leaned over to watch her sign
her name. The truth won out when her elbow brushed
against the taut sinews in question as she stepped away
from the desk. Nothing but Garth's physical presence
had been responsible for the hen scratch on the paper
in front of her. She dared not meet his eyes as she
shook each board member's hand in turn and tried
desperately to look tall as she marched out ahead of
him. Garth's height looked so imposing from her pe-
tite point of view.

"It's beautiful outside today. Do you mind walking to town? It's only three blocks, all downhill." Garth posed his question in a friendly manner that caught Katie off guard after the way he'd practically ordered her to have lunch with him.

They were standing on the sidewalk in front of the high school. It was a majestic, old edifice; two stories of weathered brick surrounded by a parklike expanse of green lawn, just beginning to turn a mellow gold. Enormous maples dotted the lawn as well as aspens and the distinctive blue spruce that grew best in the high mountains.

"No, I love to walk, especially at this time of year. Autumn is probably my very favorite season. The colors are changing and the temperature is dropping but not so much so that it's really cold yet. There's the anticipation of a new school year...I just love it."

Before they'd gone more than a few steps Garth began casually unbuttoning his red-plaid shirt. With lithe efficiency he stripped it off and tied it around his waist by the arms, then pushed up the sleeves of his black cotton turtleneck to just below his elbows. Katie tried not to stare, but the sight of strong, tan forearms sprinkled with fine black hair was an enticement her eyes couldn't resist.

Katie cast about in her mind for a nice safe topic to discuss but found herself unable to concentrate on anything except the subtly suggestive way his thin turtleneck clung to an obviously well-muscled torso. Her eyes seemed to have declared their independence from her brain as she stared at him shamelessly.

They walked along in almost companionable silence for about a block, the warmth of the Indian summer sun beating down on their faces. The sidewalk was littered with crisp, red maple leaves. The bright yellow aspen leaves were just beginning to fall. Katie kicked at them, enjoying the shushing and crunching noises under her feet. She hazarded a glance at Garth.

He had his hands in his pockets, and every once in a while he took a deep breath. The town had a smell of the mountains about it: a dry, woodsy crispness Katie could almost taste, and she took a few deep breaths of her own. In the piercing sunlight that seemed brighter up here than in Colorado Springs, she felt the tension of her confrontation with the school board melt away. It was a gorgeous afternoon, warm and clear, with the promise of winter just a tang in the air.

"That was quite a performance back there, Miss O'Connell," commented Garth, his manner disarmingly friendly.

"How so?" asked Katie, warily.

"Don't be so modest. You came on like a cross between Vince Lombardi and Gloria Steinem—a much prettier version of either one, I might add." His eyes moved approvingly over Katie's clear skin, tinted rose across her delicate cheekbones and dusted with coppery freckles over her small snub nose. Silvery eyes smiled into hazel green ones, before lingering on the soft lips that brought the word vulnerable to mind.

Individually, Katie's features were unspectacular. Taken as a whole, they formed a remarkably pretty, almost girlish face. Uncomfortable with Garth's close scrutiny, she raised her hand to smooth a few errant wisps of auburn hair curling out of her thick French braid. The action drew his attention to her hair, with its bronze and cinnamon highlights glinting and twining among the darker strands. He approved of her hair as well.

"Out with it, Miss O'Connell. What's your ulterior motive? Why do you really want this job?" He uttered the words with the same friendliness as before, but there was a distrustful, probing quality to his question. His suspiciousness annoyed Katie. She'd always prided herself on her reputation for honesty.

"Ulterior motives? A dumb jock like me, Mr. D'Anno?" She unconsciously quickened her step and moved sideways slightly to widen the distance between them.

"No one with the degrees and experience you rammed down the throats of those board members could ever be classified as a 'dumb jock,' Miss O'Connell." He matched her pace easily, closing the gap between them as his strong fingers supported Katie's elbow when they crossed the street. "Careful there. These old stone curbs are much higher than current versions, especially in mountain towns. We get quite a runoff in the spring, and half the storefronts would be flooded otherwise."

"Thanks," said Katie, her offhand tone belying the pleasurable jolt she felt at his gesture. He was such a big man, yet he had such gentle hands. His touch made her feel dainty and feminine without patronizing her the way some men did. The feeling was nice. Even if he did unjustly suspect her of harboring malignant ulterior motives.

"I'll find out sooner or later, Miss O'Connell. Save us both some time—" his voice hardened warningly

"—and some trouble. Tell me what you're really doing here."

His insistence on an answer brought out her stubborn streak. She had no intention of defending herself. "If you want to talk about ulterior motives, why don't we discuss yours? Even you must agree that $25,000 is a rather princely gift, 'old school spirit' notwithstanding."

"Okay, Miss O'Connell. I'll deal. You give me your reasons...the *real* ones, and I'll give you mine." Garth grinned suddenly, and Katie was not pleased to discover how entirely charming she found him.

"My 'ulterior motive' should be blatantly obvious to anyone with a shred of family loyalty. My twin was in a jam. I'd do anything to help him. I wasn't about to let the ill-considered prejudice of small-minded men stand in my way!" Katie watched Garth's eyes narrow at the mention of family.

"Family loyalty? You honestly expect me to believe that?"

"It happens to be the truth!"

"Come on, Miss O'Connell. Surely a woman of your intelligence can come up with a better line than that! What are you doing here?" he demanded harshly.

"I'm only going to tell you this one more time, Mr. D'Anno." Katie knew the calm she was striving so hard to maintain was in jeopardy. Refusing to let the conversation degenerate into a shouting match, she took a deep breath, expelling the air from her lungs slowly before continuing in a quiet voice. "Brian had a chance to take advantage of the opportunity of a lifetime. I had to help him. That's why I agreed to take his place if the school board would have me."

"I see. Brother Brian leaps at international coaching fame in a frenzy of irresponsibility, and you rear-range your life on a moment's notice so you can rush in and save his tail from a well-deserved lawsuit." Garth's sarcastic tone set Katie's nerves on a razor-sharp edge. "The perfect sister. Sibling devotion at its most ideal. How touching." He bit off each word an-grily, making it clear that he still didn't believe her.

"Do you have a brother, Mr. D'Anno?" she asked suddenly, her voice sharp.

Garth's face hardened into a grim mask, the strong features set in stern, uncompromising lines. "What the hell has that got to do with anything?"

"Put yourself in my place for a minute. If he was *your* brother, wouldn't you do exactly the same thing for him?"

"I wouldn't give my brother the sweat off my back if he was dying of thirst, Miss O'Connell. I'm not sure I believe you, but if 'brotherly love' is really the rea-son you're here, your brother is a master at conning you for his own advantage, and you're a naive fool who deserves all the misery he'll inevitably curse you with. As far as I'm concerned, the less said about brothers, the better." The sneering bitterness in Garth's voice shocked Katie into momentary silence. She'd never heard anyone speak such a scathing con-demnation of a relationship she'd always prized.

"Then I'm afraid you'll simply have to accept that I'm a naive fool, and let it go at that." Katie forced herself to speak lightly. She couldn't trust her tongue or her temper if she let the tiniest smidgen of anger

color her words. She'd defend her brother with her life
if necessary. Garth's words had trespassed onto
ground she held inviolate.

"Your turn, Mr. D'Anno. What's *your* ulterior
motive?" The casually phrased question cost Katie a
wealth of self-control. "Why the scholarship?"

"It's very simple. I wanted to."

"But *why* did you want to?" she persisted.

"Maybe I'll tell you one of these days...when you
decide to be a little more forthright with *me*. In the
meantime, let me give you some friendly advice.
Granby's a small town with a quiet life-style. Despite
the influx of summer tourists every year, and all the
skiers we get from Steamboat Springs, the town has
never adopted the current trends accepted as a matter
of course in more cosmopolitan areas. Don't try
grinding a feminist axe against these people's necks."
In spite of Garth's dispassionate tone, Katie heard an
undercurrent of warning. She felt unsettled, threatened, and she shivered spontaneously despite the
warmth of the afternoon.

"You insist on painting me as a wild-eyed standard
bearer for the screaming radical brand of feminism,
Mr. D'Anno. That's not true. I just don't think my sex
disables me from performing competently in a position traditionally filled by a man. Don't threaten me."
Katie spoke calmly. She realized they'd both drawn
their respective boundaries and subtly warned each
other not to trespass beyond those careful limits.

"You're an intriguing puzzle of contradictions,
Miss O'Connell. You appear to be the consummate
modern woman fashionably turned out in *Glamour*
magazine's dress-to-impress working uniform. You

claim to be a dedicated jock. But there's something about you...a certain vulnerability. It makes me wonder if there isn't a softer, more gentle woman hiding beneath all that unremitting professional toughness. I plan to spend the next few weeks figuring you out!''

Garth's expression challenged Katie as much as his words did. He'd be a formidable adversary. And such a contest wouldn't be confined to the issues raised by a woman coaching the boy's wrestling team.

"Aren't you supposed to spend the next few weeks running interference for the school board?" she sidestepped dryly. His perceptiveness was unnerving. His guess about her vulnerability hit uncomfortably close to the truth. He'd managed to put her on the defensive, and it wasn't a position she liked much.

"I don't think those poor devils realize yet how much they're going to need my mediation. Something tells me you're going to lead them a merry chase this year." His dark eyebrows knit together in a teasing frown.

"Those 'poor devils' should be dragged, kicking and screaming if need be, into the twentieth century. They don't seem entirely convinced that burning recalcitrant women at the stake as witches isn't still the best way to handle the female sex!''

Katie kicked a particularly large pile of leaves viciously for emphasis. They floated down around her ankles, one or two clinging to the hem of her pearl-gray lambsuede skirt. Courtesy of Brian and his charge cards she knew she looked her best, a fact she found extremely satisfying as she walked along beside Garth. A sophisticated gray stripe was woven through the deep-peach tones of her silk broadcloth shirt. The

material's color and sheen did wonderful things for
her skin and hair, while the perfect cut of her suede
skirt presented her gymnast's figure to its best advantage. She felt chic, confident and definitely this man's
equal.

"Relax, Miss O'Connell. These are good people,
they aren't out to get you. Your brother has forced
them into a situation that seems wholly alien to them
and unnatural. Give them time, and if you've been
telling the truth about your abilities and your reasons
for being here, it will all work out." Garth stopped and
bent over, casually brushing a bright yellow aspen leaf
from her skirt, his large hand passing over her knee in
the process. Katie felt the slight contact like an electric shock even through the buttersoft suede. His fingers were gentle and warm. "On the other hand, if
you're here under false pretenses...."

"I'm not too crazy about all this verbal volleyball,
Mr. D'Anno. If you're trying to warn me about
something, why don't you just spit it out?" As usual
when she felt threatened, Katie went on the offensive.

Since his efforts to convince the board not to hire
her had failed, Garth seemed to think he could scare
Katie into changing her mind about coaching in
Granby. He had a lot to learn about Katie O'Connell,
she thought, squaring her shoulders decisively. Even
the nuns at Bennet Hill Academy hadn't been able to
verbally intimidate her. To accomplish that it had
taken outright threats of dire punishment. Like eter-
nal damnation.

"My point is this, Miss O'Connell. A lot of unsus-
pecting employers have been targeted recently by
women's rights groups, to be the proving ground for

sex-discrimination suits. I won't let that happen in Granby,'' he warned, a dangerous glint in his eyes. He flexed his broad shoulders powerfully, as though mentally preparing for battle.

"I've already told you I'm not a feminist subversive, Mr. D'Anno."

"Then why did you threaten a sex-discrimination suit if you didn't get your way?'' Garth cocked one coal-black eyebrow, daring her to explain if she could.

"Girlish pique?" she ventured sarcastically. She was getting tired of being constantly on the defensive, her every motive suspect, her every word scrutinized to find the lie. "My skills and experience are more than adequate for this job. The board just needed a little help to realize it. A twenty-two-year old male, the ink not even dry on his bachelor's degree, with absolutely no practical experience coaching wrestling or any other sport would have received a more enthusiastic reception than I did today. What would you have done in my place?''

Garth shrugged. "You've chosen a tough row to hoe, lady. I only hope you're not too disappointed when your alleged family loyalty doesn't prove worth it."

"My family is worth any sacrifice I could make," she said with quiet certainty. "There's nothing I wouldn't do for them. Or they for me."

Garth shook his head, disdain etching a study in hard lines and harsh angles across his face. "Please, spare me the overly emotional defense of family life. I know better. The concept is nothing but a romantic fantasy. When push really comes to shove, it's every man for himself." He reached one long arm over his head and slapped a low hanging branch sharply, setting the reddish-gold leaves remaining there to shaking.

"You obviously know nothing about families!" she said heatedly, brushing a falling leaf from her hair as she passed beneath the still quivering branch.

"I know everything I need to about families. Mainly that I want no part of one. Families are no different from any other group of people except for the quirk of nature that commingles their blood." Bitter sarcasm dripped from every word with the corrosive power of strong acid. "They'll use you, lie to you, cheat you and steal from you as easily as a stranger would if it suits their purpose."

"I should have known," she said with disgust. "A cynic."

"A realist," contradicted Garth coolly. "With the experience to back up my opinions. Something you apparently lack if you still trust *your* brother."

"Frankly, I wouldn't want your experience, Mr. D'Anno." Katie couldn't help but wonder what had bred such bitterness in him and what had caused the coldness that hung over his conception of family like a dark shadow. She would have liked to pursue the subject, but his whole demeanor was so forbidding, so hostile, that she didn't dare.

Obviously, the issue of brothers was a touchy one with Garth. Fine. She wouldn't touch it. After all, she hadn't come to Granby to beat the drum about families. As long as Garth laid off Brian, and kept his sniping about *her* family to a minimum, his opinions on the topic were none of her concern. If something so intrinsically precious was of so little value to him, it was his loss. His opinions had nothing to do with her.

"If you don't watch that mouth of yours, it's going to get you into trouble," warned Garth softly. His eyes lingered on the sensuous curve of her lips, as the corners tilted upward into a smile.

"Why should I?" she asked, an air of defiance crackling around her. "I'm sure you and the school board will do that *for* me far more diligently than I would ever dream of doing."

"That was sincere advice, *Ms* O'Connell. People here aren't used to such publicly outspoken women." His expression was serious, his light eyes darkening enigmatically.

"More of that old double standard that lauds men for becoming righteously indignant while condemning women who lapse into hysterical, unreasonable anger?" Katie smiled innocently. Her hazel eyes sparkled with deviltry and merriment. There was nothing she enjoyed more than pitting her wits against someone with a truly keen mind. For pure, albeit inaccurate, suspicion, this guy was almost as good as her grammar-school teacher, Sister Mary Simon. Katie doubted he took anyone or anything at face value.

Garth appeared unruffled in the face of her rejoinders. He led her across the small main street and into the cool, quiet lobby of the old Victorian hotel where she was staying. Katie blinked her eyes several times, trying to adjust to the interior darkness, which was such a contrast after the gleaming brilliance of the afternoon sun.

"Arguing with you could become my favorite pastime over the next few weeks, Miss O'Connell. Even when I'm right, I lose! You've somehow managed to turn a few simple questions and legitimate concerns about the impact of a female wrestling coach on a small mountain town into a witch-hunt. It's not fair. Some of my best friends are women!'' Garth's feigned air of injured innocence was impossible to ignore, and Katie laughed.

"How enlightened of you, Mr. D'Anno. Somehow that doesn't surprise me at all.'' With his looks and body the trail of drool probably stretched all the way to Denver. "What do you say to a truce? Let's agree to disagree about the ability of a qualified woman to coach a high-school wrestling team.''

"Friendly adversaries?'' Garth smiled widely, placing a warm hand in the small of Katie's back to guide her toward the parlor.

"Sounds good to me.'' Katie stifled a sudden desire to wrap a corresponding arm around his waist and held herself rigidly erect.

"I just have one more question.''

"Do I need to protect my jugular?'' asked Katie wryly.

Garth grinned knowingly. "Given your obvious ability to think on your feet, and your unbelievable brain to mouth coordination, why in the world did you blush such a becoming shade of red when you first began trying to convince the board you'd be a good substitute for your brother?''

"Did I? How extraordinary,'' said Katie, remembering very well the moment she'd been caught scrutinizing Garth more closely than she would have liked to admit. "I don't think I've blushed in ten years.'' Katie managed to glide across the hardwood floor of the lobby without missing a step. Talk about lulling the enemy into a false sense of security. This guy was good, his timing was perfect.

"That's a crock! You look like the type who blushes all the time. No, despite that mouthy performance in front of the school board, I think it was something else besides pressure."

"Then tell me, Mr. D'Anno, what significance do you attach to my alleged blush?" She laid her briefcase and purse on the floor next to her, and sank gratefully onto the worn red velvet covering of the Victorian settee in the hotel's parlor.

"I don't think you're as sure you can replace your brother as you'd like us to believe. And..." Garth's clear gray eyes reflected Katie's earlier deviltry and merriment back to her.

"And..." she prompted warily. Even on short acquaintance, she'd come to recognize that taunting sparkle in his eyes. The man was about to say something outrageous. Probably chauvinistic. Undoubtedly at her expense.

"And you're scared silly someone will realize you're not as tough as you pretend to be!"

His eyes reminded Katie of the pure silver mined in the Colorado mountains during the past century. His gaze was open, honest, playful. But she'd seen his eyes only moments before when they'd looked like Toledo steel, cold and unyielding. She wasn't particularly anxious to see that naked steel again. She had to keep the conversation light.

"Mr. D'Anno, I may have been scared once or twice in my life, but I have never, not even as a child, been *silly*. Silliness is *not* compatible with my practical nature.''

"You had no giggling adolescence?'' he queried in mock disbelief.

"Maybe once, a very small smirk. Perhaps one or two practical jokes, but certainly no giggling!'' she assured him with equally mock gravity, motioning for the bell hop to send in a waiter to take their order. The dining room stopped serving lunch at 2:00 P.M., but light snacks, sandwiches and drinks were served in the cozy parlor until midnight.

"So tell me,'' Garth leaned forward, his tone conspiratorial. "Just how scared were you?''

"As a humorless adolescent?'' asked Katie flippantly, deliberately misunderstanding the thrust of his question. Did the man never let up?

"No, skip ahead to the point where you become a smart-aleck adult. I'll probably find that more interesting.'' His warm regard was an unspoken compliment, and she found herself pleased in spite of her determination to hold Garth at a distance.

"There isn't too much I'm still afraid of now that I've become a smart-aleck adult.'' She cocked her head, appearing to give the matter serious consideration. "Except maybe large dogs with sharp teeth. And skiing the back bowls at Vail. Very steep stuff.''

"I know. It's my favorite place to ski.'' His gaze became more openly admiring, and he appeared to relax. "You must be a good skier.''

"Just stubborn. I refuse to be intimidated by height.'' She gave him a meaningful smile. "Of any kind.''

A whimsical, teasing note entered his voice. "Think I'll ever be able to coax the other Katie out, the soft one?"

"I *think* you're having insane delusions brought on by severe hunger." Katie was embarrassed by the squeaky sound of her voice as she directed her comment to the waiter. The man had caught the tail end of Garth's remark and smirked.

"Not delusions," said Garth, his slow smile starting a tingling warmth that began in Katie's chest and spread out to her fingertips, "fantasies. About making friends with the other Katie. The soft one."

"Why don't you tell this nice man what you want to eat and change the subject?" Katie had a hard time swallowing the lump of excitement that had risen in her throat, and her words came out in a strangled gulp. The idea that she could fuel Garth's fantasies caused bubbles of impish delight to swirl enticingly in the vicinity of her middle. What a ridiculous paradox! She was actually feeling a surge of feminine power at the idea of Garth being drawn to the softness she'd always considered a feminine weakness. And it was sheer heresy to consider making friends with a man who held the archaic notion that a woman's options were circumscribed by her sex.

"I'll have the roast beef and cheese on whole wheat, no mayonnaise, extra tomatoes and a Coors Light." Garth rattled off his order, then slid over closer to Katie. He placed his arm along the back of the settee, his fingers just inches from her neck and shoulders.

She felt every nerve ending in her body leap to attention at his proximity. Up close his eyes were amazingly clear and light and persuasive. Persuasive? Make

that enticing, she amended. For a full thirty seconds
Katie fought to keep from reaching out to touch him
as his eyes seemed to be asking her to do. "I'll have the
same," she added absently. The waiter moved away,
shaking his head over her long delay in deciding.

"I would never have taken you for a beer drinker."

"I'm not. I can't stand the stuff. Like most of my
race, I have a congenital fondness for a shot of Irish
whiskey on St. Patrick's Day, but I absolutely loathe
beer! Even the smell revolts me." Katie shuddered,
remembering all the times she'd tried to drink a beer
to please one or another of her boyfriends. "I managed a whole glass once, and the women's restroom of
Fargo's Pizza Parlor has never been the same again."

"Miss O'Connell, you've just proved my point
about what a puzzling contradiction you are." Garth's
laughter rang out deep and rumbling, a happy, full-
bodied sound.

"Are you losing your mind? Was the walk too much
for you on an empty stomach?" Katie was plainly
confused.

"Do you see that man over there? The one coming
toward us with two beers? I have some bad news for
you. One of those beers is mine, and guess who ordered the other one?"

"I must have been thinking about something else
for a moment."

"Fantasies of your own?" asked Garth, a bold grin
breaking across his face as he reached for his beer. He
drank deeply, tilting his head back so that Katie had
no choice but to admire the strong, tanned column of
his throat.

"None that concern you," retorted Katie, jerking her eyes away from the fluid lines leading from his neck to his shoulders before he caught her in the lie.

"Could I persuade you to share them?"

"Not on a bet." She asked for some iced tea, sending the waiter back to the kitchen mumbling about lunatics.

"That sounds like a challenge. I never back down from a challenge—"

"Neither do I," interrupted Katie, hoping to get him off the subject.

"I almost always get my way," he informed her, a teasing light brightening his eyes. "Some day when you least expect it, I'm going to turn my full persuasive powers on you and learn all your innermost secrets, including your fantasies!" He rubbed his hands together briskly. "I can't wait. It should be *some* story!"

CHAPTER THREE

KATIE WAS SAVED FROM having to respond by the waiter's return. He carried a tall glass of iced tea and the sandwiches. She took a large bite of the roast beef and cheese on whole wheat, then grimaced at Garth. "Dry sandwiches, my favorite. Do you think the waiter would have a nervous breakdown, or a mere snit, if I asked for extra mayo? He seemed a little out of sorts to me."

"You mean after you specifically ordered it dry? Of course not, everyone knows it's a woman's prerogative to change her mind." Garth deftly moved out of the way of Katie's stinging swat on the arm.

"Personally, I think you'd look very attractive wearing a roast beef sandwich and this beer you say I ordered, but if you aren't in complete accord with my viewpoint, I'd suggest you keep comments like that to yourself." Katie tilted her still-full glass over his shoulder at a slight but convincing angle.

"Looking for an excuse to see how well a wet T-shirt clings to my manly physique?"

Almost before she knew what she was doing, Katie tilted her glass another inch. Before a golden cascade of ice cold beer could stream over Garth's shoulder, he grabbed her wrist, holding it immobile.

"You're quick. I'm impressed," said Katie truthfully. "Even my brother doesn't move that fast, and he was famous in wrestling circles and sororities for his fast hands."

"You two are pretty close, aren't you?" Garth took the moisture-frosted glass from her hands and set it on the silver plated tray.

Katie shot him a sidelong glance suspiciously. He was eating his sandwich unconcernedly, and she decided his question had been innocent enough. For the moment he appeared to have abandoned his efforts to intimidate her into changing her mind about coaching in Granby, and his excoriating remarks about brothers.

"Very close, even for twins. We were born prematurely and we were always the smallest kids in class. It was especially tough on Brian. He was too small for football, basketball or almost any contact sport. Small girls are considered cute, small boys are just considered weak—perfect bully bait. We were always defending ourselves."

"So his habit of letting you fight his battles stems from the fact that he was a frail little boy?" Garth's disapproval of Brian was evident from his disparaging tone.

"I never fought his battles *for* him, it was more like *with* him. He may have been the boy, but I was always more of a fighter. Even so, we were back to back when it came to fending off bullies. It wasn't like he'd run off and leave me to take care of his problems!" Katie colored. Garth's raised eyebrows spoke volumes she was embarrassed to read. He made it plain that was exactly how he interpreted the current situation, and she hurriedly continued.

"My dad introduced him to wrestling when we were seven, mainly out of fear that he wouldn't make eight if he didn't develop some way to fight back that depended more on speed and skill than brute strength."

"That's how you learned so much about wrestling?" Garth looked at Katie was undisguised curiosity.

"Actually, wrestling comes naturally to most kids. It's their primary method of conflict resolution until they go to school! My father just taught us the rules and refined our technique."

"Both of you? I don't know many fathers who would teach their daughters to wrestle! Especially since it's not a sport in which they'd ever have the opportunity to compete." Surprise colored Garth's words. He wiped his well-shaped mouth with a thick, damask napkin, set his sandwich on the blue-and-white ironstone plate, and focused his full attention on Katie.

"Sure, my brother and I did everything together. I guess my dad knew better than to try and exclude me. I'm just like my mom. The best way to harden my resolve is to tell me there's something I can't do." Katie spoke almost ruefully. "Of course, being a girl I wasn't able to compete in the AAU meets." Her tone held a hint of bitterness. "That was the first time I ever heard the word 'no' tied to the fact I was a girl. But Brian practiced everything he learned on me, and you'd be surprised at what I picked up just from going to all of his meets."

"Did it really bother you, not being able to wrestle?" probed Garth, somewhat incredulous.

"I cried my seven-year-old eyes out! In my mind, my brother and I were just exactly alike. Suddenly, there started to be a whole lot of things I wasn't allowed to do merely because I was a girl. It didn't seem fair then, and I'm afraid I still haven't learned to accept my femininity as a sufficient reason when someone tells me 'no' now." She crunched one of her pickle spears defiantly.

"When did you defect to gymnastics? I understand you were something of a state legend in that sport yourself," he complimented.

"At nine. My brother and I have similar bodies..."

"I find that nearly impossible to believe." Garth interrupted Katie in a dry voice. His eyes traveled over her womanly figure. Her breasts and hips might be on the small side, but they were arranged in a way that was purely female. She ducked her head at his frank and appreciative scrutiny.

"I mean we have similar body *types*, longish torsos, not particularly long legs and kind of broad shoulders. It gives us a low center of gravity which translates into good balance and a certain quickness. It's a matter of physics. Additionally, it let us develop disproportionate strength for our size. Brian found out he had a natural wrestler's body even though he was short, and I became a gymnast." Katie spoke objectively about her body, without vanity, almost apologetically.

As an athlete, she was proud of her skills. They had taken years of hard work to develop. As a woman, she couldn't help wishing for a few extra, critically placed inches. Secretly, she longed for the kind of statuesque womanliness that most men seemed to find sexy and attractive. Katie chafed under any male's characterization of her as cute, and resigned herself to being a friend instead of a wife or lover. She'd had her share of boyfriends in high school and college, but no relationship had ever become serious and she had not had one in a long while.

"Don't look now, but we're making progress, Miss O'Connell. We've gone from discussing your fears to discussing your body. I can't wait to see what comes next." Garth drained his beer, then leaned back on the settee with an air of expectancy. A more comfortable-looking man Katie couldn't imagine. It irked her for some reason that he should be so at ease in her company, when she was so scattered in his. She felt like a dandelion, ready to disperse into a million wispy shreds at his slightest touch.

Everything about Garth was a little too smooth to be real. Too confident, too well built, too quick, just too...smooth. Why wasn't he ugly, or boring, or clumsy? Why did he possess the kind of incisive wit and challenging intelligence she'd always found irresistible? Why didn't he have a pot belly and lousy posture like other self-respecting men his age? He appeared to be in his mid-thirties, more than old enough to start letting himself go. Yet something about the way this man carried himself—proud and tall, with a self-confident awareness of his body that fell just short of arrogance—told her that Garth was one of those men who would never let himself go.

She knew instinctively he was exactly the kind of man she could fall for, hard and fast. Yet that was the one thing she couldn't permit to happen. The town's attitude toward a female wrestling coach was one of bare tolerance. It made for a difficult climate in which to do her job. Giving in to her attraction for the leader of the opposition would make it impossible.

But those shoulders! A really decent pair had always been a particular weakness of hers. Garth's belonged on a Hunk of the Month Calendar, along with a warning that torture by titillation could be hazardous to one's health. Don't lose it over a pair of shoulders, she admonished herself sternly, focusing her attention back to his last teasing question.

"How about something really racy? Like my job?" Katie infused her tone with irony. "This was supposed to be a business lunch, after all." She spread a lavish amount of mayonnaise grudgingly supplied by the waiter on the second half of her sandwich, then took a large bite.

"I suppose that means you'd consider it a serious breach of professional etiquette if we dropped all this 'Miss O'Connell-Mr. D'Anno' stuff, and called each other 'Garth' and 'Katie'?" He sighed loudly, then stole the last pickle spear from her plate, chewing and swallowing it before she could protest.

"I think I could be persuaded to accept something like 'thief' and 'Katie'! In case you didn't notice, that was my last pickle." Katie rapped her fork across the knuckles inching back toward her plate for the solitary cherry tomato remaining there.

"I noticed. I just didn't let it stand in my way! Be nice to me, and I'll buy you a bowl of deep-dish apple pie. This eatery gets the apples from orchards in Grand Junction. The dessert is a house specialty this time of year." Garth snatched up the tomato with quick fingers and favored Katie with an unrepentant grin. She was beginning to believe his earlier remark that he always got what he wanted. "So how about it, Katie. Want to call me 'Garth'?

"What will the school board say about their champion and the enemy fraternizing on a first name basis? Underlying Katie's teasing, there was a small grain of fear that the school board would find such friendliness inappropriate, that it would jeopardize her position.

"They won't *say* anything, but what they'll think would probably curl your toes!" He gave an insouciant shrug of the shoulders Katie had spent the last four hours admiring, and she realized that he was the kind of man who didn't let the opinion of others control his actions, or change *his* opinions.

She had a sudden comprehension of just exactly what Sister Mary Simon had meant by a 'near occasion of sin.' The shrug rippled tantalizingly across the muscles of his shoulders and down his arms and chest. Swallowing the pool of saliva collecting behind her teeth became a task of monumental difficulty.

"I can't tell you how that revelation sets my mind at ease, Garth!" Katie finally found her voice. She was surprised by how much she liked the way his name sounded on her tongue. Even more, she liked the way *he* said 'Katie,' gently, easily, but with an assurance that came close to creating a sense of intimacy.

"Face it, Katie. You're in the spotlight now. As long as you don't get caught in some sort of flagrant misbehavior or blatant incompetency you won't have any problem. I don't think the two of us calling each other by our first names qualifies though, do you? After all, we'll be seeing a lot of each other until the wrestling season is over." There was no mistaking the interest Katie read in his eyes. If he looked, she knew he'd see a reciprocal, if less obvious, interest in hers.

"What points did the board want you to discuss with me?" His warm appraisal was making her uncomfortably aware of the mutual attraction between them. This kind of complication she did not need. It was far safer in the present circumstances to keep her distance from Garth. And she could still enjoy looking at him without touching, couldn't she?

"I'm afraid we'll have to discuss them later. Time got away from me. Must have been the stimulating company!" He looked at her with an expression that told her he was referring to more than her conversation. "I have a meeting with one of my foremen in about ten minutes. I can't afford to miss it." At her curious expression he explained briefly, "I own a construction company."

"Sounds impressive," commented Katie. Somehow the fact that he worked for himself confirmed her impression of him as his own person. Garth didn't seem the sort of man who'd be comfortable taking orders from anyone.

"It's small, but it's mine. I've worked my tail off for it." Pride flared briefly in his eyes before he continued. "The construction financing for Phase Two of my current project is contingent upon my meeting some pretty strict deadlines in accordance with some very precise specifications. Just before the school-board meeting, I had a message from one of my foremen that a load of crucial material has finally arrived."

"That should set your mind at ease."

"I wish. The goods are not only late, they're nonconforming." He raked his hand through the thick blackness of his hair, plainly frustrated by complications he couldn't control. "A lot of my men will be out of jobs they really need if I can't get a handle on what's causing these delays. Not to mention what it would do to my company."

Katie perceived his concern, his sense of personal responsibility for his employees and she couldn't help liking him for it. "Then you'd better go."

"Thanks. We'll do this again before practice starts for wrestling season," he said confidently. "Think hard about changing your mind. You have a few weeks before you actually have to begin coaching. In spite of your 'spunky little scrapper' attitude, this isn't the easiest job for a woman. Things could get nasty."

Katie grinned. "My greatest joy in life is doing what people say I can't possibly do because I'm a woman. There's not a prayer of a chance I'll change my mind now that the board has hired me. It's a matter of principle."

Garth studied her with a speculative air, as if trying to make some sort of decision. "A woman of principle. I'll remember that, Katie." Abruptly, he pulled some bills from his pocket, placing them on the tray with their empty plates. "Good luck with your first day of school tomorrow. You'll need it! If you think the school board was intransigent, wait until you see the kids. They've raised good-old-boy and -girl redneckism to an art form!"

"Thanks, Garth. I really appreciate your support." Katie grimaced. "If I didn't know better, I'd say you were looking forward to what you hope will be my ignominious defeat!"

"Nope. I *hope* they're tough as hell on you, but if I'm *right* you'll come out on top of what promises to be a very interesting confrontation!"

She watched him walk briskly away, puzzling over his last cryptic remark and wondering just where he really stood on the issue of a woman wrestling coach.

KATIE CHECKED HER WATCH IMPATIENTLY, sighed in exasperation at the slow passage of time and tried once more to concentrate on the teacher's edition of the algebra textbook positioned across her knees.

"Hi," said Liz Adams cheerfully, tossing a couple of cookies in Katie's lap. She let the door to the staff lounge bang shut, wiggling her eyebrows gleefully at the small act of defiance. "The principal's secretary just *hates* when I do that."

"No wonder the action has an appeal for you!" Katie shook her head in amusement, then munched the cookie, savoring the oversize chocolate chips her friend used.

Liz had a running feud with Miss Florence. The woman was outraged that Liz, a holy terror in high school, had come back to the institution in the eminently respectable, wholly unassailable position of language teacher One afternoon Liz had matched each of Katie's Sister Mary Simon anecdotes with an equally uproarious one about Miss Florence, and the exchange had cemented their friendship forever, each woman recognizing a kindred spirit in the other.

"Hiding out?" teased Liz.

"All day. I've only emerged for sophomore geometry, junior algebra, senior calculus and two quick trips to the ladies' room," claimed Katie proudly. Responding cheerfully to unmitigated hostility from students and teachers alike had taken its toll on her normally good-natured disposition. "I needed a little peace and privacy."

"This is the place to get it," said Liz, nodding her head around the luxurious room. Granby spared no expense on either its school or its teachers. The lounge was comfortably furnished with deep sofas and cushioned armchairs in muted blues and grays, library tables and even a small stereo. "You're certainly entitled after the past four weeks. *My* temper would be in shreds by now. Tell me, honestly, doesn't your mouth hurt from smiling that much all day?"

"Actually, it's my molars I'm worried about. It can't possibly be good for them to be clenched, gnashed and ground as much as they have been lately," she remarked wryly.

Liz laughed. "Hang in there, Katie. You only have one more hour to get through and you can escape back to your hotel, proud of having survived your—" she glanced at the wall calendar, making a quick calculation "—your thirtieth day."

"If I survive," said Katie ruefully, patting her rumbling stomach. "Skipping meals is *not* my favorite thing. It makes me cranky."

"Tell me about it! Why do you think I always toss you some food before saying hello? I never know if you've eaten or not." Liz's last remark was delivered as a gentle scolding.

"Foul," protested Katie. "You know I disapprove of skipping meals. It's just that the board has scheduled another of its little gatherings for this afternoon. I was too nervous to eat breakfast and too tense to eat lunch."

"How delightful. You have all the fun," Liz sighed before giving a small shudder. "Give me a call later if by some chance the board's verbal aim is off today and you manage to survive the ordeal." Hugging Katie briefly, she sped on to her last German class, remembering to bang the door on her way out.

Katie slammed her book shut in aggravation. The preferred method of explaining quadratic equations would have to wait until later. She simply couldn't concentrate. She stuffed the thick tome back into her canvas book bag and headed for the girl's gym. It was usually empty this time of day; maybe she could get in a quick workout before the meeting. She needed to release some of her pent-up frustrations.

Ten minutes later, attired in her favorite bright-blue leotard, she surveyed the girls' gym with pleasure. There were brand new tumbling mats, gleaming uneven parallel bars, several balance beams, both practice and competition height, as well as horses for vaulting and an expensive sound system to provide music for the floor exercises. Such accoutrements upheld Garth's contention that the people of Granby did indeed "take their sports seriously."

Running experienced eyes over the competition height balance beam, Katie looked for protruding bolts or gouges in the wood. Satisfied that the beam was sound, she mounted it in one light movement. In a very few minutes, the concentration that had earlier eluded her was restored as she went through one of her favorite routines. She leaped and pirouetted, executing flawless back handsprings and the daring aerials that had won her two state championships in high school and a four-year gymnastics scholarship to college.

"Yeah, Nadia, go for it!" A coolly amused masculine voice broke her intense concentration.

Instead of raising her V-sit to a stag handstand, Katie sat down hard, a very sensitive part of her anatomy coming into intimate and painful contact with the four inch wide bar of hardwood. She gritted her back teeth to prevent an expletive from getting past her lips, trying to disregard the stinging, almost unbearable pain. Her legs hung down limply as she blinked rapidly several times to forestall the tears threatening to spill in a rush over her thick coppery lashes.

"Hey, are you okay? Where does it hurt?" One look at her drawn, white face and Garth was instantly at her side.

"If you value your life, or at least your procreative abilities, stand clear of me. I'm not fully responsible for my feet at the moment. They have this uncontrollable urge to share with you exactly what I'm experiencing right now!" Katie spoke slowly, counting to ten before each sentence. Her temper was held in check by a tenuous thread she was afraid would snap at any minute.

"I think standard operating procedure at a time like this is to hold your head." Garth teased lightly, but braved Katie's feet as he lifted her off the beam in one gentle swoop and set her down on the ground. "There, that wasn't so bad, was it?"

"Are you *trying* to provoke me?" Katie decided to dispense with decorum, dignity and pride. She rubbed the tender skin high on her inner thigh, wishing Garth would disappear so she could minister to the area that really hurt. It was a toss-up as to whether or not her legs could be counted on to carry her to the locker room, so she simply stood where she was, thinking evil thoughts about Garth's lean, muscular form.

"Don't I even get a few brownie points for lifting you down?"

"Don't make me hurt you." The first shock of pain had worn away, leaving a throbbing numbness in its place. "Do you make a habit of sneaking up on people like that?"

"Sorry. I've suffered similar injury a few times, and you're right. Levity doesn't sit well." Garth cast a sly, sidelong glance at Katie. "On the other hand, I don't think you're in any condition to *sit* at all." At Katie's pained expression he threw up his hands in surrender and stepped back a few paces.

Katie contented herself with a baleful glare in his direction before moving away from the balance beam to hobble toward the wooden bleachers that had been pulled out from the gymnasium wall. She smoothed her hands over her hair, tucking an errant, auburn curl back into her braid, her movements delicate, even graceful. The vigorous exercise had painted a wild-rose flush across her finely drawn cheekbones, and Garth's unannounced entry had put a fighting sparkle in her eyes. They flashed with gold and amber lights when she turned her face to his. "I assume this is an official visit? Something to do with your position as liaison for the school board?"

"Do I have to be on official business in order to see you?" he quizzed, suddenly serious. Silvery eyes followed the motion of her hands before returning to gaze intensely at her face. His eyes lingered over her long lashes, spiky with the moisture of tears she'd earlier refused to shed, then slid down the elegant line of her jaw to rest at last on her mouth.

Katie wanted to lick her lips, but her mouth had gone suddenly dry under Garth's scrutiny. Every place his eyes had passed over tingled, as though she'd been expertly caressed. "Of course not. I see you around town all the time," she murmured.

"Two chance encounters at the bank, giving me cuts once at the post office, and a casual exchange of waves that day you roared by me in your Blazer hardly constitutes 'all the time,'" he said dryly. "I tried to track you down in the cafeteria earlier to make good on that bowl of deep-dish apple pie I still owe you. Why didn't you show up for lunch? Afraid of the cook's version of mystery-meat casserole?"

His grin was as attractive as Katie remembered. All thirty-two gleaming teeth were still impossibly white. Self-consciously, she worried the tiny, corner chip in one of her own front teeth, a souvenir of her first meeting with the uneven parallel bars.

"Heaven forfend! Don't you know all teachers have to be certified as having cast-iron stomachs before they're permitted anywhere near a school cafeteria?" She blotted her forehead and throat with a corner of the towel she'd slung around her neck. "I just didn't want anyone's blood lust to get in the way of their good nutrition. Lynching's no fun on an empty stomach."

"They've been pretty rough on you, huh?"

"Depends on what you call rough," she answered noncommittally.

"Sorry. I intended to check on you before now, but my construction project hit a few more snags, and that damn deadline hanging over my head isn't making things any easier." He clenched his fists in frustration, the veins bulging along his forearms below his rolled up shirt sleeves.

Katie felt the tension emanating from him in strong waves and knew the *snags* were more serious than he'd let on. She was surprised. He seemed to be the type of man well able to control people and situations with a smooth ease that eliminated "snags." The type of man who avoided "accidents" by careful attention to detail. She looked at his whitened knuckles. And the type to take it very personally if he couldn't. "Anything serious?"

"I don't intend to let it be," he replied tersely. "And I *didn't* come here to talk about my project." He reached over and gently dabbed her temple with a corner of the towel slung around her neck. "Missed a spot. Now, tell me all about how you've been getting along."

CHAPTER FOUR

"WELL, THERE'S REALLY not much to tell." Katie shrugged. She folded her towel, placed it on the hard bleacher seat and sat down gingerly. "After the jeering and catcalls at the assembly on the first day of school I certainly wasn't expecting any great shakes of a welcome, but neither did I expect half of my junior algebra class to actually walk out on me without a backward glance."

"They didn't!"

"Blithely!" She shifted around, unable to get comfortable. "I've never had any problems maintaining classroom discipline, but a very large, very broad contingent of football players certainly caught me off guard."

"Are you sure they were football players?"

"With those necks? What else could they be?"

"I didn't hear about that," he mused thoughtfully.

Garth seemed perfectly at ease with his long legs stretched out in front of him, crossed at the ankles. He leaned back, resting his elbows on the bleacher behind him. The stinging numbness between her legs gave way to an altogether different sort of sensation, a warmth, a melting. This man was absolutely lethal in a pair of jeans and a plaid shirt. Today he was wearing a soft flannel shirt in green and navy shades, but it molded his chest and shoulders as temptingly as the black turtleneck he'd worn the day she met him.

"Did you hear about Spit Day?" she queried mockingly.

"No, but judging from your expression I'd like to." Tiny lines crinkled the corners of his eyes as his warm smile invited her to continue.

"Half a dozen senior guys showed up in calculus class one day with enormous wads of 'chaw' wedged inside their bottom lips and carrying spittoons. They claimed it was Spit Day, and they were allowed to chew tobacco during the last class period." She'd never forget the loud pinging sound she'd heard as light-brown streams of tobacco juice hit the insides of the spittoons.

"And you believed them?" he asked incredulously, not even trying to stifle his hoots of raucous laughter.

"Hardly, but I wasn't prepared to make a federal case out of it until a tall, redheaded kid 'accidentally' missed his spittoon and hit my face."

Garth's eyes narrowed. "Greg Jenkins," he stated flatly.

"Who it was doesn't really matter," dismissed Katie.

"It had to be Greg. He's the only tall, redheaded guy in the senior class brazen enough to try a stunt like that." Garth insisted on the boy's identity with the persistence of a rat terrier worrying a bone. "I hope you came down hard on him."

"Not too hard, but I think I made my point. This student—"

"Greg," interrupted Garth insistently.

"Student X," Katie corrected stubbornly. "He has a chip on his shoulder about adult authority the size of Pike's Peak. Once I get by that, we'll get along fine. He has a real head for math; he's easily my best student."

Garth softened for a moment, but when he spoke his tone was stern. "Greg's actions seem quite a bit beyond what I could accept as normal limit testing."

"My sentiments exactly. I fell back on time-honored Catholic school tradition to make him and the others understand how unwise it was to carry their insubordination too far." Katie turned a smile of pure satisfaction on Garth. "The nuns at my high school quelled a similar insurrection when I was in the tenth grade, only the medium of rebellion was cherry bubble gum," she explained.

"What did they do?"

"The offenders had to wear the chewed matter in their ear for the remainder of the class period!" Katie's eyes twinkled mischievously, and Garth joined in her carefree laughter. It was the same happy, full-bodied sound she remembered, his broad shoulders shaking with the deep-timbred resonance.

"And they quietly submitted to that edict?"

"We-ell, the spittoon I threatened to upend on the head of the redheaded kid, and anyone else who didn't comply, proved an undeniable persuasion!"

"Greg must have loved that. Katie, you have a real knack for the unconventional!" Garth wiped a tear of laughter from the corner of his eye with the back of his hand. He pulled a small notepad and stubby pencil out of his shirt pocket, making a few notes. "Who did you say the other boys were?" he asked, still chuckling.

"I didn't, and I'm not going to. I'd rather handle this 'testing' on my own." Her chin jutted out stubbornly.

"But this is exactly the sort of situation I'm here to help you handle. I think the principal should be informed. A reprimand and a warning are very much in order."

"No. I can't be running to the principal every time my students misbehave. That's the surest way to lose control entirely." She grimaced. "Besides, the principal would probably pat them on the head for their initiative."

"Then you've considered there might be more to this than youthful resistance to a woman coach or a new teacher?" A speculative glint lit up his eyes. They were such an unusual shade of silver that Katie found herself constantly checking to see if perhaps their color wasn't just some play of light. Drawn as if by magnetism, Katie found herself getting lost in their metallic gray depths, not entirely unwillingly.

"You mean some sort of organized conspiracy to make my job so tough that I quit in feminine despair? Maybe, but since it won't work I'm not going to spend a lot of time worrying about it." Her self-confidence reasserted itself, and she was rewarded by the look of admiration she saw flash across Garth's face.

"I'll have a word with Greg, at least, since he seems to be the ringleader. He's a wrestler, so my position should have some influence with him."

"Don't," said Katie quietly, but with a firmness that carried a note of warning. She didn't intend to be crossed.

Garth raked an impatient hand through his hair. "These pranks could easily degenerate into real delinquency. The boy needs a strong hand to set him straight, and set him straight hard, before that happens."

"That's his father's job. Mine is to teach him math and coach him at wrestling. Yours is to mind your own business!"

Garth's jaw tightened. "Very well," he bit out. "For now."

Katie laid her hand on his arm, feeling the solid mass of muscle bunched tensely beneath his skin. His body heat radiated through his shirt, warming her fingertips, and suddenly she wanted nothing so much as to wrap both hands around the hard biceps, sink her fingers into the warm flesh and squeeze.

"Don't get me wrong, I think it's wonderful that you want to be so involved with the wrestling team." She made her tone conciliatory. "And there'll be lots of opportunities for you to do so. But this isn't an area where it's appropriate for you to..."

"Intrude?" Garth finished the sentence for her, a self-deprecating smile relaxing his features. He reached up and covered her hand with one of his own, the callused palm and sturdy fingers deliberately gentle against her skin.

"Assert yourself," amended Katie graciously. She slipped her hand from the warm cocoon, reluctantly.

"I hear you've also been making lots of friends among the other teachers," he remarked, the irony in his voice unmistakable.

Katie's snort was decidedly unladylike. "You must mean my good buddy Ron Luter, the football coach.

His nose was pretty far out of joint when he heard the wrestling coach was getting a bonus. The fact that the coach is a woman is really driving him nuts. I think he wants a full-fledged feud, only he's not sure how to challenge a woman to a duking out without losing some essential element of manhood!''

"He's a jerk. Just ignore him," advised Garth disgustedly. "What about the others?"

"They all love me. You can tell by the way they avoid and ignore me so I'm not overwhelmed by the magnitude of their admiration." Katie laughed, a light good-natured sound in spite of the situation that prompted it. She was gregarious, people-oriented. It bothered her to be the object of so much concentrated dislike and disapproval, but she refused to succumb to self-pity.

"I'm sorry," he offered quietly. "But the situation is exactly what I expected."

She twirled her braid around her fingers. "I'm sure things will improve when they realize I'm no threat to any of them. And I have made one friend, Liz Adams. She teaches French and German. Her sense of humor is scandalously irreverent, but she's kind and very nice."

"I know her. You're lucky to have her for a friend. For your sake, I hope the rest of your colleagues come around, but I wouldn't count on it," he warned.

"All I can do is be friendly, stay calm and get started with the wrestling team. The sooner everyone realizes I'm here for the duration, despite their best efforts to convince me otherwise, the sooner everything will settle down."

"Speaking of the wrestling team, if you're still determined to go through with this coaching business, we need to sort out a few aspects of your job. That's one of the reasons I'm here."

"I thought it was to buy me some deep-dish apple pie?"

"That's to butter you up for the recommendations the board wants me to go over with you."

"It'll take more than pie if the recommendations come from Mr. Willis and his pals," Katie retorted tartly.

"Whatever it takes, I'm happy to oblige." Garth's eyes gleamed, their silvery depths seductive with invitation and promise. "Why don't you get changed, and we'll discuss things over the sweetest fruit filling you ever tasted. Unless you prefer to go as you are?" His gaze traveled the length of Katie's bare legs, which were slim, strong and muscular. His gaze lingered appreciatively over her slender hips, trim waist and small breasts. "I certainly wouldn't mind."

She flushed under his close scrutiny. Sitting next to each other as they were, he had to be aware of the fact that she wore nothing under her leotard but her fitness. "The school board might. They have another 'Katie bashing' session scheduled for this afternoon. My presence is crucial to the festivities, so I'm afraid we'll have to postpone our discussion."

"'Katie bashing'?"

"A harmless local diversion." Her assurance was accompanied by a self-mocking grin. "The board has taken to calling informal little meetings about twice a week. The members usually content themselves with long-suffering expressions, aggravated sighs and stern exhortations to remember I'm only in Granby for the year, and only on their sufferance."

"Sounds like loads of fun."

"That's not the best part. They also manage the unfailing attendance of a few parents who haven't yet had a chance to express their total opposition to a woman wrestling coach, though one or two have grudgingly admitted their teenagers don't seem to be having their usual problems with math this year." Katie couldn't help the smug tone that crept into her voice. Her abilities as a math teacher were slowly but surely gaining her a measure of respect, if not acceptance.

"Why?"

"Come *on*. Objectively, even *I* admire the board's strategy. It gives the townspeople a chance to focus their anger on the object of their disapproval and away from the board which might otherwise have to deal with it."

He shook his head, a frown knitting his dark brows. "No, I meant why do you continue to attend? Strictly speaking, the board can't force you to go along with that sort of thing."

"Maybe not," she agreed calmly. "But if I don't go, I'll never be able to persuade people to change their minds about me, about what I'm doing here. Sure, I've taken a lot of criticism, but I've also had a chance to express my point of view, to meet people face-to-face. If they don't know me, they can only judge me by their prejudices. This way they have to make a more objective assessment. Attending the meetings hasn't been easy, but it's a valuable exchange for both sides."

She turned an earnest face to him, searching for some sign of understanding.

"Did you ever stop to think that the people who live here, and I'm talking about women, as well as men, are perfectly content, even happy, with the status quo? That it might be somewhat presumptuous for a thoughtless *outsider* to barge in, insisting we adopt changes we may not want?" He leaned forward, his expression intense, almost angry.

"I'm not insisting anyone do anything but listen to another point of view with an open mind." Katie was taken aback by his vehemence. The possibility that the townspeople, that *Garth*, saw her as a thoughtless and arrogant intruder stung. Once more, he'd managed to put her on the defensive. "Why are you so threatened? Are you afraid the women of Granby will demand a change in the dynamics of their relationships with men if they see a woman succeed here in a position traditionally filled by a man?"

"What do you know about Granby, or the dynamic of relationships between men and women here?" Garth got to his feet abruptly, forcing Katie to look up at him, his voice rising rapidly by angry decibels as he paced the gym floor, like an animal staking out his territory.

"Plenty. I've experienced life in Granby firsthand for a month now. Maybe a 'presumptuous outsider' is what this place needs to change outdated complacent attitudes about a 'woman's place,'" she replied coolly, flinging her braid over her shoulder with a toss of her head.

"You sound so damn condescending when you talk about changing people's attitudes in that cavalier tone of yours! Are you so positive you won't do those boys more harm than good?" He lowered his face until it was inches from her own. *"Did it ever, for one minute, occur to you that you might be wrong?"*

Katie met his furious glare steadily. "It did...but I'm not," she said with quiet conviction.

Disappointment tickled the edge of her emotions, but she wasn't really surprised. Garth had made it clear from the beginning of their friendship, that he didn't think a woman had any business coaching a boys' wrestling team. His mind appeared firmly and permanently closed to any other point of view on the subject. Nor would he give her a chance to present her calm, reasoned arguments against what she considered an arbitrary prejudice; he just kept trying to convince her to give up before she'd even started.

So why was his good opinion of her so important? She'd never felt the need to explain her actions or justify them to anyone before. And certainly not to someone whose opinions and beliefs were so stubbornly contrary to hers. Now, her desire to change Garth's mind amounted to a near compulsion. It felt strange to be worrying about whether or not he approved of her, and even more strange to crave that approval when it wasn't forthcoming. Strangest of all was the odd, inexplicable energy between them, a spark promising to burst into a nice cozy flame every time they were together.

"Your mind is nailed shut," he snapped, scowling fiercely. "It's damn aggravating!"

"Funny, I was thinking the same thing about you," said Katie evenly, glowering back at him.

"You don't give an inch, do you?"

"Nope."

"Get changed. We'll negotiate the terms of compromise over pie," he said disgustedly, jamming his hands into the pockets of his jeans.

The confrontation had stripped away layers of control from both of them. Awareness crackled freely between them like static electricity before a lightning storm. Katie met his eyes for a moment, then looked quickly away, not sure she wanted to acknowledge what she saw there.

"I already told you I have an audience with the school board," she repeated.

"Your 'audience' is with me. The board arranged this meeting so we could work out the final details of your mandate. Which is exactly what we're going to do. Over pie. If it chokes us!"

SEATED AMID THE VICTORIAN OPULENCE of the hotel's dining room sometime later, Katie happily contemplated the biggest bowl of deep-dish apple pie she'd ever seen. Thick rivers of French vanilla ice cream just beginning to melt oozed over a golden pastry that looked even flakier than her mother's prize-winning pie crust. She plunged her spoon through the crust and found a wealth of tiny raisins and finely chopped nuts hiding among the thick apple wedges. A rich, sweet syrup heavily laced with cinnamon surrounded every bite, sliding down her throat with pleasurable ease.

"This is fabulous!" She closed her eyes, sighing blissfully. "All that cinnamon...those crunchy little nuts...luscious. If you have any bad news, tell me now. I'm weakened!"

Garth laughed. "I told you this dessert was a house specialty." After swallowing several large bites, he set his own spoon aside and sipped the strong coffee he'd insisted was a necessary accompaniment from the blue-and-white ironstone cup. "Tell me, what are you planning on wearing to wrestling practice?" He asked the question almost too casually.

"What the ancient Greeks wore, of course...not much," teased Katie.

"The school board has asked me to settle this point with you. They've agreed to abide by my decision."

"They're doing a lot of that lately," she muttered rebelliously. "What difference does what I wear make?"

"As long as you don't show up in a singlet or anything else too skimpy, I don't think we'll have a problem." There was a warning look in Garth's eyes. Their color once again had begun the transition from warm gray to steely pewter.

"You're serious, aren't you?" Her enjoyment of the pie dissipated, and Katie pushed the bowl away from her. "Frankly, I think that's outside the board's jurisdiction. There hasn't been a dress code for *students* in ten years!" A slow anger began to build as she realized the board intended to insinuate itself into an area she considered basic to self-expression.

"The board is concerned with the boys' reaction and that of their parents. It's bad enough the new wrestling coach is a woman. You've seen the opposition firsthand. You show up for practice flashing your body around, and things will go from bad to impossible."

"I am *not* a flasher!"

"Too bad for me!" Garth grinned. "I suggest warm-up pants and a long sleeved T-shirt, but I'm willing to listen to any other ideas you might have." He faced Katie calmly with the sort of reasonable superciliousness that always made her want to scream.

"The board had a chance to negotiate a mandatory dress code as part of my contract over a month ago. You tell them I'll wear whatever I please to practice. Probably a leotard and tights."

He shook his head firmly. "Too revealing. Look at it from the parents' point of view, Katie. You'll be dealing with very impressionable teenagers. The board insists the proprieties be fully observed."

"Give me a break! The board is looking for a way to harass me into quitting. No one in their right mind would believe that a bunch of teenage boys, no matter how hormone activated, could be stirred to heights of uncontrollable lust over my body if it's not swathed in fifty layers of padding. You can assure the board that whatever *I* choose will be perfectly *appropriate*, but they are *not* going to dictate what I wear!" Katie set her chin at its most stubborn angle.

"My binding arbitration says they *are*!" retorted Garth, apparently unaffected by her doggedness. Though his voice was firm, there was a barely perceptible twitch of his upper lip that told Katie he was on the verge of laughter.

"Think this is real funny, do you? How am I supposed to demonstrate moves if I'm hampered by too many clothes?"

"That brings up some other points."

"Which are?" she asked suspiciously.

"No physical contact between you and any member of the team, and—" he drew a quick breath "—you're to stay out of the boy's locker room."

"That's insulting. I'm their coach, not some desperate Mrs. Robinson! Aside from the fact that at twenty-eight they'll probably think I'm too far over the hill to be worthy of their amorous attention, what possible interest could *I* have in some barely pubescent teenage boy?" The implication of Garth's words stung. Katie loved coaching, and it hurt to think the very benevolent interest she bore her students wasn't immediately apparent to the school board. Did Garth share their opinion of her? The notion bothered her. A lot.

"I should think that the interest the board is worried you might inspire would be obvious. Trust me, you're not over the hill." Garth allowed the twitch around his mouth to break into a full-fledged smile. "In fact, I doubt you've even reached the summit yet."

Katie ignored his statement. "We're not talking about indiscriminate groping here, Garth, just the neutral touching any coach is permitted. And that bit about staying out of the boys' locker room. Don't they give me credit for any judgment at all?"

He didn't answer.

"I see." Disgust twisted her mouth. "The only time I'd go in there would be in case of injury to one of the boys, or if a fight broke out, or some similar circumstance!" She fiddled with her braid, her aggravation manifesting itself in the way her slender fingers repeatedly wound the thick rope into a large, tight curl, then let it free fall almost to her lap.

"Ignoring the part about the locker room for now, can't you explain the moves you want to teach, then let the boys practice on each other?" Garth's voice was gentle.

"Possibly, but it won't be nearly as effective. They need to see and feel the physical dynamics of a move before they can duplicate it."

"Can't you use some sort of substitute during demonstrations?"

"You mean like one of those plastic dummies they make the kids practice mouth-to-mouth resuscitation on in health class? Maybe, but I can't make it respond to commands, or show cause and effect the way I could if I demonstrated each move on the boys themselves." She stabbed viciously at the pie with her spoon, making mush out of it, but thinking of no way to circumvent the board's strictures. "I'll give it a try, but I'm warning you, if using the dummy doesn't work I'm going to demonstrate on the boys. If the board doesn't like it, they can just go...hang themselves!"

"We'll work something out, don't worry." The pensive note in Garth's voice gave way to a naughty quality that promised mischief. She suspected she ought to worry about what he intended to "work out," but there were too many other things on her mind.

"I'm delighted to be the source of such amusement for you, but I've never in my entire teaching career had to submit to this kind of nonsense." Katie's whole body quivered with righteous indignation.

"You've never been a wrestling coach before. If you'd stuck to coaching girls' gymnastics, you wouldn't have these problems." Garth's eyes caressed Katie from across the narrow table, then he reached out and tugged on her braid. "Somehow, I have the feeling that this is the first time you've ever had to *submit* to anything, period!" He wound the dark auburn coil around his hand, pulling her face closer to his. "Am I right?"

"No touching allowed, remember?" Katie tried to resist the magnetism impelling her forward, using the table separating them for leverage. Garth simply scooted his chair around next to hers without releasing her hair from his grasp.

"Ah, but I'm not a member of your team, Katie. We can touch each other all we want." His deep voice had taken on a husky timbre. "And I think we want to, quite a bit."

She could feel Garth's voice resonating through her body, causing little frissons of excitement up and down her spine. If he came another few inches closer he would kiss her, she was sure of it. She couldn't wait. She couldn't dare allow the intimacy.

"It won't work, Garth. You won't get me to compromise myself so easily. Obviously, I'm attracted to you, but surely you don't think I'm so dumb, desperate or indiscreet I can't see through what you're trying to do?" Katie faced him tremulously. Why did the first really likely prospect in a long time have to be a man whose motives she didn't dare trust?

"Why don't you tell me what you think I'm trying to do?"

"Don't play innocent with me. If I kissed you the news would be back to the school board in five minutes. They'd call my response to you moral turpitude

and have just the excuse they need to fire me legiti-
mately. Isn't that what you had in mind when you
couldn't convince me to quit on my own initiative?''
Katie winced slightly as Garth gave her braid a nasty
tug, not hard enough to be painful, but enough for her
to know he was angry.

"The members of the school board might be somewhat behind the times, but even they know that it
takes more than a kiss to prove moral turpitude! I
don't know about 'desperate,' I doubt 'indiscreet,' but
you're doing a wonderful display of 'dumb.'" Garth
spoke softly, the lethal softness of true anger just
barely contained as he tossed her words back to her.

"Angry at being caught out?" she taunted.

"Think it through, Katie. Small-town morals don't
exactly smile on the kind of behavior you've just accused me of. In spite of your gamine good looks and
the probably enviable level of sexual experience im-
plied by your advanced age of twenty-eight, I am not
about to risk what I hope will be a very satisfactory
return to Granby for the sake of a kiss motivated by
anything but the purest, most personal self-interest. I
have far too great an investment at stake."

Mocking scorn turned the handsome charmer she'd
felt so attracted to before into a harsh-featured adversary with whom she felt intensely ill at ease. She re-
treated farther against the needle-pointed back of her
chair, suddenly feeling an urgent curiosity about
Garth's background. She'd assumed he'd spent his
entire life in Granby.

"Don't worry," he said derisively. "I think better
of myself than you apparently do. I prefer to save my

kisses for women who combine whatever attraction they feel for me with at least a modicum of trust.''

A long, tense silence followed his words, while Katie tried to think of something to say. "Does this mean I don't get another piece of deep-dish apple pie?'' she asked winsomely.

"Sorry, Katie. I don't like 'little girls' either. Just women...warm, honest, fully grown women. I thought you might be one when you didn't try to deny the sparks that have been flying between us from the minute you walked into the principal's office a month ago. Guess I was wrong. Our relationship will be more correct in the future.''

She badly wanted to believe in him. He seemed honest. But what could she say now that would undo the damage of her earlier mistaken conclusions?

"Don't be so prissy, Garth. All right, I misjudged your motivation, but under the circumstances can you blame me for being suspicious? Granby hasn't exactly welcomed me with open arms, and you *are* the board's handpicked champion. You've been after me from day one to pack it in and go home. Let's agree to bury the hatchet somewhere other than each other's backs and start over. I'll even buy the second round of pie.'' Katie bestowed her warmest, most winning smile on Garth; the one guaranteed to provoke a short, vulgar expletive from Brian because of its nearly one hundred percent efficacy.

"Will you spring for double ice cream?''

"Don't push your luck.'' Katie motioned to the waiter to bring them each another bowl of pie and ice cream, feeling relieved. Though the earlier promise of intimacy was gone, things were back on an even keel.

That knowledge pleased her more than she liked to admit.

Garth scanned the loose pages he held in his hand. "I doubt you'll like these last recommendations, but they seem reasonable so I've agreed to enforce them. First, you'll wear a bra while coaching."

"Hold on! Whether or not I wear a bra is no one's business but my own!" Katie couldn't control her outburst. "Aside from the small matter of verifying compliance, even *you* must see that requirement is a total invasion of privacy?"

"I'm getting damn tired of the way you challenge every damn word I say, Katie," he snapped impatiently. "If I have to verify the fact myself, you *will* wear a bra at all practices and wrestling meets. Do I make myself clear?" His flint-edged tone could have cut a diamond. It had very little problem slicing through Katie's resistance, nicking her tender, burgeoning feelings for him in the process. She felt the sheer force of his will pour over her, obliterating even the desire to oppose him.

"Very well." She simply acquiesced. Getting to know Garth was a novel experience. Always before, the mere fact of being *told* instead of asked to do something had been enough to make Katie refuse on principle. But something about Garth, maybe the fact that his strength was so completely without violence, made her accede to his demand. He exercised a raw power in its purest form that compelled her without threatening or frightening.

"Secondly, all out of town or overnight trips with the team will require a chaperon." If Garth was surprised at her easy agreement he gave no indication.

"I think that's a good idea. Riding herd on the entire team by myself while trying to coach them at a meet is no small job. I'll be glad of some help. Maybe a couple of parents?" suggested Katie, nodding her approval in subdued fashion. Five years of coaching high-spirited teenagers had taught her the kind of trouble they could stir up away from home.

"The chaperon is not for the team. It's for you." Garth uttered the words softly, as though recognizing the indignity of his last demand. He seemed almost sympathetic, and she almost forgave him for agreeing to enforce the list of petty rules.

"I see. Does this...affront have your unqualified seal of approval?" Anger still pounded impatiently in her veins, but it was tempered now by a steely determination not to buckle and give way to her ire. No matter what further humiliations the board had in store for her, they wouldn't make her quit.

"Not for the reason you think. I told the board I didn't think such a policy was necessary to protect the morals of the boys involved. But frankly, I think it's the best thing they could have done to protect *you*. With a chaperon along, no one will be able to start any wild rumors about improper behavior on your part."

If she didn't know better, Katie would have sworn he was trying to be nice. "Very well, Mr. D'Anno. I'll get you a list of out-of-town and overnight trips so you can line up a chaperon for *me*. If that's all you have to say, I believe I'll say good-bye." She rose from her seat and stalked from the dining room.

Garth caught up with her in the lobby. "Don't take it so hard, Katie." The tender way he said her name made a mockery of her attempt to go back to a more formal mode of address, as did the delicate way he enfolded her hand after reaching out to clasp it in both of his. In spite of herself, Katie felt comforted, but her principles were still not satisfied.

"Unfortunately, I can't take it any other way. I've always been a very respected, very *respectable* teacher and coach. All these restrictions...they...hurt. I know the board is having second thoughts about hiring me. They expected the community's opposition to their hiring a woman wrestling coach to have died down by now, but it hasn't. I suspect they're trying to pile on so many stupid, ridiculous rules I'll quit in frustration or louse up, so they can fire me. I'm telling you now, it won't work." Cool, implacable determination underscored her words.

Her reasons for coming to Granby flashed through her mind and a sudden realization surprised her. Now that she'd spent some time in the town, teaching in its small but excellent high school and planning for the upcoming wrestling season, she liked the place. Her loyalties quickly had become engaged without her knowing quite how it happened. Strange as it was, considering her reception so far, Granby and its students were suddenly as important to her as helping Brian and owning the gingerbread house. She thought longingly about the state wrestling trophy, wishing she could help them win it. She'd have to see what she could do about obtaining college wrestling scholarships for the boys with true promise.

Her tone hardened. "None of you nice people realize it yet, but those boys *need* me and what I know about wrestling. Nothing, I repeat, *nothing* will make me turn my back on my responsibility!"

Katie strode across the lobby without giving Garth a chance to respond. She stepped through the lacy grillwork of the old-fashioned elevator and slammed the interior glass door shut. The noisy reverberations were only partially satisfying.

CHAPTER FIVE

"EXCUSE ME, MISS O'CONNELL, but Mrs. Adams asked me to bring this to you." A slender sophomore smiled timidly, embarrassed at interrupting Katie's senior math class. "She asked me to wait for an answer." The girl handed Katie a folded note, then ducked her head, blushing at the long, low whistle from a boy in the back row.

Katie looked up sternly. "Don't be rude, Jim."

"Sorry, Miss O'Connell. Reflex reaction." He delivered his apology in a voice that sounded anything but sorry, leering at the girl. "She's such a fox, I couldn't help myself."

"Knock it off, Bradley; she's just a kid. Leave her alone," warned Greg Jenkins. The redhead, usually one of Katie's more troublesome students, scowled fiercely at Jim Bradley, before smiling a gentle encouragement at the pretty brunette messenger. The girl shot him a look of grateful relief, then shyly lowered her eyes.

Katie restrained a smile, wondering if she was witnessing a budding romance. Usually Greg Jenkins displayed the same mad-dog truculence in class that his father had shown at the school-board meeting the day she was hired six weeks ago. It was gratifying to discover the boy had a few gentler emotions tucked away somewhere inside. She unfolded Liz's note.

Dear Katie,

  I am being held captive by a group of crazed Francophobes who are torturing my ears with their deliberate mispronunciation of the most beautiful language on earth. I've bribed them into understanding the imperfect tense by promising to dismiss French class five minutes early. Join me in sneaking off for coffee somewhere?

Liz

Katie scribbled her agreement beneath Liz's signature. "Thank you, Marie." The girl took the note, then left quickly, stealing one last look over her shoulder at Greg Jenkins. He winked, then leaned back in his desk chair with a confident ease that reminded Katie of Garth.

"I'm going to let you out five minutes early today, people." An excited undercurrent traveled through the room as her students grinned at each other, shuffling around expectantly in their seats. "So pay close attention while I go through this equation one more time."

The remainder of the hour passed quickly. "Okay, that's it. See you all on Monday. Jim, Laurie and Karen, try to keep your homework away from your little brothers and sisters," she said with a wry smile. Errant siblings had been the excuse of the week for incomplete assignments.

As the kids began noisily gathering up papers and books, anxious for the weekend to begin, Katie remembered one more thing. "Those gentlemen interested in wrestling this year, don't forget the first practice will be a week from Monday at three-thirty."

"How could we forget? You've been counting it down every Friday since school started," muttered Greg Jenkins, not quite under his breath.

She ignored his remark. "Wear your singlets, don't be late and come prepared for a good workout."

"That's what you always say." Greg glared resentfully at her, slamming his books into his knapsack.

"Greg, please stay behind for a moment. I'd like to speak with you."

The other students filed past him, sympathetic expressions on their faces. When the last of them had gone, he turned a sulky face to Katie. "What do you want?" he challenged.

"It was nice of you to stand up for Marie. She's a little shy, and it must have been pretty tough for her to walk in on a senior math class. Jim's remarks didn't make it any easier. I appreciate what you did."

"No big deal," he said off-handedly. "Anyway, I didn't do it for you. Can I go now?"

"In a minute. Tell me, are you coming out for wrestling this year? I understand you did quite well last year. You'd be an asset to the team this year," she said forcefully.

"With a girl coach?" Greg smirked insolently at Katie. "I was hoping to get the recruiters from a really good wrestling school, maybe Ohio State, to notice me this year. Now, I might as well forget it."

"If you need a scholarship, maybe I can help, get my brother to put in a good word for you with his contacts. He wrestled at Ohio State."

"Everyone knows about your *brother*."

"Then I'll see you at the first practice?"

"I'll think about it."

"Good. Meanwhile, I'll talk to my brother and see what he can do."

"Don't bother. I don't need anything from you, or anyone else," he said with surprising vehemence. "My mom's old man set up a college fund when my parents adopted me. I can pay my own way. All I want is a place on a really good team. I want to be a coach, like your *brother*!"

"Show up a week from Monday, and you'll have a place on a really good team," retorted Katie. "Have a good weekend, Greg."

He left without a word.

"Is it safe to come in?" teased Liz Adams, her fluffy brown hair and warm brown eyes peering cautiously around the doorjamb.

"Yes," laughed Katie, waving her friend in.

"I'm the one Greg has a problem with. He doesn't approve of a woman wrestling coach."

"How original of him!"

"Yes, isn't it?"

"Still, it's a relief to know I'm not the only teacher whose students have an attitude problem. All my sophomore boys have decided that learning French is wimpy. That means all the girls who are trying to attract their attention have to hate the language too. It could be a very trying year!" Liz erased the blackboard and started packing up the books on Katie's desk. "Come on. Let's get out of here and go somewhere they don't allow kids. I need an immediate fix of adult company."

"Sounds great. What about Gerry's Café? They make great coffee."

"Perfect. No teenager would be caught dead in there. We'll have to sneak by Miss Florence, though; I haven't turned in my insurance forms yet." Liz wrinkled her nose in distaste. "Fifteen pages of enforced disclosure of all my deepest secrets, like weight, height and age."

"Fate worse than death," agreed Katie. "We'd better use the fire escape stairs."

They crept surreptitiously out the back way and covered the short distance to town on foot. A biting wind reddened their cheeks, and they laughed like schoolgirls at having escaped early for the weekend.

"We'll probably get our first snow tonight," remarked Liz dismally, pointing out the unbroken mass of low hanging gray clouds that made it seem as though the sky had dropped to just overhead.

"Great," answered Katie with enthusiasm, pulling off one bright-turquoise mitten to turn the handle on the door to Gerry's Café. "I love snow. We never get enough in Colorado Springs for my taste. Winter in the high mountains is one of the things I'm most looking forward to this year."

Liz shook her head in disbelief. "You're a sick woman, Katie O'Connell. Tell me that again when you've been waist deep in it for six months straight."

They seated themselves at a window booth and flagged down the pink-uniformed waitress. A few minutes later they wrapped their numbed fingers around steaming cups of coffee brewed from freshly ground beans, savoring the rich fragrance and the welcome warmth.

"Looking forward to the start of wrestling season, or are you nervous about it?" asked Liz, stirring a spoonful of sugar into her cup.

"A little of both, I think," answered Katie honestly. She took a tentative sip of her coffee, then added more cream. "You should hear all the rules I have to follow." She recited the board's list for Liz.

"Garth was right. They are keeping you on a tight rein." Liz's face bore traces of sympathy.

"Don't talk to me about that man."

"You don't like him?" Liz sounded surprised. "Troy and I had him to dinner the other night, and he gave the impression the two of you were friends. In fact, I wondered if there might me more brewing, at least on his side." She grinned naughtily. "His date was not at all pleased, but I was thrilled. You'd be great for each other."

"We'd kill each other." Katie blew at the steam rising from her cup, then sipped her coffee thoughtfully. "Believe me, if you think he's nursing a secret *tendresse* for me, you're mistaken."

"I know the expression I saw on his face when he talked about you. Garth is definitely interested. You won't find a nicer guy. He is smart, witty, hardworking, and with his looks, especially those wonderful shoulders, not too many women would kick him out of bed on a cold night!" She looked pointedly at Katie.

"Liz, please! I scarcely know the man and, except for his shoulders, what I *do* know I'm not sure I like. He's so irritatingly dogmatic in his opinions, I want to smack him. Sometimes I find myself contradicting him just to disagree even though my own opinions aren't all *that* different or untraditional!''

"Garth's a self-made man. Everything about him is strong," agreed Liz fondly. "Strong opinions, strong emotions, strong loyalties. He can seem abrasive to those who don't know him, who don't realize what enormous odds he's overcome to get where he is today."

"Well he certainly abrades me!" said Katie feelingly.

"Beyond the fact that he opposes you as wrestling coach because you're a woman?"

"No. Mad as that makes me, he has plenty of other opinions that rub me the wrong way," countered Katie, a defensive note in her voice.

"Like what?"

"Family, for one thing. My family is everything to me. You should hear Garth on the subject. His comments are either caustic, cynical or both." Katie frowned, remembering his worst barbs. "And he's got a real burr in his hide about brothers, mine especially. He seems to think that anyone who's part of a close family, anyone who loves and trusts a brother is a naive fool blind to reality. And that infuriates me."

Liz chewed her lower lip pensively. "Cut him some slack, Katie. He didn't grow up with the best family in the world. Or the best brother."

"Don't worry," breathed Katie earnestly. "Even the mere words 'brother' and 'family' have become taboo between us!"

"He wants to get to know you better." Liz paused, as though uncertain of whether or not to say more. "I'm sure he'll explain why he feels the way he does at some point. Don't judge him too harshly until you know the whole story.''

Katie thought of her family, missing them. She thought of the closeness and mutual support. And love. She'd come to suspect that there was more to Garth's attitude than mere cynicism. Liz's remarks confirmed her suspicions. Now, sympathy for the unhappy childhood her friend hinted Garth had suffered welled up in her, warring with the self-protective instincts urging her to keep him at a distance.

''I know him as well as I intend to,'' she said finally. Caution had won out. ''We're too different to be anything more than casual friends, and I'm not even sure we can be that.''

Liz leaned back against the printed cotton damask cushioning the restaurant booth. A speculative gleam twinkled in her chocolate brown eyes. ''But would you kick him out of bed?''

''I just got through telling you...''

''I know what you told me, but sometimes the kind of chemistry between two people you describe usually means the start of an exciting relationship.''

''It's exciting all right,'' said Katie, rolling her eyes. ''We get along for about ten minutes, then we're at each other's throats.''

''Like I said, chemistry!''

''Like *I* said, the combination is too explosive. And truthfully, I don't understand why.'' Her last comment was uttered in a perplexed undertone, more for her own benefit than Liz's.

''What don't you understand?''

Katie groped for the right words. ''I've never had such a...such an *adversarial* relationship with anyone before. You'd never know it from my encounters with Garth, but it's not as though I don't know how to get along with men. All my life my brother has been my best friend, and all of his friends liked me, too. They considered me one of the guys."

"Maybe that's your answer," murmured Liz, hiding a tiny smile behind the rim of her cup.

"What is?"

"Garth doesn't consider you one of the guys."

"You're right. He doesn't. He considers me one of the enemy!"

"That doesn't sound like Garth. Sure you're not being oversensitive?"

"Maybe." Katie sounded doubtful. "All I know is that our views on practically everything are completely opposite..."

A loud knock on the window interrupted her. She looked up and started guiltily. Garth stood outside, a strong wind whipping his dark hair around his face, emphasizing his lean, hard features. His shoulders looked even broader encased in the shearling jacket he wore. It was unbuttoned, and he seemed impervious to the cold. A wide grin softened the rugged planes of his face, then he shivered theatrically, pointing inside and raising his coal black eyebrows questioningly.

Liz nodded eagerly. "Katie, I've got to run. I just remembered at least six vitally important things I have to do." She scooted out of the booth, pulled on her coat and left with a gay wave. "Enjoy the weekend!"

"Don't do this to me, Liz," called Katie.

"Don't do what?" asked Garth curiously, slipping into the booth Liz had vacated.

"Uh, leave me with...the check." Katie drank in Garth's presence, all her senses sharper suddenly, now that he was seated across from her. He seemed too large, too vital to be contained by the narrow confines of the tiny booth. Anticipation hummed along her nerve endings, making her eyes sparkle and her skin glow. She sat up straighter, inexplicably glad that her soft angora sweater displayed her curves. The thick wool looked infinitely touchable, and the soft rose color flattered her.

"You look pretty. Cold weather must agree with you." Garth casually shrugged off his jacket, briskly rubbing his large hands together several times trying to warm them.

"Don't you have gloves?" asked Katie, refusing to acknowledge his compliment, but pleased nonetheless.

"I forgot them at the site. I was in a hurry to get to the bank before it closed." Garth reached for her hands, folding them around his own. His fingers were long, strong-looking and icy cold. "Warm me up?"

"Sure, I'll buy you a cup of coffee." She tried to disentangle her hands from his, but Garth tightened his grasp. A quivering sensation tickled the area around her breastbone at the contact.

"Not exactly what I had in mind." He nodded a greeting to the waitress who brought another cup of coffee at Katie's request. "Still, I have hope. You know the old saying, 'cold hands, warm heart'!"

Katie managed to snatch her hands away, but only because he permitted her to. "*You're* the one with cold hands."

"Want my warm heart, too?"

"I didn't want your cold hands!" She laced her fingers protectively around her own cup. *He's only a man,* she repeated silently to herself. *There is nothing to get so excited about.*

Garth ran the tip of his index finger around the rim of his cup, inhaling the fragrant steam with an appreciative sniff. "This might be the first cup of coffee a woman ever bought me."

"You probably never gave a woman the chance," said Katie tartly, fascinated by the caressing motion of his blunt-tipped finger against the thick ceramic cup. "You'd probably let a woman make you a cup of coffee willingly enough, but I bet you'd scream bloody murder if one ever tried to buy you a cup in a restaurant!" His finger continued its rhythmic circling, and Katie clasped her own cup more tightly.

"Not true. You're the first woman who ever offered. It's kind of a nice feeling, someone wanting to treat you," he said quietly. "Thank you."

"Just drink it before it gets cold."

She was surprised and confused. He seemed sincere. Suddenly, she felt special. Over a simple cup of coffee. Because Garth thought it was a treat. She flicked her braid over her shoulder nervously. Things were getting way out of hand.

Garth raised the cup to his lips and drank deeply. "It's delicious. Strong and hot." He set the cup in the saucer and licked his lips. Katie found the action totally unnerving.

Say something, anything; just say it fast, she told herself. "Maybe there's hope for you yet."

"With you?"

"That wasn't what I meant. Not only are you letting a woman buy you a cup of coffee, you appear to be enjoying the experience."

"Katie, you insist on painting me as a wild-eyed standard bearer for the strident, radical brand of male chauvinism. It simply isn't so!" he said ingenuously, widening his eyes.

"Good one, Garth. That remark drew blood!" Katie laughed at his paraphrase. Opposites they might be, but the man had a wicked sense of humor she couldn't help enjoying.

"It wasn't meant to," he said warmly, clasping her hand across the table. He had working-man's hands—callused, rough and weathered, with small nicks and healing cuts. Yet, despite its texture, Katie felt only gentleness in the hand holding hers.

"'God bless the hands of a working man,'" she murmured half under her breath.

"What's that?" His sharp ears picked up her remark.

"A line from an old song my mom used to sing to my dad when I was small."

"I thought you said once your father was a college professor? That's hardly likely to leave him with working-man's hands," he said disparagingly. "Unless it was your mom's way of needling him about having a soft job?"

"Not at all," said Katie defensively, annoyed by his continued sniping. "After Brian and I were born, my dad used to work construction jobs in the summer. It paid more than teaching summer school, and we needed the money. He'd come home every night for the first few weeks with his hands all torn up with cuts and riddled with thick splinters. My mom used to pick them out, kiss his hands and sing to him. Every night. Every summer.'' Her eyes misted in remembrance of the loving rapport she'd witnessed between her parents as a child.

''Charming,'' he said carelessly, as if he meant the exact opposite.

''I take it back.'' She set her jaw stubbornly. ''There's no hope for you except as my adversary. And probably *not* a friendly one!''

Garth shook his head, laughing softly. ''The fact that I won't indulge your romantic fantasies about family life means nothing. The fact that I know better than to believe blood is thicker than water—especially concerning brothers—means nothing. I think you're just using our conflicting opinions as an excuse to keep me at a distance.'' He leaned forward, lowering his voice as if to tell her a secret. ''We're not as different as you're trying so hard to convince yourself we are.''

''Wrong! We are complete opposites. That's why I'm keeping my distance.'' Katie's heartbeats quickened. Garth's words struck a nerve; one she hadn't even known existed. ''Anyway, I don't need an excuse. I'm here to work, not romp.''

''Can't you do both?'' he queried playfully.

''Probably not in Granby, given the circumstances, and certainly not with you.'' She couldn't risk acknowledging their reciprocal attraction.

''I thought you said there was hope for me?'' His voice was teasing but with a low, sexy quality she imagined was perfect for whispering endearments in the dark. He had a bedroom voice. That's what it was. A bedroom voice.

She had to remind him exactly how different they were as people before things got *irretrievably* out of hand. "You don't think a woman can coach a boy's wrestling team. I do. Remember?"

"So?"

"So, that means you probably have other obnoxious notions I don't agree with."

"A mere difference of opinion makes me ineligible for consideration as romp material?" He feigned shock incredulity. "Katie, Katie," he said shaking his head. "I thought you were more open-minded than that."

"Not when the difference of opinion in question is something along the lines of 'women belong at home, in the kitchen.'"

"That's not the only place I like to find them," he murmured, beginning a caressing motion across her palm with his index finger. He stroked tiny circles on her skin. The movement was hidden from any casual observer by the position of their hands.

His forthright admission bothered her, but not nearly as much as his touch. She was drowning in the sweet pleasure of his touch. Struggling to breathe in steady cadence, she filled her lungs with slow, deep breaths. "And you undoubtedly think the only other place for us is the bedroom!" She was annoyed that she could respond physically to a man with whom she disagreed so strongly.

"The ultimate chauvinist, hmmm?" His callused finger rasped across her skin. She tingled, resenting her response...loving it.

"Right!"

"Wrong! I like women in the kitchen, but only if they want to be there, and only if they can cook. I like them in the bedroom, again, only if they want to be there, and if they're at least willing to learn to...'cook.' I also like them in law, medicine, business, in fact, I like them almost anywhere their individual talents enable them to be. And that includes, but is not limited to, the kitchen or the bedroom!"

Katie wrenched her hand from Garth's grasp, nearly upsetting her still half-full coffee cup. "But it *excludes* coaching a boys' wrestling team, right?"

"I'm afraid so."

"Because you don't think a woman can do the job." Her voice simmered with indignation.

He hesitated. "Because there's a great deal more at stake than you realize."

She folded her arms obstinately across her chest, a resolute expression emphasizing the defiant angle of her forward-thrusting chin. "Then help me realize. From where I'm sitting, it sounds like pure, unmitigated prejudice."

Katie noticed several diners casting surprised looks in their direction and she lowered her voice. "If you really believe everything you've just said about women being able to do whatever their talents enable them to, why are you so opposed to me?" She leaned forward, her voice quietly earnest. "You really don't believe a woman can do the coaching job, do you?"

She knew she was stupid to ask. His answer could only hurt her, but she had to hear his reply. His answer would be the shield she needed to protect herself against the overwhelming strength of his personality and the magnetic attraction that pulled her far too powerfully for her own good. It would help her get Garth out of her mind once and for all. Yet knowing the truth would hurt.

"Do you?" A perverse tenacity made her repeat the question insistently.

"There's a world of difference between *can* and *should*, Katie."

"You're splitting hairs, Garth."

"Am I really? Think about it. I'll grant that on paper you appear well qualified for the job. Your knowledge is extensive, your coaching experience impressive and your background unique. So what? Do you honestly believe that's enough?"

"Yes!" she answered heatedly. "That's as much as any man could bring to the position."

"No, it's not. A man brings a role model and a confidant as well."

"In principle, so do I."

"Katie, don't let your stubborn insistence on principle blind you to reality!" His strong hands clenched into frustrated fists with nothing to do but rest incongruously tranquil on the pink Formica table. "No matter how willing you are to listen, do you seriously believe the boys will confide in you?"

"Once I've gained their trust, I see no reason why they shouldn't." Her words were confidently spoken, but the self-assurance she'd always taken for granted wavered for a moment, the passionate intensity of Garth's verbal assault a powerful brunt.

"About the things that really trouble them?" He laughed, but it was a brittle, hollow sound. "You're being naive again."

"And you're being insulting!" snapped Katie, bristling into rigidly erect posture. "Coaches are uniquely positioned to advise and guide the members of their team. It may take a little longer, but in the end it won't be any different with the boys in Granby than it was with the girls I coached in Colorado Springs."

"Lady, if you believe that, then you know a damn sight less than I originally gave you credit for! A coach is usually someone a boy looks up to and respects, someone whose opinion he values and who has the necessary objectivity that a parent or friend may lack. Above all a coach has to be approachable." Garth's tone was stinging, each comment flaying precious strips off her self-confidence.

"I'm always available to the kids on my team." Her words tumbled over each other in a furious rush to be spoken. "They know from day one that they can call me *anytime*, about *anything*, and be sure that I'll be there for them! Believe me, I know all about approachability."

"Maybe from the *coach's* standpoint, but not in the *boys'* eyes! The issue here isn't only your right to a job for which you may be qualified. There's also the question of the boys' right to have the best coach for them determined on the basis of *their* needs."

Misgivings hit Katie with the force of a powerful blow to her midsection. Her own vague doubts about the wisdom of taking her brother's place as coach suddenly crystallized. The arguments she'd asserted so confidently to others now rang less convincingly in her own ears. She couldn't help but wonder if the claims she'd been making were really as frivolous, vain and selfish as Garth was making them sound.

He pressed his stand. "How comfortable do you think those boys will feel approaching a woman coach, from their unique perspective as *male* adolescents, with problems or questions about sex, girls, drugs, or parents?"

"I'm not sure," admitted Katie miserably.

"Sports are one outlet teenage boys use to test their masculinity. How fair do you think it is to saddle them with a woman coach when doing so leaves them particularly vulnerable to attack from their friends, or teams from other schools, or even from their own self-doubts?"

She had no ready answer. The napkin she'd been twisting in her hands was now a small mound of ragged, pink shreds. Garth had shown her another side to the whole issue. She was ashamed she hadn't thought of it herself.

"I'm going to have to give what you've said some serious thought." She spoke in a soft, low voice. "But nothing can change the fact that I'm going to coach the wrestling team this year. Making sure the boys don't suffer in any way because of it is going to be my top priority." She dug down deep into her psyche, searching for a hidden reservoir of confidence to help convince Garth of her sincerity. "All I can do is my best. Whether that will be good enough remains to be seen. No man could do better, or guarantee more."

Garth drained the last of his now cold coffee. "For everyone's sake, you'd better be right." He slid out of the booth with a pantherish grace, slinging his jacket over his shoulder. "Thanks for the coffee. It was a real treat. See you a week from Monday."

"You plan to observe the first practice?" Katie tried to sound nonchalant, but she knew she'd feel self-conscious her first time out as a wrestling coach. Garth would be a distracting audience.

"I'll be observing as many practices as my schedule permits until I'm...satisfied—" he hesitated just long enough to give her the impression that he was interested in more than her ability as a wrestling coach "—that your skills are equal to the task."

"As liaison for the board," she stated in a flat, uncompromising tone of voice. She had to make him understand that their future encounters would be cool, neutral, and not in any way personal. Definitely not like the fiery encounters they'd had so far.

"Partly as liaison," he agreed in a slow drawl. "And partly because the sight of you working out on the balance beam was the sexiest thing I'd seen in forever. I can't wait to watch you exercise with the wrestling team!"

"No, Garth."

"Yes, Katie," he mocked gently. "You excite me. I think the feeling is mutual." He laid the palm of his hand against the smooth curve of her cheek. She received a shock of static electricity that started an excited current of an entirely different kind running back and forth between them. "See?"

"Your hands are cold."

"There's nothing cold about the excitement that crackles and snaps between us. You're feeling it now, aren't you?" He stroked the velvet soft skin, smiling as he felt her tiny involuntary quivers.

"We're too different." Her tone was tinged with regret as she laid her hand over his for a moment, then pulled away from him. "The things we disagree on...families, brothers, women's roles, they're too fundamental. This afternoon proved that."

"All this afternoon proved is that no difference of opinion in the world is strong enough to override what sizzles between us." His voice was a husky growl. "We're like magnet and iron, hot and cold, good and bad. The very things that make us different attract us to each other. Wouldn't you like to find out how the things that make us *alike* feel?"

The rough timbre of his voice, the confident strength of his powerful body, the latent sexuality that directed each lazy smile, his essential masculinity—everything about this man tempted her. Still, she remembered her delicate position.

"It's not possible, Garth. Things can't get personal between us."

"It's going to get very personal between us, Katie. It's inevitable. I'm looking forward to it." He stroked his middle finger across the seam of her lips, then down over her chin to tilt her head up. "I'm sorry if I hurt your feelings this afternoon. I'm sorry we disagree about your job and about...other things. But I'm not going to let any obstacle get in our way."

He sauntered off with a peculiar, rolling gait Katie found vaguely familiar without being able to pinpoint exactly why. No matter. She ran her fingers across her lips. Garth's electric touch still lingered on her mouth. She was in deep trouble. Yes indeed, she was in deep, probably inextricable trouble. Coaching would begin a week from Monday. She couldn't wait for a week from Monday.

CHAPTER SIX

EVEN THOUGH SHE WAS BONE TIRED, Katie couldn't sleep that night. As she twisted in the sheets, Garth's words turned over and over in her mind. One part of her wanted to follow him down whatever garden path of sensual delight he chose to wander. But the more principled side of her nature intervened, demanding that she make him understand once and for all that a relationship between them was impossible.

There could be no scandal, not in a town as small and conservative as Granby, not with her brother's big break depending on her keeping her job. There could be no compromise of the principles that prevented Katie from becoming involved with a man who wanted to put limits on what she could do because she was a woman.

She'd been so sure when she first came to Granby that what she was doing was right, that she had a lot to offer and a lot to teach the students, both in the classroom and on the wrestling mat. Now the uncertainties she'd experienced when Brian first outlined his scheme were intensified by the potent logic of Garth's arguments. There was no doubt in her mind she had the skills and experience necessary to be a decent wrestling coach. On the other hand, she was swayed by Garth's insistence that the boys on the team needed more than what her technical expertise alone could provide.

Her own concept of a high-school coach's role mirrored Garth's. Maybe at the college or professional level a coach's job was merely to win, to get the best performance out of his team regardless of the cost to each individual. At the high-school level Katie felt a coach owed his team more because each boy counted so much. She was racked by the possibility she might fail the boys in one of the auxiliary areas because she wasn't a man.

And if she wasn't absolutely sure she was right, how could she be sure Garth was wrong? Having acknowledged the merit in his argument, didn't she also have to acknowledge that his opposition to a female wrestling coach wasn't merely an unreasonable prejudice? Or was she simply reaching for an excuse to justify her attraction to the man, to make it right for her to allow a personal relationship to develop between them?

Katie thumped her pillow energetically, then wrapped herself around it, trying to get comfortable. Blast the man anyway! He'd stirred her finely tuned conscience into a maelstrom. She hated doing this kind of tortured analysis over something that originally had seemed so simple—a lark, really. And blast Brian, too, for getting her into this!

A quick peek at the luminous dial on her travel alarm relaxed her features into a mischievous smirk in the dark. At this hour on a Friday night, Brian was generally teaching a new sex kitten the finer points of some wrestling move. Flicking on the bedside lamp, she reached gleefully for the phone intending to dial up the coach's quarters at the U.S. Pan-Am Wrestling camp.

She stopped. No. Not this time. Not when the problem she wanted to discuss was so inextricably intertwined with her feelings for Garth. Those feelings were too new, too jumbled to bring out in the open, even with Brian. They seemed too personal, somehow. For the first time in her life, there was something Katie truly couldn't share with her brother. The realization shocked her.

She and Brian had always felt a strong sense of connection. For twenty-eight years she'd defined herself in terms of being his twin. Until this moment there'd never been a thought she couldn't discuss with him, an opinion she couldn't express to him, or a confidence she couldn't share with him. Even when she was physically absent from him, her sense of being linked to him kept her from feeling alone.

And now, her feelings for Garth had severed that connection. She felt bereft, adrift and uncertain. This was something she had to work out completely on her own. Alone. The realization was painful.

Katie replaced the phone with a small sigh. For the first time in her life, she felt utterly lonely.

"Miss O'Connell!"

Katie let her hand drop from the handle of the teacher's lounge door and turned with a sigh. Two more feet and she would have made it to sanctuary.

"Telephone message." Miss Florence thrust two slips of pink paper into Katie's hand, then marched off down the hall in military cadence without giving her a chance to respond.

"'Miss O'Connell is to meet me at my construction site at noon. Give her directions. Tell her Mr. D'Anno says this is *not* a request. It concerns the wrestling team.'" *Wonderful,* thought Katie dryly, crumpling the paper into a tight ball. *Well, that means no lunch today.* The not-so-faint stirrings of rebellion churned in her stomach. She was tempted to treat Garth's imperious summons with imperious disregard, only he'd baited the hook too well. If his command concerned the wrestling team, there was no way she could refuse him.

Katie looked at the crude map drawn on the second slip of paper and hurried toward her classroom for her coat and purse. According to the directions the site was at least twenty minutes away, and the was already eleven-thirty.

"Where's the fire?" Liz stuck her head in the lounge door, grinning.

"Command performance at Garth's construction site at noon to discuss the wrestling team." Katie started to grimace, then realized in surprise that her true reaction to Garth's order wasn't the irritation she normally felt when *told* to do something. She was actually pleased to have an excuse, any excuse, to see him.

"He's being bossy again, huh?" Liz laughed, a silvery tinkle that always made Katie think of crystal windchimes. "Things must be getting hectic down at the site if he can't even spare the time to come into town. You're not going dressed like that, are you?"

"Why not?" Katie looked down at her wool challis skirt, the soft teal and gray folds flowing just over the tops of her gray leather boots. She pushed up the sleeves of her teal cashmere sweater, enjoying the feel of the soft fibers sliding on her arm. "My down coat is warm."

"I wasn't thinking of the cold. It's still a mess out there. Jeans would be better."

"I haven't the time to change. I've got to be there by noon, and according to this map, my hotel is in the opposite direction from the site." Katie was worried. She'd do a lot for her team. But the new clothes she'd acquired on her spending spree with Brian's charge cards did a lot for *her*. She hated the thought of ruining them.

"Tell you what. My house is on the way. If we hurry, you'll just have time to borrow a pair of my jeans. Just make sure to keep your coat closed so you don't snag that beautiful sweater on any random nails."

Katie breathed a sigh of relief. "Thanks, Liz. I really appreciate this."

"No problem, we're about the same size."

Katie dug her aerobics shoes out of her gym bag by the desk and held them up to her friend. "Good thing I'd planned to work out after school. I'd die, no, I'd kill someone if I scratched these boots."

"So would your brother, considering what he must have paid for them!" Liz said, laughing.

Katie made it to Garth's construction site with a minute to spare. And wearing a pair of the tightest jeans she'd ever wiggled her way into. She liked her jeans snug. The firm rear and decent legs which enabled her to wear them like that seemed a just reward for over fifteen years of practicing gymnastics. But Liz's jeans...Katie sucked in her breath, well, they flaunted every single one of the five pounds she had on the pert brunette.

A flurry of wolf whistles and suggestive comments ended her intention of slipping in to see Garth unobtrusively. Instead, she simply walked on toward the trailer that she hoped was Garth's office, carefully picking her way over lumber, equipment and mud holes. She shivered as the wind bit right through her clothes to the skin.

"Hey, lady, looking for somebody?" A husky voice pealed confidently through the cold, clear air.

"The boss. Seen him around?" she quizzed playfully, turning a bright smile in the direction of Garth's voice. All the stern warnings she'd given herself about keeping her distance from this man were ignored when her eyes lighted on the tall, lean-hipped figure swinging easily toward her.

"You're looking at him." Garth jerked a thumb toward his chest. "Come into the office and get warm. Sun's bright as hell, but it's cold enough to freeze—"

"Anything off anything I'm sure," finished Katie hurriedly to forestall his imagery. Knowing Garth, what he'd been about to say was liable to be colorful, graphic and chauvinistic.

"Coffee? I owe you a cup." He tossed his hard hat on a durable-looking sofa, which together with an oversize metal desk and the swivel chair behind it completed the furnishings, and raked one large hand lazily through his thick, dark hair.

"Thanks." She accepted a heavy red mug from him, then moved toward the sofa, enjoying Garth's smooth, spare movements.

Garth settled into the swivel chair, tilting it back and resting his booted feet on the desk. "Take your coat off. Stay awhile," he invited with a smile.

Katie drew her down coat closer around her, grateful its bulk hid the revealing jeans. "I think I'll keep it on. I'm still cold." But she was getting warmer fast. The man had the kind of broad shoulders and wide chest that were only accentuated, not camouflaged, by his heavy turtleneck and the inevitable plaid shirt.

"Those aren't jeans I see peeking out from your coat, are they?" The swivel chair shot forward and his feet hit the floor with a loud thud as he leaned over the desk. "Give a guy a break. Take off your coat."

Katie's throat constricted. He was too vital, too handsome, too damn everything. Garth. He melted all her resistance, turning it into liquid acquiescence that ran honey-sweet through her veins, softening all her hard edges.

"Please?" he coaxed.

Silvery lights gleamed in his eyes as he let his gaze caress her through the thick down coat. Suddenly, she was suffocating, and her hand came up to drag the zipper slowly down. The action was difficult, like running through molasses. She almost couldn't move her fingers.

In fact, she *couldn't* move her fingers. The zipper was stuck on a fluff of down padding.

Garth moved around the desk to the sofa, sitting close, then leaning forward so that he was even closer. "Allow me."

"That's okay, I can do it."

"Really, it's my pleasure." His breath stirred the wisps of hair escaping her braid, and he brushed a curling strand out of her eyes, tucking it behind her ear. For a moment, his thumb lingered on the sensitive area there, before returning to work the zipper.

No, it was definitely not *his* pleasure. It was *hers*, to have those long, strong fingers moving carefully just inside the coat's neckline, brushing across the soft cashmere of her sweater so that the delicate skin beneath flushed with the desire for more intimate contact. His fingers were gentle and warm, and Katie knew they'd be gentler and warmer if it was her bare skin he was touching. She couldn't speak or protest; she didn't even want to. All she could do was experience the incredible sensation of his featherlight touch.

"There. All done." He drew the zipper down the length of her body.

Well done, mused Katie whimsically. Very well done. His touch almost scorched. "Thanks."

"Believe me, the view is more than enough thanks! Do all your jeans fit this way?"

The jeans. Blast. No wonder she couldn't talk. The stupid things were cutting off her circulation. "These aren't mine. Liz loaned them to me so I wouldn't ruin the clothes I wore to school."

"Funny, I don't remember them looking like that on Liz." His teasing regard made its way back to her face. "They're a perfect fit. She should give them to you."

"And *you* should tell me what's so important to the wrestling team I had to miss my lunch."

Garth picked up the hard hat he'd discarded earlier and pulled it down over Katie's forehead. "Let me show you instead." He opened a small closet, grabbed another hat for himself and, folding Katie's hand into the warmth of his own, led her outside.

They started toward a complex of buildings that appeared to Katie to be perhaps three-quarters of the way complete. The various crews at work watched their progress toward the complex with undisguised interest.

She glared at two men straddling a girder, nodding and grinning in her direction.

"The first man to open his mouth gets one of these two-by-fours across the face," she informed him, pointing to a pile of lumber partially covered by a large tarpaulin.

"You're with me. They wouldn't dare say anything off color." They stopped in front of the complex. "Year round, time-share vacation condos," he explained with pride. "Seventy-two units, all with top-of-the-line carpeting, drapes, furniture and fixtures, and state-of-the-art appliances. Completely solar heated, sauna and jacuzzi in each unit, and the best building materials available used throughout."

"These will be gorgeous when they're finished, Garth." Katie couldn't help but be impressed. Painstaking care, thoughtful planning and meticulous attention to detail were evident everywhere. The setting itself, nestled near the banks of Grand Lake and surrounded by evergreen forest, would be worth whatever price Garth demanded. "But what does this complex have to do with my wrestlers?"

"There'll be a community center with rooms for meetings or parties, tennis courts, stables, horse trails, a nine-hole golf course and an Olympic-size heated pool with an air-supported bubble top that comes off in summer for outdoor swimming. The water source is one of several hot springs located on the site. The others will be maintained for use in their natural state."

He spoke faster as he shared his plans for the project. "All building and landscaping has been designed according to ecological principals and with environmental protection the top priority. When I'm done, this place will not only be one of the most luxurious projects built in the last ten years, it will also be an example of how mountain recreation areas can be developed in harmony with nature."

"My wrestlers, Garth," reminded Katie, astounded by the scope of his project. "Where do they fit in?"

His tone was low, impassioned. "I can make a difference in the future of mountain development if I bring this project in on time and according to specs. I need apprentices to take over some of the grunt work so my experienced crews can concentrate on the job itself. Think your wrestlers might be interested in part-time jobs with me? I pay well, it would be great experience for them, and I'd work their hours around wrestling practice and school."

"Are you kidding? Every boy on that team will jump at the chance!"

Garth shook his head. "Greg Jenkins turned me down flat when I saw him in the drugstore the other day. He wouldn't even put the word out to the other wrestlers."

"I'll mention it to the other boys at our first wrestling practice," she assured him.

"I particularly want Greg," persisted Garth. "He's the team leader. If he comes, they all will."

A new thought occurred to Katie. "You'll take special precautions for their safety, won't you?"

"I take special precautions for *all* the men on my job sites. Don't worry." He grinned wryly. "Right now, the best precaution I can take is getting you out of here. You're becoming quite a distraction. Distracted men have accidents."

"Annoyed women *cause* accidents!" she retorted, stepping around a pile of scrap material. "Don't let my team pick up any bad habits from your crew."

"Word of honor," he promised solemnly. "I'll handle their instruction personally.

THE DAY OF THE FIRST wrestling practice dawned bright and early. Too early, as far as Katie was concerned. The questions to which she still had no definitive answers had kept her awake most of the night. Now the moment of truth had arrived. She resolved simply to do the best coaching job she knew how, keep an open mind about Garth and apply the under-eye concealer with a heavy hand.

Knowing that a good breakfast would go a long way toward curing the lethargy that lack of sleep had induced, Katie ordered the works from room service and stumbled toward the bathroom, hoping a long, hot shower would do its part in her revival. She'd just finished plaiting her French braid, when a knock at the door accompanied by a cheery "Room service, Miss O'Connell!" and the ringing of her telephone simultaneously demanded her attention. She rapidly donned clean underwear, then slid into her short robe.

"Come in," she called out, flinging herself across the bed on her stomach to answer the phone with a breathless "Hello."

"My God, you sound almost cheerful! Don't you realize what time it is? You're supposed to be snarling and swearing." Brian's cocky humor fell on Katie's ears like balm on a wound.

"I think you may have the wrong number. Who's calling, please?" she asked with courteous formality, waving in the bell boy without turning around.

"Katie? It's me, your twin."

Katie absently patted the bed so the bell boy would know where to put her tray. "Do you mean the one who hasn't called me in six weeks? The one with whom I've had no communication the entire time I've been stuck in Granby doing him a favor?"

"I sent you two postcards!" he protested.

"And very effusive they were, too. One said 'Love and miss you,' and the other one said 'How's it going, Boo-Boo?' You didn't even sign your name!" Katie felt the bed give way under the weight of a heavily laden breakfast tray, and she reached over for one of the two croissants she'd ordered to go with her sausage, eggs and fresh fruit cup, after signing the bill she found there.

"Don't nag long-distance," pleaded Brian. "I've missed you like crazy. How *is* it going?"

Katie heard the door close softly, and silently commended the unobtrusive efficiency of the hotel staff. She munched the flaky croissant, drank some hot coffee, then scooped a forkful of sausage and eggs into her mouth. Flexing her toes, she languorously crossed and uncrossed her ankles in the air. "Let's just say I'm thinking of all the broken gingerbread trim you promised to fix on the house I want to buy, and I'm smiling. Broadly."

"Shi..."

"Don't say it. My team will run laps for swearing."

"Thank God I'm not on your team!"

"Really, with your garbage mouth you'd spend all your time running instead of wrestling." Katie spooned some fresh mixed fruit into her second croissant and took a blissful bite.

"I take it you've settled in at Granby and done your usual job of making everyone love you?" His question was teasingly, pridefully affectionate, as though the answer was a forgone conclusion.

"Not quite. As a matter of fact, if the townspeople had a place to hide the body, chances are strongly in favor of your becoming an only child."

"I can be on the next plane, Katie," said Brian, suddenly serious.

"Don't you dare. I'm counting on my half of your bonus money when the U.S. wins that gold medal." She recognized the protectiveness in his voice, and smiled around a succulent mouthful of fresh strawberries. Trust Brian to turn her life upside down with a crazy stunt like this, then at the first sign of trouble for her, rush in like the cavalry.

"I thought you said I could keep the entire bonus."

"That was before I got a look at the guy who donated the money to improve the wrestling program."

"A real gorilla?"

"A real hunk," said Katie dryly. "The school board made him their liaison with me."

"Is that drool I hear you wiping from your mouth?" asked Brian, chuckling ribaldly.

"It's strawberries," responded Katie airily.

"Ri-i-ight. I might have to make a special trip out to see this guy. He's probably got shoulders like King Kong."

"Conan the Barbarian," she corrected. "But I won't quibble over a few feet."

"Anything going on you'd like to tell me about?" Brian's tone conveyed equal parts of concern and discomfort. "Anything...interesting?"

"'Interesting'?"

"You know exactly what I mean, Katie. Watch out for this guy. You've waited a long time...what I'm trying to say is...guys like that are usually all muscle and no tenderness...hell! Just be careful..."

"I don't want to talk about it, Brian," she interrupted impatiently. They'd been having similar versions of this conversation for a long time. Listening to her brother squirm over the warnings he felt compelled to give her had always been the best part of such talks. Now, his discomfort made her uncomfortable.

Katie's feelings for Garth, confused feelings she wasn't sure she could verbalize, even for her diary, were intensely personal. And her sex life, or lack thereof, was no longer a subject she could discuss with Brian. Once more she felt a painful psychic rending separate them.

"If you're thinking along the lines I suspect you may be, you could get hurt," he warned.

"Don't worry, Brian. He may be a hunk, but he's also one of those die-hard chauvinists I refuse on principle to fall for."

"He got on your good side right away, did he? Good. That should be some protection. You'll be there until June; that's a long time."

"I know," she said wistfully. Maybe too long where her feelings for Garth were concerned. They seemed to be growing. Independently of her strictures. And their tender nature absolutely refused to be affected by her better judgment.

"You know, Katie, I could probably swing a weekend off in a few weeks. Care to hit the slopes at Steamboat with me?"

"Maybe we'd end up in Granby for dinner?" She managed to suppress her laughter. Just barely. Brian at his most transparent was convinced he was his most devious.

"Great idea!" he enthused. "Maybe we'll run into Conan, and you can introduce me."

"'Maybe'?" she asked archly. "Are you bringing your high-intensity search lamp and the bloodhounds?"

"Have I been found out?"

"Definitely," replied Katie firmly. "You're on the wrong track about this man, Brian."

"Time will tell."

"Time! Brian, I have got to run this minute, or I'll be late for school. Thanks for calling. I love you."

"I love you too, Boo-Boo Bear," answered Brian quietly. "See you soon."

"'Bye." Katie replaced the receiver, popped one last orange slice in her mouth, and rolled off the bed.

She walked straight into Garth's waiting arms.

"You! How did you get in here?" Quickly, she pulled her short robe more tightly around her.

"Boo-Boo, is that any kind of reception for an acknowledged hunk?" He locked his arms around Katie, drawing her against the firm strength of his broad chest.

"If you don't let go of me, I'm going to tell you exactly what substance I think you're a hunk of!" She strained against the arms holding her prisoner, but struggle was useless. Garth was as strong as he looked.

"Tsk-tsk. You wouldn't want to fine *yourself* laps around the football field, would you?"

"Okay, you've got what you came for. You've eavesdropped on a *private* conversation with my brother..."

"Your brother." Garth made it sound like a vulgar epithet. "Two postcards and one phone call in *six weeks*? Tell me some more about how much your *brother* loves you."

"Done the peeping Tom bit..."

"Sounds to me like once he conned you into saving his miserable hide, he left you on your own to sink or swim without a whole lot of regard for which outcome it would be."

"*And* copped a feel; now would you *please* get out of here so I can get dressed?"

"What's wrong? Can't those sentimental fantasies about your wonderful brother stand a little objective scrutiny?" The sneer that curled around Garth's narrowed lips was hard to ignore.

Do not rise to the bait, she commanded herself. *Brothers are this man's blind spot, it's nothing personal. Ignore his silly remarks.* "I don't have the time to stand around and shoot holes in your 'objective' observation. You're going to have to accept it on faith that it would be painfully easy to prove how wrong you are about my brother.''

"I don't take anything on faith. Start talking.''

"I can't be late today. It would be just like Mr. Penrose to fire me for dereliction of duty before I even start as wrestling coach. Or did you forget that the first wrestling practice is today?'' Embarrassment shortened and sharpened Katie's tone. She was going to curl up and die. Why did she have to say all those things to Brian? And why did Garth have to hear her say them? If it was the last thing she did, she was going to buy a long, heavy bathrobe. With feet. And a hood. And she was never going to order from room service again.

"No, I didn't forget.'' Garth relaxed his hold on Katie, but he continued to confine her in a loose grip. "And I didn't come by to sneak a peek, or cop a feel, as you so indelicately put it. Garbage mouths must run in your family! And you seem like such a ladylike little thing for all your tomboy tendencies.''

Again, Katie heard that slightly sarcastic emphasis on the word family. It nettled her into a sharp response. "I especially hate it when men refer to women as 'things,' ladylike, little or otherwise!''

"You know us die-hard chauvinists.''

"What are you doing here?'' Obviously Garth had no intention of releasing her, nor of doing anything but maximizing her evident discomfort over the fact that he'd overheard her conversation with Brian.

"I brought you something by way of a peace offering.''

"What?'' asked Katie warily, drawing back as far as she was able against the steely strength of the arms encircling her.

"A little good-luck charm, in honor of your first day as wrestling coach. Heaven help us all!" he murmured in an undertone, before bending down to brush her lips lightly with his own.

A joyous warmth filled her at the soft contact. His lips were soft and gentle. The kiss was over in the wink of an eye, and Katie hated herself for wanting it to continue.

"That was very nice. I appreciated it. Thank you." She tried to think of all the most boring ways she knew to get her blood pressure back to normal, but not even the prospect of beginning a Trollope novel and reading every single word was enough to slow the rapid beating of her heart after Garth's light kiss. "You can leave any time now."

He laughed, and it was a low, seductive sound. "The kiss wasn't for you. It was for me." He dropped his arms, abruptly releasing her. She stepped back in reflex, though her instincts were urging her forward, toward Garth. "*This* is for you." He picked up a small china pot with a tiny plant inside. It had soft green leaves, and one delicate, star-shaped flower bloomed in pale, lavender-blue splendor.

"Oh, how lovely," she breathed, reaching out to take the glazed pot. It was a deep periwinkle. "What kind of a flower is this?"

"Don't tell me a paragon like yourself doesn't recognize the state flower?" he teased. "That's a columbine. Despite its fragile appearance, it's amazingly tenacious. I found it growing in a protected niche between two rocks over the weekend, alive and thriving in spite of the light dusting of snow we got Saturday. Somehow its feisty nature reminded me of you." He stroked down the line of her jaw with his knuckles, leaving a tingling trail in its wake. "Good luck, Katie girl."

She looked up, her thoughts a complex confusion. Joy and appreciation shone on her face with an almost painful intensity. There was something else there in her expression too. Gold flecks sparkled in her eyes, warming their hazel color until they seemed to glow. "Thank you, Garth."

"You're welcome." His tone was gruff, almost as if he was embarrassed.

He'd done this for her, she marveled. Seen the columbine, picked it, chose the darling little pot in a beautifully complimentary color. Something was wrong. Some realization was tugging at her memory. He picked it, picked it...*he picked it*! The warmth of her eyes became a blazing fury of indignation. "You picked this!" she accused, not quite able to bring herself to throw the pretty thing at him. She cast around for a substitute, her eyes lighting on the remains of her fruit cup.

"Don't even think it!" warned Garth, following the line of her sight.

"There's a *$500* fine for picking columbines in this state, Mr. D'Anno, and another $500 fine for having picked columbines in one's possession. This is a $1,000 good luck charm I am holding, Mr. D'Anno, and *I'm* the one who's going to end up paying the fines!" The gory details of the Lives of the Saints flashed through Katie's mind as she contemplated a suitable way to murder Garth.

The twitching around his lips that she'd learned meant imminent and uncontrollable laughter on his part began once more. "I can always tell when you're mad at me, Katie. You immediately revert to calling me 'Mr. D'Anno' in a voice I'm sure you intend to be prim, but which never quite makes it; that little touch of fury always spoils it!"

Deep, booming, irritatingly fractious laughter filled the room with sound the way the bright, after-snow, Colorado sun filled the room with light. His unchecked chortles ignited the besieged temper held sorely in check for six long weeks.

"Out, Mr. D'Anno, I'm warning you. I am not a nice person when I lose my temper. My ire is going to reach critical mass in seconds, and when it does, so help me, I'm not even going to try to control myself!" Her fists began clenching and unclenching at her sides.

"Relax, Katie girl." Garth's voice was soothing and smooth as hot caramel melting on a sundae. "I dug the whole plant up, but only after I'd called a friend of mine in the forestry service for permission."

"You must have some clout if they let you *dig up* the state flower," she retorted, mollified in spite of herself.

"More like a quid pro quo. I promised to scatter a couple of hundred dollars' worth of columbine seeds next spring," he informed easily.

"Then I can keep it?"

"Of course, I'm flattered that it means so much to you." Garth moved toward the door, then turned back toward Katie, a confident smile once more enhancing the handsome planes of his face. "Great view earlier, by the way, and *cute* outfit. Wear it for me again some time? Now that I know what a hunk you think I am, that is."

"Out this minute!" ordered Katie, pointing toward the door, her equilibrium restored. Garth had to be the most irritating, contradictory, appealing...hunk of man she'd ever met. Not even Brian got under her skin the way Garth did, or made her laugh so much. Or made her so blasted mad!

"I'm gone! See you this afternoon." He opened the door and ducked out with amazing speed.

Katie stroked a gentle finger over one soft petal, then dressed and dashed off to class, a lavender-blue columbine in a tiny, periwinkle china pot tucked carefully into her canvas gym bag. She would put Garth's gift on her desk at school.

CHAPTER SEVEN

BY THREE-FIFTEEN THAT AFTERNOON, Katie was more than ready to coach her first wrestling practice. The tense, edgy uncertainty of the week before had melted away, leaving behind a firm determination to make things work out. She stroked the delicate petals of the columbine, gracing the corner of her desk, for luck, then grabbed her canvas bag and strode down the hallway toward the gym. Thinking of the small addition to the uniform Garth had suggested a couple of weeks ago, she felt the beginnings of a mild anxiety attack.

He'd probably say something nasty and scathing, but realistically he couldn't do anything about it since she'd followed his instructions to the letter. She laughed aloud, swinging her bag. Too bad for him; Katie O'Connell was ready to take on the world. Or at least Granby.

Running across the gym, still empty of wrestlers, Katie had a moment's panic that none of the boys would come out for the sport this year. She descended the stairs to the girls' locker room two at a time. They'd come; they *had* to. After checking to see her hair was securely braided, she slipped quickly into a thin pair of burgundy plastic sweatpants and gold T-shirt. Maybe she'd score a few points with the team by wearing the school colors.

Brian had discovered plastics in college about the same time he discovered that his fondness for pasta was totally incompatible with his need to make weight during wrestling season. He'd worn them during work-outs when he needed to sweat off a few extra pounds. Plastics resembled parachute material, lightweight and durable. Katie knew they'd be less cumbersome than regulation sweatpants.

She wound the small addition to her practice clothing in her towel, then, anticipation beating a staccato rhythm in her brain, gave the door to the gym an enthusiastic push with the palm of her hand. Garth was standing just inside. Then she saw the boys standing in the center of the gym. Their uncompromisingly hostile expressions almost floored her.

Animosity emanated from them, striking her with an almost palpable force. For a few seconds she recoiled protectively, then a cold, creeping fury wound itself around her better sense, and the trembling that warned her friends to tread carefully around her temper began. She was not about to be intimidated by a group of teenage boys, no matter how surly or uncooperative.

Katie squared her shoulders and walked to the center of the gym with the confident gait gymnasts use to approach their apparatus. Head held high, back arched proudly, she moved with an elegant grace that highlighted her body's lean strength. The effect her stance had on judges was well-known in gymnastic circles. Now her team would learn it meant "watch out," because the first boy to mouth off was going to bear the full brunt of a fully justified righteous anger that had been building for weeks.

"Gentlemen, welcome. Before we get started, let's clear up a few administrative details." Her tone was curt, each word clipped. She gestured toward Garth with a forceful sweep of her hand. "I'm sure Mr. D'Anno needs no introduction. He'll be attending practice and accompanying us to meets as his schedule permits. Make him welcome when you see him."

Garth moved closer to Katie, nodding amiably at the scowling boys in acknowledgment of her introduction. He leaned down to whisper in her ear. "Cracking the whip right from the start, hmmm?" he murmured in an undertone. Before she had a chance to reply, he moved away in the direction of the bleachers.

He pulled a newspaper out of his back pocket and proceeded to read it, apparently oblivious to the tense undercurrents of teenage challenge thickening the air. Katie could have kissed him for his sensitivity. She wanted to kiss him period. That was the problem. Against her better judgment, and against every principle that denounced what she knew to be his 'type,' she liked the man himself.

She glanced at him from under lowered lashes. He held the newspaper between both hands, leaning forward to rest his forearms on his thighs. The position only emphasized the breadth and strength of his upper torso. She didn't dare let her mind wander farther down his body than that. A wise woman knew her limitations. She turned her attention back to her team.

"We all know each other pretty well already from math classes. Greg, I'm glad to see you at practice."

"Is *he* going to be here every day?" asked Greg, nodding in Garth's direction, his expression as surly as his tone.

"If you're lucky he will be," shot back Katie, impatient with the boy's attitude, and angry on Garth's behalf. "Mr. D'Anno made a very generous donation to our wrestling program. Now, he's showing his interest in each of you by the even more generous gift of his time."

"You want us to write him a thank-you note?" Greg said, smirking.

"A simple handshake and a sincere 'thanks' will be fine." Katie set her lips in a thin line. Greg was pushing the limits, as if taunting Garth to respond. "Mr. D'Anno has also offered an apprenticeship on his construction project out near Grand Lake to any interested wrestler. The pay is excellent, and he'll work the hours around wrestling practice and school. I'm sure you all realize what an incredible opportunity that is, especially in terms of experience. The plan has my full support, and I hope many of you will take advantage of it."

She looked at each boy in turn, but not one of them met her eyes. "Now, administrative detail number two is to get a few rules out of the way. Why don't we take a seat on the bleachers for a minute?" Katie strode over, choosing a seat a few feet from Garth.

Garth looked up and smiled, then went back to reading his newspaper, seemingly unconcerned. Even so, Katie could tell she had his absolute, if surreptitious, attention. About half the boys had followed her, seating themselves around her. The other half, led by Greg Jenkins, remained in the center of the gym, identically truculent expressions smeared across their faces. Katie knew the trial by insubordination was on.

"The third administrative detail is that when I say move," she began in a pleasant, well-modulated tone addressed to the boys around her, *"you move it!"* She permitted her voice to raise by several decibels and whipped her head around to fix a steely glare at the group still standing. The boys deferred to Greg, who returned Katie's look with an insolent one of his own. The others quickly followed suit.

Katie rose slowly, walking over to stand in front of Greg. It was one of those times when she most wished to be half a foot taller than her tiny five foot three.

"Sit down, Greg." Her voice was firm, but low. The gym was as silent as a church on a weekday.

"My dad says I don't have to take orders from a girl wrestling coach!"

Katie could tell he wasn't quite sure of standing his ground in the face of her show of strength. "If you don't plan on taking direction from the wrestling coach, what are you doing here?"

"I'm the captain of the team. They do what I say." He jerked his thumb at the other boys with a belligerent air.

"If they want to play on *my* wrestling team, they do what *I* say. Now, are you here for practice, or aren't you?"

"I guess." He answered her with the enthusiasm of a spy compromising national security.

"You're the heavyweight, right, Greg?" asked Katie conversationally.

"Yeah."

"Ever win the state championship in your weight class?" A little preliminary research had given her the answer, but like Brian always said, "get their attention, *then* tell them what you have to say."

"Nope. What's it to you?" His defensiveness was apparent to Katie.

"Would you like to?"

The boy gave a derisive snort. "I don't have a chance with you as a coach."

Katie swallowed a sharp reprimand. There must be something in the water besides the fabled Rocky Mountain purity. Every single male she had so far encountered in Granby had that same cocky, aggressive attitude. If she could control her almost Pavlovian antagonism to it, maybe she could make it work for her team's advantage. A little aggressiveness in a wrestler was a good thing. So long as it wasn't directed at the coach.

"Anyone in this room ever win a state championship in any sport?" Katie looked around at the boys, then casually began walking toward the bleachers. Unconsciously, some of the boys began following her before they realized they were doing so. She suppressed a triumphant grin when they stopped, then continued on toward the bleachers, as if realizing that once they'd committed themselves in one direction, they would look foolish if they turned around and went back. Greg Jenkins was left standing alone in the center of the gym. Katie ignored him.

"Not one person in this room has won a state championship?" She saw the boys exchanging perplexed expressions before shaking their heads. From the other end of the bleachers Garth winked and nodded his approval. "Well, I have. Two, as a matter of fact. True, my trophies were in gymnastics, but the qualities it takes to win a trophy in any sport are pretty much the same. And let me tell you, athletic ability is only part of it." She was gratified to see that at least she had their attention, though their expressions were still skeptical. "Anybody have any ideas about what those qualities are?"

"It doesn't matter what they are. You can't help us get them! We need a real coach for that." Greg Jenkins chimed in as if on cue, as infuriatingly arrogant as Garth D'Anno at his best, or rather, his worst.

Katie pinned him with an uncompromising stare. "Greg, you have to make a decision. Either you're on this team, in which case you better move your tail over here with the rest of us; or you're off the team, in which case you have to go home. I'll wait about three seconds for you to decide."

"I'll stay...for today." He sauntered over and sat down.

"Not good enough, Greg. We have to be able to count on you every day, not just when you feel like it. That's what being part of a wrestling team is all about. Sure, you go out there and compete individually, but the score is a team score. Everyone has to put out 110 percent of their best effort if we want to win any meet, let alone the state championship."

"Like, you really have 110 percent to give!"

"Greg, you multiply 110 percent by the number of boys on this team, and that's how much *I* have to give!" she assured him earnestly. "I can teach you as much as you can learn, but the most important quality you'll need to win that state trophy is commitment."

She paused, took a deep breath and continued. "Today I want a commitment from each of you to stick together, help each other, learn from each other and trust me to do well by you. You give me that commitment, and mine to you is this, by the end of the wrestling season, whether we win the team trophy or not, each one of you will have become a damn good wrestler—much better than you are right now."

Katie looked at each boy in turn, letting them consider her words. Finally, she walked down the bleachers to stand in front of them. "Will you each give me your hand on it?"

"We didn't want a woman coach!" Greg's frustration tugged at the sleeves of Katie's sympathy. Her concern flowed out from her in unrestrained waves. She'd been in Greg's position, wanting something so badly she could taste it, only to have fate and circumstances intervene to deprive her of it.

Her expression softened, and when she spoke, her voice was gentle. "Things don't always work out the way you want in life, Greg. Sometimes, all that matters is what you have to work with. This year, you have me, and I don't think one person in this room is stupid enough to give up wrestling without giving me a chance." She turned questioning eyes on the boys seated around her. None of them spoke, or nodded, but none of them were walking out, either.

"Even those of you who cut out of my math class the first week of school aren't that stupid, and believe me, when I'm done making you run extra laps for that, you're going to feel pretty stupid!" Katie smiled at the boys in comradely fashion, then held out her hand. "Come on, Greg. Be a good leader; that's the captain's job. Give me your hand on it."

Greg looked uneasy. The other boys didn't move. They sat quietly and just watched him, waiting. Even Garth had abandoned his pretense of reading to regard the tableau being played out on the gym floor. Finally, Greg shuffled over to where she stood. "I don't think you'll be much of a coach, but okay." He took Katie's proffered hand limply.

"You just watch me, Greg." She spoke confidently, shook his hand firmly and slapped him on the back. One by one, the other boys descended, coming forward to shake Katie's hand. She gave each boy a firm handshake and a slap on the back, the small action taking on ritual significance. She was peripherally aware of Garth, but didn't dare break the tenuous rapport she'd established with her team to meet his gaze.

"All right. Let's get the rules straight. Be on time for practice. No swearing. No smoking or drinking, it's bad for your health, not to mention illegal at your age. And if I catch anyone taking drugs of any kind, that person better have a prescription from his family doctor in his hand to show me. No one gets below a C+ average in any class or he's off the team until his grades improve. Understood?"

The boys rolled their eyes at each other. The gesture pleased Katie; she could sense in it the first faint stirrings of team spirit. "And most importantly, no skipping class." Katie gave them all a wide smile. She was rewarded by several sheepish grins and bowed heads. "Any questions? No? Then let's get to work."

"I thought we were supposed to wear practice singlets...Coach."

"That's right." Katie repressed a smile at the way Greg almost choked on the title.

"Then where's yours?"

Katie unfurled her towel. "Right here." Holding up the burgundy singlet she'd "borrowed" from Brian before leaving Colorado Springs, she waved it defiantly in Garth's direction when his head snapped up at her remark.

Ignoring him, Katie slithered into the one piece wrestling garment, pulling it on over her plastic sweat pants and T-shirt. The singlet had a low U-neck, a deep V-back and was held up by two narrow straps over the shoulders. Made of stretchy nylon, the garment hugged Katie's slender curves snugly, outlining the gently rounded breasts she'd always wished were larger, flaring in at her small waist, and easing smoothly over her slim hips before ending halfway down her thighs. She shrugged several times to get the fit right, and looked up to see Garth coming toward her, a murderous expression on his face.

"Gentlemen, get the wrestling mats out of the store-room, and set them up at the far end of the gym," said Katie calmly. Her team moved away to do her bidding, and she turned to intercept Garth, an equally murderous expression on her own face.

"Garth, before you say one word, I want to make one point very clear. Don't you ever come stomping over to reprimand me in the middle of practice, or countermand my authority with my team. If you have something to say, you raise your hand, or *very politely* ask to speak to me in the hall. Understood?"

Katie spoke in a low voice, but indignation and outrage emanated from her.

"Agreed," he bit out.

"Very well. What's your problem?"

"I said no singlet, Katie." Garth made his statement flatly, his own anger at her seeming disobedience coming through clearly. Katie guessed it was simmering at nearly boiling point slightly below his surface calm.

"You said nothing about wearing a singlet *over* the uniform you specified. If anything, I have on more clothing than you suggested, only now I have freedom of movement as well." Katie demonstrated her point by taking a tumbling run across the hardwood floor, executing a trio of perfect back handsprings.

"That singlet outlines every curve on your body. You're asking for trouble, if not from the boys, then from their parents."

"No one can say anything about my wearing a singlet this way, Garth. It's perfectly appropriate. Besides, many *male* wrestling coaches wear them this way." Katie moved a few inches away from the growing anger, mingled with frustration she saw reflected in the glittering silver mirrors Garth's eyes had become.

"And we both know you're not above threatening a sex discrimination suit to get your own way, don't we?" He seemed ready to reach out and shake her when the boys came trooping back into the gym, halting when they saw Garth and Katie standing so close together. "Wear the singlet for now, *Coach O'Connell*, but we'll discuss the matter after practice. You're not off the hook yet, so help me!"

"We'll see, *Mr. D'Anno*, we'll see." Katie shot her retort at Garth's back, unable to ignore the fact that his shoulders looked even broader from that angle. Or maybe, she pondered, it was just that his hips were so lean.

As she watched him walk away from her, she was struck once more by a sense of familiarity. She knew there was something about him she recognized; she just hadn't been able to place it yet. No matter, she would. As Brian had reminded her, she had until June.

Moving to the far end of the gym, she directed the placement of the thick, gray wrestling mats and started the exercises of her first wrestling practice.

"That was quite a workout." Garth pointed sympathetically to the boys straggling silently, fatigued, and considerably chastened, in the direction of the locker room. They'd come up to him after practice in small groups of two and three, offering an awkward handshake and a diffident "thanks." A fair number had even accepted his job offer. But not Greg. He'd made a point of heading straight for the showers, ignoring Garth's attempt to engage him in conversation. "Those poor kids did everything but jump through hoops. You worked them pretty hard."

"They're young and strong; they'll live. I needed to find out the level of each boy's skill."

He grinned. "Sure you weren't exacting a little vengeance for the past few weeks of hell they've put *you* through?"

"We-ell, I admit I enjoyed sweating those cocky attitudes out of them, but I really was trying to determine where each boy needs the most help." Her earlier irritation with Garth had disappeared. She mopped her face and neck with her towel, then walked over to the drinking fountain. Garth followed, holding the faucet handle for her while she drank her fill.

"I owe you an apology, Katie," he said quietly.

"You owe me a million!" she teased, dipping her fingers in the arc of water and flicking a few drops in his face. "If this is about your near tirade at the beginning of practice, forget it. It probably looked like I was flouting orders, but I wasn't. Not merely for the sake of flouting them, anyway."

"Really?" Garth cocked his eyebrows in a droll fashion, his tone dry. "It looked amazingly like you were waving a red flag in front of a bull."

Katie laughed, a tinkling trill that subsided on a more serious note. "Okay, I'll admit to that, but truly, that wasn't the reason I wore the singlet." She seated herself on one of the bleachers, breathing deeply, enjoying the sense of tired well-being she always felt after a strenuous workout. "A coach has to walk a fine line between establishing the psychological distance from his team which permits him to coach them, and fostering the sense of identity which lets them accept his authority."

"Katie, I hate to disillusion you, but not even wearing a singlet to practice is going to convince those kids you're 'one of the boys'!" Garth snapped one of the straps on her singlet lightly for emphasis.

"It's not supposed to. Wearing the singlet reinforces my position as their coach. It says we're all at practice for the same reason...wrestling." She brushed his fingers off her shoulder, then gave him a meaningful look.

"That's pretty subtle psychology."

"Don't underestimate the power of symbols. Uniforms are for the purpose of unifying a team. I can't place myself outside that unity and expect to inspire the same respect for my authority, or the same acceptance for what I want to teach them."

Garth considered her words, then nodded. "Okay. The singlet stays. But do me a favor?"

"If I can," she equivocated.

He signed. "Don't surprise me with any other additions, or deletions, from the uniform we've agreed upon." His long-suffering look became a sly smile. "Watching you exercise is still the sexiest thing I've ever seen. I can just barely stand it, dressed as you are now." He ran his thumb under the strap of her singlet, gently caressing her shoulder through the thin T-shirt. "I make no guarantees about my self-control if you show off any more of your body!"

He twisted the stretchy, nylon strap around his thumb, drawing her body to within inches of his own. For a moment Katie thought, even hoped he would kiss her, but he only ruffled a few curly wisps of hair around her face with his breath, then rose and strode purposefully out.

She leaned back against the bleachers and exhaled slowly. The man was trouble. Deep, *definitely* inextricable trouble. And she was very much afraid the cost of wanting him would be her principles.

CHAPTER EIGHT

KATIE GLANCED AT the large, round clock over the basketball hoop in the gym. It was four o'clock and there was still no Garth. He'd quickly become a familiar sight at practice since that first day, and her wrestlers now took his presence in stride.

Not that such a hunk of male animal was a sight *she* ever expected to be able to take in stride, Katie mused ruefully. Indeed, the almost daily appearance of Garth's lean, lithe, hard-muscled proportions could best be described as stirring. The few times he'd missed practice, like today apparently, Katie had been annoyed to discover she felt keenly bereft of his presence.

Katie sensed his eyes constantly upon her during practice, ever watchful. Afterward, he would tease her about working the kids too hard, or sometimes offer a carefully respectful suggestion, which, considering he knew nothing about wrestling, demonstrated surprisingly shrewd insight. Even more surprising was the fact that she'd come to honestly welcome his comments. Well, most of them anyway. He'd thought some of her flexibility and balance drills were ridiculous, only he'd phrased his criticisms more pithily.

"They looked like a bunch of goddamned cranes!" he'd exploded after the third day of practice when

Katie had coached the team in an exercise designed to help them find and maintain their center of gravity for minutes at a time. "How the hell is *that* going to turn them into better wrestlers?"

"Garth, you've seen them. They move like their feet are glued flat to the floor," she stated baldly. "There isn't a boy on that team who doesn't need to develop a better sense of balance. They've got to be instinctive and quick by the time they start competing in matches, otherwise when they shoot their moves they're going to fall flat on their faces. Wrestling doesn't just have to do with strength. It's about agility, speed, balance and flexibility."

"They need to be learning *moves*, Katie, not standing around on one leg with one leg stretched out behind them and their arms flailing around like airplane wings in a storm," he'd protested, flapping his arms in mocking demonstration.

"Tell you what," she'd said evenly, rising up delicately on the ball of her right foot. "Why don't you come over here and try to pull me off balance?"

She smiled, remembering how Garth had come at her suddenly, pulling her right arm forcefully. She'd merely rotated her weight, dipped her left shoulder and recovered her balance. He'd been surprised, and tried again several times to unbalance her, coming at her from all angles. Eventually, he'd succeeded; she'd toppled over, but not before her point had been made.

"Okay, I understand what you think this will accomplish," he'd admitted grudgingly. "But I still say they looked like a bunch of goddamned cranes!"

He'd walked her to her hotel that day, after she'd showered and changed, and it seemed the most natural thing in the world that they should continue their discussion about wrestling over deep-dish apple pie in the cozy hotel parlor. It seemed even more natural that their conversation would range wider, covering a broad selection of topics before the last bit of pie and ice cream had been consumed. Of course, by that time it was the dinner hour, and Garth had offered her a meal in the hotel's excellent restaurant.

Over dinner—thick, corn-fed Colorado beefsteaks grilled over a mesquite flame, and baked potatoes drooling butter, sour cream and tangy fresh chives— Katie had discovered that she and Garth not only had a lot to argue about, they found a lot of interesting things to discuss, even agree about, as well. Like the fact that they both loved strong, full-bodied wine like California Cabernet, a bottle of which had gone a long way toward mellowing the evening.

Several days later, they'd had a disagreement about Katie's decision to incorporate a few gymnastics limbering exercises into the team's daily calisthenics.

"Maybe that crane thing serves a purpose, Katie, but those little, flirty gymnastics routines have to go!" he'd insisted.

"They stay," she'd argued uncompromisingly.

"Look, you heard the flak the boys took when the football team trooped through the gym on their way to the weight room. It's not fair to subject the wrestling team to that kind of ridicule because that's the kind of exercise their coach is most familiar with."

"I'm trying to lay a proper foundation for them. They need to get in shape with basics. The season has barely begun. I don't want them rushed because I want them strong *and* healthy."

"So far during wrestling practice the boys have listened to you discuss the physical dynamics of motion until *I* was ready to upchuck, flapped around like dying swans, and done the most sissified collection of conditioning exercises I've ever had the misfortune to see forced upon a group of teenagers I can only describe as 'all boy,'" he'd fumed. "When do you plan on getting to moves, defenses, strategy, and technique?"

"I'm making them do gymnastics exercises be cause I think they're the quickest, most effective method of improving flexibility and coordination, and not least because they're safer and put less stress on still-developing teenage joints than some of the traditional wrestling exercises I've seen done," she'd blazed at him. *"They stay!"*

"Well," he'd replied, somewhat mollified. "I think that about settles *that*!" Garth's look suggested he was trying to appear properly humble and suitably penitent. "Pie and forgiveness?"

"At least pie," she'd replied with a smile, unable to stay angry with him.

Katie glanced up at the clock once more. It read four-thirty. She tried to stifle her disappointment. She'd thought he'd be at practice today, of all days. The team was going to start weight training with programs she'd devised especially for each boy.

Except for Greg, she knew the boys would be disappointed by Garth's absence, too. Little by little he'd managed to win their liking and respect. He praised them after especially good workouts, encouraged them to persevere with difficult maneuvers and teased them all with the easy jocularity of a favorite uncle.

Only Greg resisted all Garth's friendly overtures, maintaining a stubborn, icy reserve that made Katie want to shake him. He'd eventually accepted a job on Garth's project, but only after making it clear that his sole reason for doing so was to buy a home computer and some video games for his two younger brothers for Christmas. Katie shook her head, bemused. Greg might be ornery and hard to handle, but he had a real soft spot for anyone younger, smaller, or weaker than himself. Especially, she'd learned, the two little boys born to Mr. and Mrs. Jenkins several years after they'd adopted Greg.

It was four forty-five. She couldn't delay any longer. "Okay, guys, take a ten-minute break, then meet me in the weight room."

The boys dispersed from their positions on the wrestling mats scattered around the gym, one or two making the usual deprecating comment about the gymnastics exercises they all despised.

"You mean we finally get to do something like the guys who play other sports?" asked Greg Jenkins with barely veiled sarcasm.

"The only thing that could stop you is your smart mouth, Jenkins," she shot back. "How does the idea of running laps in twenty-eight degree weather appeal to you?"

"Come on, Coach, it's *snowing* out there!" pleaded Jim Bradley.

"Coach Luter's team runs every day, regardless of the weather," Katie offered mildly.

"Coach Luter is a sadist," groaned another boy.

"Come on, man, let's just get out of here before she changes her mind. This is the best thing we've had the chance to do since wrestling started!'' Tommy Jones, a little 105-pound sophomore, affectionately called Flash by the team, hustled them out.

"And don't forget your weight belts," she cautioned.

Several of the boys raised their arms languidly in response without turning around, the four inch wide straps of stiff, thick leather with the heavy buckles dangling from their hands.

Katie watched them laughing and teasing each other, a proud fondness welling up in her. These boys really were good kids. A little rebellious, certainly mouthy, but basically good kids. Too bad Garth was going to miss today's practice.

He'd been surprised to discover how adamantly in favor of weight training she was. Only a couple of days earlier, when she'd mentioned that weight-lifting was the next thing on her agenda for the team, he'd pretended exaggerated shock, but Katie knew she'd caught him off guard with her plans.

"What?" he'd drawled in feigned amazement. "You're actually in favor of a coaching technique as traditionally macho as weight-lifting?"

"Sure, as long as the training program is tailored for each boy, I think weight-lifting is a fabulous way to build strength and confidence," she'd responded enthusiastically. "I just don't want my team to use strength as a crutch, so that the boys are merely muscling their way through the moves."

"I thought you admitted that strength was an integral part of wrestling?"

"There's always going to be someone stronger out there," she'd shot back quickly. "But form and technique are great equalizers. Having learned the basics, the right way, with no bad habits, it's time for my team to start concentrating on strength and those tricky moves you've been after me to teach them. My way, they'll have it all.''

"I can't wait to see this." Garth had grinned, crossing his arms over his chest in a way that emphasized beautifully developed biceps and forearms. His muscles were long, what her brother called "cut," the veins bulging beneath his short-sleeved T-shirt.

"Be here on Thursday at four-thirty," she'd quipped.

"I wouldn't miss it for the world!" he'd averred.

So where was he? She wanted to share her team's first weight-training session with him. An unspoken rapport seemed to be growing between the two of them that didn't depend on words to communicate thoughts or feelings. Except for her twin, Katie couldn't ever remember feeling so closely attuned to another person. It was disturbing, distracting, and it worried her.

Slowly, she made her way to the weight room, hoping it wasn't another problem with his project that was delaying him. He'd had far too many; the project was already at risk from the construction deadline edging ever closer.

At the weight-room door, Katie took one look at the long faces of her team and knew there was a problem. The boys were muttering among themselves, and some of them were slumped dejectedly against the wall.

"Come on, you guys, I know some of the things we've done so far have been a little unusual, but I thought you were all hot to pump iron?"

"It's going to be just like last year," bemoaned Jim Bradley. "He's not going to let us anywhere near those weights."

"And *you* won't be able to *make* him share the weight room!" said Greg Jenkins accusingly.

Two steps forward, eight steps back, she thought, the fact of her womanhood a censuring specter hanging heavily in the air. "Will someone please explain why you're all moping around like sick puppies? Greg...Jim...somebody?"

Andy McFarland, the heartthrob of the girls' cheerleading squad, stepped forward, his famous smile hidden behind an even handsomer scowl. "Coach Luter acts like the weight room is his own private club. He won't share it. Last year, he let the football team cut into *our* scheduled practice time a little longer every session."

"Yeah," interrupted Greg. "It finally got so bad, we had to use the weight room on our lunch hour instead of eating, or in the morning before school. Coach Luter wouldn't let us in there during our scheduled time, and our old coach didn't want to fight with him."

She heard Greg's unspoken criticism loud and clear. The old wrestling coach *wouldn't* fight with Coach Luter, and the new one was a woman who *couldn't* fight him.

"Let's go. It's our turn to use the weight room," she said crisply, turning the handle of the weight-room door. It was locked.

That fact was all it took to get her Irish up. She balled her hand into a fist and started banging on the small glass pane in the center of the door. "Time's over for the football team, Coach Luter. Open up. Now!''

"Ah, Miss...Coach O'Connell, what are you doing here?'' Luter's tone was patronizing.

It was a bad mistake for him to have made. Katie drew herself up even straighter: five foot three inches of righteous indignation fully outraged. "I've reserved the four-thirty to five-thirty slot on Tuesdays and Thursdays for the wrestling team, Coach. It's past that time now. Have your team wrap it up.''

"The wrestling team doesn't need the weight room as much as my football players do.'' He looked disparagingly at her team before remarking maliciously, "I understand you've instituted the same program you used for *girls* before you came to Granby.''

Katie could hear the football team sniggering in the background, but she ignored Luter's remark, pushing open the door and marching confidently into the room. There wasn't a weight belt in sight, except on her team, and the football players had staggering amounts of weight locked on the ends of their barbells. "No weight belts, Coach?'' she quizzed coolly.

"My men have got much stronger arms than your wrestlers,'' he replied condescendingly.

"It's not the strength of their arms that weight belts are designed to protect,'' remarked Katie tartly. "I hope none of them herniate themselves beyond a doctor's ability to repair. It would be a shame if there wasn't a future generation available to carry on Granby's glorious football tradition.''

An angry flush rose in Coach Luter's thick neck to suffuse his bald head as he registered the aspersion Katie had just cast on his team's masculinity.

"Greg, you and Jim start your upper body program with the free weights. Frank, I want you, Brett and Martin to start on the Universal machine. Do the leg workout. The rest of you help Coach Luter's team get their stuff together so we don't waste anymore of *our* time."

Katie's team looked at each other uncertainly, then moved hesitantly to take up the positions she'd instructed, only to be blocked by the grinning, arrogant faces of thick-necked football players, who refused to budge. She met Coach Luter's self-satisfied smile, his bull-dog tenacity washing over her like an unpleasant smell.

She could either run or brawl. Catching sight of the disappointment etched on the faces of her team, she sighed. There *was* no choice. She was their coach, the only one able to stand up for them against the Neanderthal Luter, the only one who had equal status and authority. Brawling it would have to be. *Thank God Garth wasn't here.*

"Maybe we should let the teams settle this, Miss…Coach O'Connell. How about a tug-of-war with the winners getting exclusive use of the weight room?" Coach Luter smiled. His expression was nasty, smug and gloating.

"I think not. After all, this is really between you and me, isn't it, Coach?"

"What are you suggesting, Miss…Coach O'Connell?"

Katie could swear he kept calling her "Miss" on purpose. She could swear, period. "What else? A weight-lifting contest. Whoever lifts the most weight wins," she said calmly, her tongue thick in her mouth from nerves.

"Exclusive use of the weight room?"

"Winner's option."

"Sure you want to do this, Katie?" asked a familiar voice, deep, husky and concerned.

Garth. The man had arrived as if on cue, with his usual impeccable timing. She turned to face him. "Don't you think I can win, Garth?"

"I'm not sure. Can you?" An enigmatic expression clouded his face.

"We'll see." Katie noticed his frown and pursed lips. The last time she'd seen that kind of look on his face there'd been trouble at his project site. Two pieces of expensive equipment had been vandalized, and the replacement parts had been difficult to come by in the small, mountain town and very expensive to boot. "Trouble at the project?"

He shrugged. "It's not important now. Maybe we'll talk later."

Greg Jenkins tugged at her arm. "If you blow this, we won't get to use the weight room at all this year," he hissed in an angry whisper.

"Interesting choice of the word 'if,' Greg. It implies you think there's a chance I might win. Thanks for the vote of confidence."

She caught Garth's eyes. They traveled the length of her slim body, his eyebrows rising slightly as his view passed over her thighs. He smiled at her, then leaned back against the wall, his hands jammed nonchalantly into his pockets.

Katie turned to Tommy Jones, the boy closest to her own weight. "Toss me your weight belt, Flash." He beamed, obviously pleased that she'd used his nickname, then he did as she requested.

Katie buckled on the belt. "Shall we weigh in, Coach?" she asked, stepping onto the scale. "That's 112 pounds for me and it looks like 240 for you, Coach."

Coach Luter moved over to one of the benches, put 100 pounds on each end of a barbell, then lay down, barrel belly up.

"Only 225 pounds?" asked Katie, trying to conceal her excitement. "You weigh 240. You're not even going to bench press your own weight?"

"No need," was his smug reply. "That's one pound over twice your weight, and I *know* you can't bench that." Quickly, smoothly and easily he lifted the barbell off the stand. For several tense seconds, he held it over his head, then in rapid succession he lowered it to his chest, raised it in the air and replaced it on the stand.

"Way to go, Coach."

"That showed her." The football team praised him loudly.

Katie moved to the chalk box, dipping her hands in to chalk her hands and forearms.

"Let me," said Garth quietly, chalking his own hands, then gliding them gently along Katie's forearms. The smooth rasp of his touch shot adrenaline and excitement in equal measure into her veins. "Are you going to do what I think you are?"

Katie glanced down at her thighs, then over to Coach Luter's arms. "Sure am!"

"I'm buying you dinner after this. With champagne." Garth's voice was warm, admiring. He encouraged with his eyes and his smile, as well as with his words. Katie had a sensation of being caressed, as if his whole personality had somehow reached out and gently enveloped her in a hug.

Confidence surged through her body apace with her rapid heartbeat. "You can buy the champagne, but I'm buying dinner."

"Deal. Poor Luter."

Katie snorted, then walked over to stand toe-to-toe with her adversary, her legs planted firmly about a foot and a half apart. "Sure you don't want a chance to bench press 240?"

"Don't need to."

Before he finished speaking, Katie quickly bent her knees, keeping her back straight. She wrapped her arms around the man's thighs and locked her hands together, lifting him off his feet in one smooth motion with a loud grunt. She swung around in a half circle, letting the inertia of their combined weight carry her, then put him back on his feet. She couldn't contain her triumphant grin, and gave the thumbs up gesture to her wildly excited team. "The keys, Coach Luter. If you please."

The man's astonishment was not a pretty sight to see. His face purpled, then contorted. "You cheated!"

"I most certainly did not! We said whoever lifted the most weight would win; there was nothing said about *how* we'd each lift." She glanced at her team. The wrestlers deserved a little vindication of their own. "As my men know, the brain is more powerful than any muscle in the body. I may not have done it the way you expected me to, but you can't deny that I out-lifted you.'' Her team beamed, at her, at each other, and most especially at the football team.

"She beat you, Luter. Give her the keys." Garth's voice brooked no disobedience, and the man handed Katie the keys.

"Like I said, Coach, the weight room is reserved for the wrestling team from four-thirty to five-thirty on Tuesdays and Thursdays. That's all the time my men will need."

The football team shuffled out, with Coach Luter behind them. She turned to her own team members who were jabbering excitedly about her victory. "Okay, you guys, remember what happened here today. My thighs are thicker and stronger than the arm of the biggest guy in here. The same principle holds for each one of you. Remember it when your man has biceps like the ones on Coach Luter's football team. Don't forget to use your legs."

The boys went at their weight-lifting with a vengeance.

"It's all in the legs, hmmm?" asked Garth softly in her ear. "I'll remember that. I'll definitely remember that!"

"No, Brad, that's not what I meant. Do it like this." Katie sighed impatiently and reached for the plastic dummy in disgust.

Looking at the blank faces around her, Katie felt the rush of frustration that had been her off-and-on companion since wrestling practice began. The wrestling move she'd been trying to teach them was a relatively simple takedown. Clean, precise, effective and, unfortunately, useless if she couldn't get the physical dynamics across to her team.

"Let's take a break from this for now, guys. Give me six laps around the football field, then come on back, and we'll try the move again." The boys rose from their positions and started toward the door. "And no dogging it, either!"

Katie marched angrily over toward Garth. "I told you using this dumb dummy wouldn't work. When they get back, I'm going to start demonstrating on *them*." She thrust the rubber surrogate into Garth's lap.

"Is there something you want me to do with this?" His mild tone was at odds with the naughty twinkle in his silvery eyes.

"Very funny. You may think this is all a big joke, but I've hit the proverbial wall. There are a few boys on the team who have terrific potential, and I can't do enough to bring it out. My hands are tied by that *stupid* rule!"

"Those requirements were a condition of your employment," warned Garth, his voice firm. "You'll think of something. Even I admit you're a natural coach, in spite of all that weird stuff you made the boys do at first." He placed the dummy on the bleacher behind him.

"I'm afraid my coaching ability is not doing my team much good at the moment," said Katie dispiritedly.

"Hey, where's my 'spunky little scrapper'?"

"She was beaten into the ground by Mr. Willis and his cronies." Katie slumped over, her chin cupped in her hands, her elbows resting on her knees. "Diagrams, the dummy...nothing works, not even our old home movies of my brother's college meets. They *need* to see an actual demonstration where one party knows the move!''

"Come on." Garth stood abruptly, and held out a hand to Katie.

She shook her head. "I can't simply leave. I'm in the middle of practice."

"I don't want you to leave," he said, removing his shoes and socks, then taking up a position in the center of one of the gray practice mats spread out over the gym floor. "I want you to come here and explain the move that I'm going to help you demonstrate when the kids get back from their run." Garth's loose-limbed stance told Katie she'd been right, he was an athlete. The sinuous way he rotated his hips as he began to limber up suggested that football had been his sport. *Too bad he wasn't a wrestler.*

"Look, Garth, I appreciate what you're trying to do, but I can't teach you how to wrestle in five minutes, even if I *can* do a hands-on demonstration with *you*!" Her tone conveyed a regret she told herself was due to the futility of his offer, not to any thwarted desire to take advantage of what would have been a perfectly legitimate excuse to touch Garth's broad shoulders and powerful arms. And thighs.

"You won't have to teach me anything, just explain what you want me to do so I can help," he said matter-of-factly, continuing his warm-up. He placed his hands behind his neck, raising his elbows to shoulder height and bending alternately to his right and left, forward and backward. The action of his shoulders and lateral muscles strained the seams of the blue work shirt he wore. In one quick motion he stripped it off, then continued as before.

Katie sucked in her breath at the sight of taut muscles undulating beneath smooth, still-tanned skin. She closed her eyes for a moment, trying to erase the disturbing view of fine black chest hair narrowing down a firmly muscled abdomen to disappear into tight jeans riding dangerously low on slim hips. He was beautiful. Absolutely beautiful. "Trust me, it won't work," she said earnestly in a voice curiously short of breath.

"Trust *me*, it will!" Garth lunged forward suddenly, driving his right leg between Katie's thighs. He wrapped both arms around her body, clasping his hands at the small of her back in a viselike grip that pinned her arms helplessly to her sides. She was stunned.

Garth nuzzled her spontaneously. She felt his warm breath against her stomach when he exhaled, and a skittering excitement shivered through her body. He lifted her a couple of feet in the air and swung her around. "Bear Hug...from the Russian series. 1964 Olympics. The Soviets really wowed the world with those moves. They had quite a grudge match going against the Japanese." Garth was in superb condition. His heart hadn't skipped a beat; his breathing was easy.

Before she could speak, Katie found herself flat on her back, pushing vainly against the broad hand trying to force her left shoulder to the mat. Even if he'd been as ignorant of wrestling as she'd mistakenly assumed, theirs would have been a plainly unequal match. His greater size and strength alone would have been sufficient to subdue her, but her stubbornness urged her on. Refusing to bend to his physical superiority, she feined a relaxation of her muscles, and when Garth eased his hand in reaction, turned in his grasp like an eel and slithered away.

"Nice try. I'll give you the points for an escape."

From the agile, practiced grace of Garth's movements it was obvious he'd been to the mat more than once or twice in his life. Suddenly, the nagging sense of familiarity about his walk that she hadn't been able to place rang bell-like tones of crystal clear recognition in her mind. He had a wrestler's walk! That peculiar, rolling, balls-of-the-feet way of moving that Brian had.

He was a wrestler! He'd been one for a long time. That walk wasn't something a wrestler developed in a day. Dignity demanded she protest. Loudly, volubly and with particular creativity. Garth scarcely gave her the courtesy of time to draw breath before grabbing her right arm and pulling her toward him. The action unbalanced her, in spite of her expertise at "the crane," and she nearly fell into his waiting arms.

CHAPTER NINE

"FACE-TO-FACE COMING UP. You can do a single- or double-leg takedown to achieve the position. Personally, I think my double-leg from here is better, at least it used to be in high school, but the single-leg version is so much more exciting." He snaked his right arm between her legs, reached his left arm over her shoulder and down her back to clasp his hands together, then raised her straight in the air.

Katie finally found her voice. It was not a pleasant sound. "Put me down immediately! What if someone sees us, you fool!" She twisted on Garth's forearm, trying to get away. She fought more than the enforced intimacy, though having a man's arm in contact with that particular portion of her anatomy wasn't something she was used to. It was her response to Garth that alarmed her. They'd been dancing around each other for weeks, flirting with flicking the spark of awareness that existed between them into a raging blaze. Suddenly, she longed to have done with the game, to yield more to him than the impromptu wrestling match. That fact alone made her double her efforts to wriggle free.

Her movements were useless to gain her release, but they were more than effective to start a warm ache at the juncture of her thighs, rubbing against the corded strength of Garth's arm. She was melting everywhere his body touched hers. He paused and carefully rotated his arm to get a better grip. The movement felt like a caress to Katie, but she dismissed that notion as pure fantasy when he swung her into a horizontal position against him and put her down on the mat, hard. She landed on her back with a loud thump. Garth was resting heavily upon her.

"If done correctly, the result should be a face-to-face position on the mat." He imprisoned her flailing hands in his, holding them over her head. Without warning he closed the remaining centimeters that separated them, and his lips softly touched hers. The glancing contact was light and sweet, leaving a tingling warmth behind. "Apparently I've done it right this time since we are, indeed, face-to-face."

Not to mention chest to chest, stomach to stomach...everything else to everything else. Katie licked her lips once to wash away the feel of his mouth pressed against hers. It didn't work. She shook her head quickly in an attempt to clear her mind, and her senses, of the pleasure stealing languorously over her. She restrained a wanton desire to writhe freely beneath him and return his kiss with a deeper one of her own. Principle demanded she neutralize the sexual awareness between them. And she must do it while she still could.

"You are mashing my...a very sensitive part of my body!"

"I know." Garth grinned wickedly, then boldly rubbed his naked chest against her breasts. Her thin T-shirt and the nylon singlet were no protection against the tantalizing friction that turned her nipples into small, hard pebbles.

"Do you think you could possibly let me up? I'm suffocating." Idiocy. This entire experience was pure idiocy, but she was loving every moment. And judging by the hardening body above her, she wasn't alone.

"After all I went through to get you in this position?" mocked Garth gently. His long legs were stretched out the length of her own, and she squirmed, trying to break the close contact. Her resistance only made him press down on her all the more. She could feel every muscle, most of his bones, and a healthy amount of his desire. "I thought I'd show you my Cradle next."

"Don't you dare! Let me up, Garth. The team will be back any minute!" She said her last words with something akin to desperation. The awareness of sensuality was growing between them, like a taut thread spun from his heart to hers, knotting them irrevocably together. The wrestling was becoming a mere guise for increasing intimacy. If they didn't break apart soon, Katie feared that all her concerns about the inappropriateness of this time and place would vanish, and they would please each other in the way promised and sought after by their straining bodies.

"You just want to quit because you're losing. You're afraid of the riding time I stand to rack up here."

"I'm not afraid of anything, except possibly broken ribs and punctured lungs, you oaf!" She bit his chin sharply, writhing free when her painful surprise broke his hold.

"You don't actually think you can defeat me, do you?" Garth sounded amused. "Get serious! I only wanted to demonstrate my casual acquaintance with wrestling so you'd take my offer to help seriously." He grabbed her knees before she could stand, dragging her back toward him. "Now I have to all-out win!"

Katie twisted free and stood, facing him. "*Casual* acquaintance? Ha! 'Russian Series...moderately difficult...not for beginners,'" she mimicked, trying ineffectively to grasp his hands which seemed to be everywhere at once.

"Hand control, Katie, hand control. It's vital! Isn't that what you've been teaching your team?" He chuckled, slapping at her hands, taunting her with his wrestling ability.

"I'm trying, blast you! Why didn't you just coach the team yourself!" she said sarcastically.

"I couldn't score as high as you did on the wrestling coach exam."

"I believe *that* like I believe the witch pushed Hansel and Gretel in the oven by mistake!"

Garth laughed. "Besides, it's been a long time since I managed to stumble my way through a couple of wrestling seasons in high school, even if I do still compete in the AAU freestyle competitions in the spring," he said modestly.

"I'll just bet! You're probably one of those 'old guys' with the 'weird' moves that all the college kids are afraid of."

"Merely a matter of timing," he dismissed, circling around her, looking for an opening. "Timing is everything." He made another fast move, and she found herself once more on her back.

Katie turned quickly onto her stomach. She tried to crawl away, only to feel herself tightly pinioned once more beneath Garth's considerable weight. His legs were positioned firmly on either side of hers. The full breadth of his bare chest crushed her to the mat, his hot breath fanning the wisps of hair escaping her auburn braid.

"Let me up!" she hissed.

"What'll you give me?" Garth ground his hips against her bottom, and she felt the throbbing strength of the hard, wanting male above her.

"A thump on the head if you don't!"

Garth laughed heartily. "I've been promised a lot of things by a lot of women in similarly compromising circumstances, Katie, but not one has ever tried to bribe me with a 'thump on the head'! Try something a little less bloodthirsty."

"This isn't funny anymore. Let me up!" Katie panicked. Her team would be walking through the door at any moment. More importantly, Garth's proximity and warmth and not-so-subtle teasing were having an unbearable effect on her. She hadn't known she was capable of feeling such hunger for a man.

"Keep wriggling that delectable little rear of yours. It adds a whole new dimension to that wrestling move called the Saturday-nite ride. I've never enjoyed riding time this much, or found it so stimulating! In high school I thought the maneuver was a rather inglorious way to win on points." His voice was gravelly and low, even huskier than usual. It raised to a rolling boil, the excitement Katie was trying so hard to tamp down. "I've since learned to win any way I can."

Garth finished the move as Katie suspected he might. He kept his thighs wrapped firmly around her hips, then tucked his legs under the front of her thighs. He lifted his ankles which pressed the back of her thighs to the front of his and rocked gently. Their bodies were, if possible, even closer than they had been before.

For a few seconds, they both just lay there. Katie was afraid to move. Afraid her slightest motion would telegraph to Garth how very much she wanted him.

"Turn over and I'll show you my very best riding time position...the honeymooner," said Garth softly, seductively.

"I'm...familiar with the position." Katie managed to choke out a response.

"It's just like the Saturday-nite ride, only you'd be on your back. When I grip your hips with my thighs, the strongest part of me embraces the most delicate part of you. It can be very...effective with the right...opponent." He traced the petal soft outline of her ear with his tongue, and she shivered.

"Please, Garth," she begged tremulously.

"Please what?" he murmured, his tongue moving lazily from her ear to her neck, leaving a moist trail in its wake. He moved her thick braid aside and bit the back of her neck gently. He continued giving her little nipping bites that drew forth small moans Katie couldn't smother.

She trembled under his expert mouth and yielded to the pure pleasure he gave. She half turned in his arms, reaching for him. Her lips were warm and pliant and more than ready for his kisses. The heated core of her searched for the source of her release, for the strongest part of Garth. Suddenly, she felt a blast of cold air and heard the chattering racket of her team coming back. In a flash, Garth had raised them both to their feet without her quite knowing how he had done it.

"Gentleman, Coach O'Connell has convinced me to help her demonstrate the takedown she was trying to explain earlier. We've been practicing, and I think I finally understand what she wants." He gave Katie a look that promised glorious fulfillment. "Coach, I'll turn it over to you."

"I will get you for this if it's absolutely the last thing I ever do!" she spat out in an undertone. She couldn't still her quaking body, which refused to acknowledge Garth's abrupt withdrawal.

"I hope so, Katie. I certainly hope so." His unsteady voice and the flush coloring his high cheekbones were the only indication that he was similarly struggling to control his own full-blown desires.

The team trooped in obediently. The few snickers and fresh remarks some of the boys made were quelled by Garth's threatening scowl. Katie had no choice but to continue practice, exercising a ruthless force of will to bring her shaking limbs and uneven breathing back under control. "Okay, guys, pair up according to weight and take your positions on the mat," she said weakly. It was going to be a long afternoon.

KATIE WOKE SLOWLY, resenting every second of her increasing consciousness. Morning was not, and had never been, her best friend. She hovered on the brink of full awareness and semi-slumber, unable to make the decision to open her eyes and answer the brave fool banging on her door.

"Later," she managed to say groggily. Why did the hotel maids insist on cleaning her room first every morning? The steady pounding became a rapid staccato increasing in volume by the second, demanding that she respond.

She threw off the quilt with one violent motion and stumbled blindly toward the door. She was going to kill the maid. No, she thought with pleasure, first she would torture her, *then* she would kill her. It was that simple. She was going to spend the rest of her life languishing in the State Pen at Canyon City, she prophesied morosely. Because when she opened that door she was going to strangle, or throttle—it made no difference so long as it was mortally—whoever stood behind it.

She flung open the door then stepped back in confused surprise, her hands dropping limply to her sides.

"Aren't you going to invite me in?" asked Garth with a jaunty grin that, for all its attractiveness, exuded far too good a humor for Katie to stomach first thing in the morning.

"What are you doing here?" She ran her hand quickly over her braid in a self-conscious attempt to subdue the escaping bronze wisps she knew from experience would be sticking straight out.

"What the hell have you got on?" demanded Garth suspiciously. Pushing Katie aside, he entered the room with a purposeful stride.

"This?" she responded, bewildered by his obvious irritation. "A pajama top. Why?" She hitched the maroon pinstriped material back onto her left shoulder. The darn thing kept slipping down, exposing an uncomfortably large expanse of creamy skin. She decided his irritation stemmed from a belief that women should wear flowing, frilly nightgowns to bed. Such a credo would be right in character for him. "Why?" she repeated patiently. He didn't answer, just looked around the room intently.

"Okay, I know I'm not *Venus Rising* first thing in the morning, but neither am I some monster from the deep," she continued defensively. "And I'll admit I'm a trifle grumpy if I'm not sipping hot coffee within thirty seconds of opening my eyes, but you're the one who barged in here, waking me from a perfectly delicious sleep..." Her voice trailed off as she realized he didn't even hear her.

His silvery eyes scanned her hotel room, missing no detail. She saw him register the rumpled bed with its white linen sheets, her few personal possessions scattered about and the remains of last night's room-service meal on the table in the alcove. His eyes flicked over the pile of neatly folded clothes resting precariously on the bentwood rocker, the picture of a teenaged Katie exuberantly embracing her twin holding pride of place on the nightstand, and the stack of paperback mysteries resting on the floor beside the bed—their grim titles and lurid covers a bright splash on the dove-gray carpet.

"Are you alone?" he asked fiercely.

"No, I've got the Denver Broncos' entire defensive line cowering in fear in the bathroom. That's why it took so long to answer your knock," she retorted. When Garth glanced speculatively toward the bathroom, Katie rolled her eyes and shut the door behind him. "Of course I'm alone."

"That looks like a *man's* pajama top."

So that was the problem. Garth was jealous. "It is a man's pajama top." An irrational joy that he was bothered made Katie's voice softly seductive as she fingered the solid maroon lapel caressingly. "Not that it's any of your business," she continued demurely, "but my brother gave it to me. I have about eight more in various colors."

"Your brother? Right." Garth sounded skeptical.

"My brother," repeated Katie firmly. "Every year my grandmother makes him a pair of silk pajamas for his birthday, and every year he thanks her profusely, then gives them to me. He thinks they cramp his style with his girlfriends."

Garth considered the explanation. "Do you save the bottoms for your boyfriends?" His rakishly arched eyebrows signalled the return of his earlier congenial mood.

"I usually make dustcloths out of them, or use them to polish silver."

"You make dustcloths out of pure silk pajamas?" he asked incredulously. At her prosaic nod he burst out laughing, the sound falling harshly on Katie's sensitive morning ears. She cringed in pain.

"Now will you please tell me what you're doing here so I can get back to bed?"

"Is that an invitation?"

"Hardly."

"I was afraid that would be your answer." His disappointed sigh sounded almost real. "In that case, let me remind you that today is Rent-a-Wrestler Saturday."

Katie glanced at the travel alarm on the nightstand next to the picture of her and her brother. "Not at 7:00

A.M. it's not." She pointed toward the door. "Come back around noon, and I'll spend the entire afternoon doing your chores. Right now, I'm going back to bed. Alone."

"Afraid not," he said in a forceful tone. "After all, this stunt was *your* idea. 'It will do the boys good to earn their way to the Intermountain Wrestling Meet in Denver. It'll build character,'" he mimicked.

"I don't think *my* character is in need of any building." Katie turned crisply on her heel and started toward the beckoning comfort of the bed.

"That's debatable if your marginal civility first thing in the morning is anything to go by," responded Garth, catching hold of her arm and swinging her around in the direction of the bathroom. "It's also irrelevant. I paid $500 for your services today, and I intend to get full value for my money. Go shower, and here—" he thrust something into her hands— "—wear these."

Katie looked at a brand new pair of what she knew would turn out to be very tight fitting jeans. "Dream on," she said, pushing them at Garth's chest. She tried to ignore how well the heathery tones of his blue crewneck sweater became him. Her fingers brushed against him, and she knew the sweater could only be cashmere. The muscles it covered could only be called rock hard.

"You have no choice. Jeans are the uniform of the day." Garth's eyes twinkled merrily. "Besides, I want to see if I finessed the fit correctly."

"Finessed?"

"It's a French term meaning 'have my friend Troy Adams steal a pair of his wife's jeans for me, then buy a new pair in exactly the same size, brand and style, and get the originals back in Liz's closet before she realizes they're gone.'" Garth grinned boldly.

"I'm sure if I ask Liz she'll verify that you left a tiny nuance out of an otherwise word-perfect definition," rejoined Katie, inspecting the jeans reluctantly.

"What nuance?"

"The one indicating 'you must be crazy if you think these will fit me.' You picked these up in the children's department, did you?" she remarked disparagingly, her thumb and forefinger dangling the offending garment in front of Garth with delicate disdain.

"No, but I might try there next if these aren't tight enough!"

"Cute. You rented the services of a temporary employee, Garth. You didn't buy a slave girl at an auction."

"You like that game, too?" A lazy, speculative gleam shone from his eyes as he warmly surveyed her scantily clad form.

Katie was suddenly aware of just how short the pajama top was, and the length of smooth bare leg it exposed to his view. The deeply slashed neckline did a lot more than hint at what it purported to cover. And the blasted shoulder was slipping again. "Forget it. Arguing with you is too strenuous without coffee. I'll wear the stupid jeans." She beat a hasty retreat into the bathroom, grabbing clean underwear and a kelly-green turtleneck on the way.

Once inside she let a steady stream of water as hot as she could stand sluice down her body until her skin started to tingle. Or maybe, she thought, the tingling was due to the anticipation of spending the entire day with Garth. Lathering her body generously with her favorite lily-scented soap, she refused to probe that possibility too deeply. It was getting harder and harder to deny their mutual attraction. But there were too many differences between them, too many things that blocked the way to anything more than casual friendship.

Garth was willing to put limits on what a woman could aspire to achieve. Katie had always despised the notion of limits, period. *Especially* if the reason was her sex. The result was their tug-of-war over her position as wrestling coach. And a personal tug-of-war in Katie. It went against every principle she lived by even to consider a deeper relationship with Garth so long as he couldn't see beyond her sex to her abilities. Yet, the attraction was still there, hard to ignore, and daily softening her, impelling her surrender to the feelings he inspired.

But the surrender was incomplete every time she crashed into the impregnable wall of cynicism about families he'd erected in the dark shadow of his bitterness about brothers. She couldn't understand his feelings, get around them or probe the reasons for them. The most neutral reference to "her family" or "Brian" caused Garth's silent withdrawal into a cold formality she hated. A loving mention of her twin's name was greeted with a spate of caustic remarks she couldn't let pass unchallenged. And the subject of *his* family was entirely taboo. The few times she'd broached a careful question he'd simply walked away from her without a word.

Their differences were deep and defined, and to her mind, seemingly insurmountable. And yet the attraction between them still grew. Katie could see the longing in his eyes when he looked at her, silvery, watchful, quietly intense. She could feel his need in the casual touches for which he found an excuse more and more often. She could feel her own desire. Every day she had an increasing awareness of herself as a woman. Like a newfound muscle, she flexed her femininity whenever she was around Garth, glorying in his immediate and positive response to a quality she was only just beginning to understand and appreciate.

Back and forth their battles went: his refusal to accept a female wrestling coach was anything but an unfortunate, and temporary, aberration; her insistence women not be bound to traditionally female occupations. His cynical denigration of families; her conviction they were the most important thing in life. They were engaged in a personal and professional tug-of-war. By some tacit understanding, they'd managed to maintain a kind of cautious equilibrium. They kept their relationship light. Both of them were aware of what was happening but neither one was daring enough to delve into the stronger emotions just below the surface.

So far their relationship had worked. They'd become friends, learning to respect that each held differing opinions on certain matters, but carefully backing away from confrontation on seriously divisive ones. And if they were occasionally uneasy with the strong physical attraction that often flared spontaneously between them, one or the other managed to subdue the errant emotion with a healthy dose of humor. Or food. Katie reached for the shampoo, remembering the quantities of deep-dish apple pie they'd consumed in the restaurant downstairs. Either sublimation worked—so far.

"Hurry up in there. You're on *my* time today." Garth began a rhythmic pounding on the bathroom door, and Katie, knowing by now that he could continue indefinitely, did as he asked.

Half an hour later they were zipping along an unfamiliar road in Garth's Volvo. "Great car for the mountains and snow. Unbelievable mileage, safest thing on wheels," he'd boasted, when she'd teased him about not driving a truck like other self-respecting construction workers. "Ah, but I *own* the company."

"Where are we going?" The road was clear, though remnants of the last snow were piled into gray-brown mounds on either side. Katie expected more snow from the low-hanging gray clouds and biting cold air heavy with moisture.

"Slaves shouldn't question their masters about such things."

"Slaves apparently aren't provided much in the way of breakfast either." The man had the most infectious grin even when he was saying the most outrageous things. With an exasperated sigh, Katie reached for the second of the jelly donuts she'd badgered him for, on spying a light in Gerry's Café. The first donut was now a memory, demolished immediately with the large coffee she swore she couldn't start the day without. She sipped her second large coffee appreciatively, trying to make the donut last by taking small bites.

Garth held out his hand for her coffee cup, and she felt a curious intimacy, both in his unspoken assumption that they'd share it, and in the way he turned it around to drink from the exact spot she had.

"I suppose I'll spend the day catching up on the housecleaning you've let slide, hmmm?" She took the Styrofoam cup from his hand, holding out the donut to offer him a bite.

"Not exactly, but you're warm. It has something to do with houses." Strong fingers circled her wrist lightly as his white teeth bit into the powdered sugar confection. He licked the raspberry jelly oozing down her thumb. His tongue lingered over the small pulse point he found at her wrist, and he smiled when he felt it quicken under his gentle laving.

"Watch the road!" she exclaimed.

Garth stroked his thumb across her palm and kept driving. A few minutes later he turned into a residential neighborhood located along the banks of nearby Grand Lake. Katie grew suspicious when he pulled into the driveway of a small cabin-style house with a large For Rent sign out front.

"House-hunting? That's what you have in mind for today? No way. I'm supposed to do chores for you. This one doesn't qualify." Katie shook her head regretfully. Visions of her stereo and records, her needle point pillows, her books and all of her plants washed over her with a wave of longing, but she ignored the images. Not even the thought of her favorite china teapot and its matching cups delicately painted with tiny blue cornflowers, or the sterling silver demitasse spoons Brian had given her for their twenty-fith birthday could sway her. A deal was a deal. She owed

Garth a day's work. Fulfilling a commitment was a matter of principle.

"Looking at the house will take your time and energy, and it's as much for me as for you," explained Garth patiently. "Doesn't that sound exactly like the definition of a 'chore'?"

"How is this for you?"

He looked around furtively, then leaned over and spoke in a low whisper, his warm breath brushing Katie's ear. She shivered with delicious sensation before giving his words her full attention.

"Do you realize that every time I stop by the hotel to see you it's all over town in about forty-three seconds? That old Miss Hackathorn down at the front desk probably keeps exact records of the time you enter and leave? That I don't intend to pursue you under the watchful eyes of the town's most morally upright citizens? That your reputation is in dire jeopardy unless you find your own place immediately, because I intend to keep seeing you? That I..."

"Stop. Enough. I'm convinced. We'll spend the day house-hunting." Katie laughed aloud with the sheer joy inspired by the promise implicit in Garth's words. She scurried up the sidewalk, carefully avoiding a slippery patch of ice.

Ten minutes later they both hurried outside holding their noses and gasping for breath. They skidded together on the ice, clutching at each other precariously as they attempted to regain their balance.

"It smelled like somebody died in there!" cried Katie, taking deep, cleansing breaths of the frigid air. Her words swirled around her head in clouds of frost.

Garth muttered a rude expletive. "I'd heard it needed some fresh paint, maybe a few touch-up repairs. But that place needed a wrecking ball!"

"And all that garbage lying around, and that...that..." She couldn't finish. The filth had been indescribable.

"We should probably get the authorities out here to pick up that goat before someone gets hurt." Garth brushed a soft kiss across the top of Katie's head before opening the car door for her.

"Someone did," she laughed.

"I'd like to see how funny you think it is the next time some damn goat tries to take a bite out of *your* hide. I can't believe the animals people keep for pets, or the way they just abandon them." He pushed the lock down before slamming the door. The gesture made her feel protected, as though he cared about her safety. The kiss was nice, too—sweet, promising, but not presumptuous.

They spent the next several hours inspecting a series of houses, duplexes and apartments for rent. One was too far from town, another was too expensive. A large Victorian house that reminded Katie of her dream house out near The Broadmoor was too large. Even Garth admitted it would have taken a family of at least twelve to do justice to the place, though he'd teasingly offered to take one of the bedrooms off her hands. All the apartments they saw lacked a minimum degree of warmth or charm, and Katie knew she'd be miserable spending a whole year in any of them.

They'd stopped to review Garth's list of available rentals, and Katie was dismayed by the page of thick black lines drawn firmly through the list of addresses. She was tired, depressed and still homeless. "There's only one left," she said without enthusiasm.

Garth drove back toward the lake, then followed the road along its bank for a while. He cut through an old neighborhood they'd passed earlier to double back over some winding trails Katie refused to call roads. She tried to orient herself, but it was a difficult task since she wasn't that familiar with the entire region yet, and the houses, like those in many mountain areas, weren't arranged in neat patterns of parallel streets. After fifteen minutes she surrendered in hopeless confusion.

"I give up, Garth. Where are we?"

"Hang on, Katie. We're almost there." Garth turned onto yet another back road. Unlike some of the others, the snowplow had cleared this one.

A snow-covered meadow ringed by tall pine trees spread out on either side of the road. They drove through the trees, and ahead Katie could see a small, neat A-frame cabin. It was built of clear-heart cedar planks sealed with a varnish that made them glow a warm, golden yellow. Diamond-paned windows shone even in the minimal light of the darkening afternoon. She noticed the cobblestone chimney with delight, thinking of the fires she would build, and then smiled in surprise. Without even seeing the inside she'd decided that the tiny cabin was where she'd live.

"Hurry up, Garth, please," she begged. "I have a feeling this is *the* place!"

The inside of the cabin more than fulfilled the exterior's promise of perfection. It was one huge room with a sleeping loft above reached by rustic stairs of smooth-finished natural oak. Katie ran her hands appreciatively over the painstaking handiwork before taking the stairs two at a time to view the loft. A row of tiny, diamond-paned windows overlooked the snow-covered field below, and a skylight promised she'd stargaze herself to sleep on clear nights. Dark-blue carpeting would cushion her toes in its plush warmth on cold mornings. A side door led to a pretty blue-and-white tiled bathroom containing an over-size, clawfooted bathtub surrounded by a greenhouse window and warmed by a small Franklin stove.

"It's perfect! I can't believe it," she exclaimed, hurrying to see the rest.

Downstairs, polished hardwood floors gleamed with a patina Katie knew only paste wax and elbow grease could achieve. An enormous stone fireplace rose in the center of the back wall, and on sunny days she knew the room would be drenched with sunlight from the two tall windows on either side. Built-in floor-to-ceiling bookcases covered one wall, and Katie realized that even her voracious reading habit could be contained within their confines. One end of the open room served as the kitchen, which, although complete with every modern convenience, maintained an old-fashioned country charm enhanced by the deep, glass-fronted cabinets and a cast-iron gas range.

"I love this place, Garth. Please say the rent is something I can afford!"

Garth consulted his list, then named a figure well within her budget. "It's yours if you want it. I can give the agent a call for you later and square away all the paperwork."

"This is too good to be true."

"You haven't seen the best part yet." He grabbed her hand and led her out to the snowy field comprising the backyard.

"Where are we going?" She picked her way carefully over slick rocks scattered over the partially shovelled pathway.

"There!" Garth pointed triumphantly toward a small body of water protected from the bitter wind on three sides by tall pines and majestic blue spruce. Curling mists of thick steam rose from what looked to be a dark pond or miniature lake. "It's a natural hot spring that's deep enough to swim in."

His hands swept the mountain panorama with pride, taking in the spring, the meadow and the steep, snowy peaks rising around them in the distance. Deep purple shadows were beginning to creep across a gray chiffon sky back-lit by the sun. The result was a luminescent dusk glowing softly, intimately, as the sky embraced the Rockies.

Katie took a few deep breaths of air so cold it pierced her throat and lungs like tiny icicles, and so pungent with the scent of pine and spruce she could almost taste them as a flavor. She crossed her arms, hugging them to her side, and surveyed the beauty and quiet peace that was hers for the next year.

Delight became a surging happiness impossible to contain. Spinning around with an uninhibited whoop, she threw back her head and flung her arms out wide as if to gather the scene close. She felt weightless, euphoric. And as she came full circle to meet Garth's eyes another feeling settled over her. A subliminal discord that she hadn't realized existed within her resolved itself, and she knew a strange, intensely satisfying sense of coming home.

CHAPTER TEN

THE FOLLOWING SATURDAY Katie commandeered the services of a few of her wrestlers and moved into the cabin.

About twenty cartons had been moved from the basement of her hotel to her new home, their contents unpacked, unbroken, and in an amazingly efficient manner. By way of thanks to the team she'd served a huge pot of chili, which together with several pounds of hamburger, several pans of corn bread, and two enormous chocolate cakes had been pronounced by her team as "enough to tide them over until dinner."

When the last boy left she looked around the cabin in satisfaction. She was going to be happy here. Very happy. Just as soon as she recovered from all that bending, lifting, carrying and unpacking. In spite of all the help, it had been an exhausting day, and the idea of a long, hot soak in the tub was beginning to seem like heaven on earth. Starting toward the hand finished oak staircase leading to her sleeping loft, she stopped groaning long enough to smile with delight. Ah, she thought—the hot spring!

A few minutes later, seated on a flat rock and slouching down so that she was covered to her neck with almost hot, slightly effervescent water, Katie decided she could happily spend the rest of her life lazily soaking. Her only exertion was a periodic glance at the mountains in the distance. "Gorgeous, absolutely gorgeous," she sighed, closing her eyes.

"I couldn't agree more. I don't know what looks more inviting, the hot spring or you in it."

Katie's eyes snapped open to take in the sight of Garth standing on the gravel path not ten feet away, hands on slim hips, strong legs planted firmly apart. "What are you doing here?" she asked, surprised but not displeased. With the winter sun setting behind him, silhouetting the man against the mountains, Garth seemed a natural, almost elemental, part of the setting.

"If you knew the kind of day I've had you wouldn't ask, you'd just invite me to share that spring. Not only was there a large absentee rate among my apprentices today, a major piece of equipment broke down mysteriously as well. I had to fix the miserable piece of—" he grinned mockingly at Katie's raised eyebrows "—rat doo-doo in the mudhole where it decided to quit on me and then work all day in triple time to keep on schedule." He shrugged, flexing his arm. "I'm dead tired and sore as hell, so how about it? Sharing?"

Katie's eyes darkened to a deep olive at his seemingly innocuous request. *She* had on a bathing suit. A nice, demure one-piece bathing suit. In a very pretty shade of blue. Knowing Garth, he intended to crawl into the hot spring wearing nothing at all. The idea was entirely too appealing. Not to mention dangerous. Treacherously so. She was tired, but relaxed. Her resistance ebbed to an all-time low just thinking about the interesting possibilities that sharing the hot spring presented.

"Sure, come on in. The water's fine." She kept her eyes on Garth's face, liking the way his eyes glittered silver bright at her throaty response and the small tick in his jaw. He placed his jacket on the same rock her own clothes were draped over, and slowly unbuttoned his shirt before tugging it out of snug jeans caked with dried mud. She closed her eyes for a moment, taking a deep breath. When she opened them again, the jeans were gone.

And he was wearing long underwear. In a very pretty shade of red. She knew her expression registered her disappointment when his knowing smirk chased the tired hollows from under his slanted cheekbones and eased the tightness of exhaustion from around his eyes and mouth.

"I like that look," he said, sliding into the spring until the heated water covered most of his tall frame.

"What look?" When did her voice develop that seductive tone? She'd lost every bit of practical good sense she'd ever had. In fact, if she was honest with herself, she'd started throwing it away two handfuls at a time the minute she'd heard his deep-throated, gravelly rumble.

"The one flashing in your eyes along with those little gold lights. It's naughty. Inviting. I like it," he repeated, moving slowly toward her through the water.

She flicked a handful of water at him, then darted playfully to the other side. She was flirting. It was unbelievable. After her father and Brian, Garth was the most confirmed chauvinist she'd ever met. He thought families were the scourge of the earth. How could she even *like* a man like him? Easily. He possessed intelligence and sharp wit to spare. He exuded strength and solidity. And he had the fittest body she'd ever seen, even in wet long johns. Especially in wet long johns. And that face. Not exactly handsome, but ruggedly male in a way that made Katie shriekingly aware she was female, and glad of it.

"How does beef stew, loaded with carrots and simmered in burgundy, accompanied by whole-wheat rolls slathered with honey-butter sound?"

"Wonderful, but I've already fed the Mongol hordes once today, thank you. The menu was chili, hamburgers and chocolate cake with milk, and there's not a crumb left."

"If I tell you it's already cooked and throw in a bottle of Beringer's best Cabernet?"

"Just let me get *my* Mongol pony!" Katie started toward the edge of the spring, reaching first for her snow boots. Her wet body could brace the icy chill for the ten seconds it would take to pull on her boots, but there was no way her feet would step out of the hot spring if they had to stand barefoot on frozen pebbles covered with snow for *any* number of seconds.

"You have some kind of party today?" asked Garth, his voice quiet, curious.

"Uh-uh." Katie held her boots high in her right hand, her jeans and kelly-green sweater in her left. "Some of the wrestlers helped me move into the cabin today. Feeding them seemed the least I could do." She halted at the ominous darkening in Garth's eyes.

"*You* preempted my apprentices today?" he growled in a way she couldn't be sure was teasing.

"I didn't realize it would put you in such a time crunch if they took a day off," she replied hastily. Garth was moving inexorably across the pool, the threat of dire consequences written all over his face. "They're *my* wrestlers, after all!"

"They're also part of *my* construction company. You realize, of course, that only torture can even the score at this point, don't you?" He lunged for her, grabbing her around the knees and tumbling her back into the spring. Her boots hit the water with a loud splash, then disappeared beneath its dark surface.

Katie came up sputtering, grasping at him blindly. "My boots, where are they?" she gasped, groaning at the sight of her jeans and sweater floating on a bubbling eddy, the water slowly seeping through.

"At the bottom by now," replied Garth equably, lounging back against a smooth rock.

She flung her wet sweater and slacks back over a rock. "And just how do you suggest I get across this meadow in the snow with no boots?" she asked, dangling his shearling jacket over the water by way of emphasis.

"Drop that coat and there won't be enough left of you to worry about it, that I promise."

Katie lowered the coat another few inches nearer the water.

"Okay, okay. I know when I'm licked." Garth grunted in disgust, then heaved himself out of the spring, helping himself to Katie's towel before pulling on his own boots. He turned his broad back and bent down near the edge of the spring. "Hop on. I'll piggyback you home so you can change out of that wet swimsuit before dinner."

Katie tossed one last fleeting handful of practical good sense over her shoulder and climbed onto Garth's back, locking her ankles around his tight belly, and sliding her arms around his neck. Even in the near freezing weather, his bare back radiated warmth, and she snuggled against him. "Brr-rr! Once you get out of the spring you really notice the cold! Hurry, okay?"

"Here, I'd rather carry you than these." Garth handed her a bundle of clothes, his and hers mingled together in a dripping jumble. "Wrap my coat around you." He ran his thumbs absently over her thigh where he held her, the small action subtly teasing. Little tremors of excited response raced along the surface of her skin everywhere it touched the smooth warmth of Garth's. Closing her eyes, she gave in to temptation and nuzzled with her chin the vulnerable area where his strong neck flowed into his broad shoulders.

Garth had loped perhaps a quarter of a mile in the opposite direction from her house before Katie realized they were going the wrong way. "My house is that way," she protested.

"Who said anything about going to *your* house? I'm taking you to my house."

"Your house is near mine?" A mutinous light glistened in her eyes.

He hoisted her higher on his back. "Actually, it's my guest house. I rent it out sometimes." As she gathered her resources to protest, he hurried on, firm conviction resounding in every word. "Don't worry. It's perfectly appropriate. Not even old Miss Hacka-thorn can say much. The main house where I live is about a mile and a half from your cabin, and thank

God, only another few hundred yards ahead through those pine trees."

Katie felt in no condition to argue. The cold and wind bit through even Garth's fleece-lined jacket, and her bare legs were covered with goose bumps despite their proximity to his tautly muscled belly. Or perhaps because of it. "What do you propose I change into once we get there?"

He turned his head around, a wolfish grin on his face. "I'll try real hard to find something suitable for you!"

Garth's house was a larger version of the guest house Katie rented. It was made of the same, clear heart cedar planks, varnished and glowing the same golden yellow. Identical diamond-paned windows, lit from inside, gleamed invitingly, and a huge floor-to-ceiling stone fireplace dominated his living room as well. The only difference was in size. And in the fact that the hand finished oak staircase led to a second floor with a full complement of bedroom suites and bathrooms, instead of the single loft that comprised the sleeping area in Katie's house.

Katie slid down Garth's back, clasping trembling arms around her body. "Any chance on getting a fire lit in that fireplace?" She could hardly get the words out for her chattering teeth.

"Not soon enough to suit me!" Garth pulled an attractive moon-and-stars patterned quilt off the back of a raisin-colored velour sofa. "Here. Wrap yourself in this and toss me your wet clothes. I'll put them in my dryer as soon as I've changed and brought back some wood. Get comfortable, rest awhile. I'll bring dinner in here." He went through a doorway toward what Katie assumed to be the back of the house.

She pulled off her wet swimsuit and wrapped herself in the quilt, luxuriating in the sensation of being warm. Cuddled into a corner of the sofa, legs tucked up under her, she unbraided her hair and let her head drop back drowsily. In no time at all the day's exertions caught up with her and she was asleep.

A series of small pops and a low hiss awakened Katie sometime later. She stretched, rising on her elbows to inspect the source of the pale glow lighting the otherwise dark room. A large fire burned cheerfully in the stone fireplace, sending out waves of welcome warmth.

"You're awake. Good. Now we can eat." Garth's voice was low, controlled, but with a husky intensity that made Katie want to scratch the surface of that control and expose what lay beneath.

"Thanks. It's been a while since anyone fixed dinner for me." She struggled to achieve a sitting position, tangled as she was in the quilt.

"God, you are so beautiful!" Garth spoke the words almost reverently. His eyes were drawn to her hair, curling and tousled now that it was loosed from the habitual braid. Bright coppery highlights gleamed softly in the flickering firelight. His eyes dropped lower to the quilt slipping down her body, exposing her naked breasts to his hungry gaze. He hastily placed the tray he carried on a side table and moved toward her.

Embarrassed by his frank scrutiny, Katie pulled up the moon-and-stars patterned coverlet, tucking it securely under her arms. "Did I miss something?" she asked primly.

"The fun hasn't even started," he assured her teasingly.

"Are my clothes dry?"

"All except for the undies I found in the pocket of your jeans. Pretty skimpy. I was afraid to put them in the dryer. For half a lace handkerchief and six ribbons, why bother with it at all?"

"Who are you to have any say about my choice of underwear?" She'd always been somewhat self-conscious about her lingerie. It was her sole expression of a femininity she hungered to claim, but felt was beyond the grasp of a small, athletic tomboy.

"I'm the guy who intends to have *all* the say about it from now on...as in, 'wear the flimsy red one with the strategic cutouts'! I swear the stuff now gracing the edge of my bathtub is enough to turn a normal, red-blooded man into a slavering pervert!"

"Pretty sure of yourself, aren't you?" She'd always hated men who came on strong and bossy, sounding like jealous children guarding their toys when talking about what "their women" could and couldn't do. Coming from Garth the command sounded very nice, very right and very adult. It also sounded surprisingly...loving.

"No, I'm not. There's a powerful attraction between us, Katie. I'm not sure where it's going, but I'm tired of pretending it doesn't exist. I can't fight my feelings anymore, they're stronger and truer than I've been giving them credit for. I think you feel the same way about me."

Katie's heart lurched at the tender expression she read in his eyes, but weeks of hiding her growing attraction made it difficult to tell him of her feelings openly. An unaccustomed shyness stilled her tongue.

"I'm right, aren't I? The attraction *is* mutual, isn't it?" His eager eyes raked her face apprehensively.

"Yes, Garth, it's mutual." Katie's soft admission eased the tightness around his eyes and mouth. She saw how much her words meant to him in the warm, relaxed smile he now bestowed on her, and her earlier reticence disappeared. "I've been so obsessed with our differences. And there are still a lot of differences between us, Garth," she said quietly. "We can't simply ignore them."

"We can't ignore the way we feel, either! I care so much for you, Katie. I tried hard not to, but I can't help myself. You're beautiful and strong—a potent combination." He smiled ruefully. "Your intelligence, your common sense, the vulnerability and sweetness you disguise with tough talk, your stubborn persistence in upholding principles, those are all qualities I admire very much. Can't we put aside our differences? Try and work them out for the sake of what we feel for each other?"

She had never seen him more earnest. "Do you really think we can?"

"It won't be easy. We both have strong personalities, and we're both leaders," he admitted honestly. "It'll be tough learning to take turns following, but I'm willing to give it one hell of a try."

"We could hurt each other, Garth."

"We could, but I don't think we will. Come on," he said persuasively. "Take a chance with me. Take a chance this could be...something special."

She hesitated only a moment. "Okay." She felt a little frightened by the enormity of feeling, commitment and exposure to risk contained in that one word of simple acquiescence. But one thing was certain, she'd give their love one hell of a try herself.

"Then you'll humor the decidedly possessive streak I'm developing about you?" he asked gently, leaning over to stroke his index finger down the line of her jaw with feather lightness. He tucked a long auburn strand of hair behind her ear.

"I think it could be arranged. In fact, I'll probably love it."

Garth wrapped his arms around Katie, quilt and all, and kissed her softly, warmly, lingeringly. The sofa gave way to accommodate his weight as he pressed her more deeply against the overstuffed cushions. His hand rubbed slowly up and down her arm, and she felt his tenderness. With a low moan she gentled under his touch and gave herself over to his kiss.

His tongue played tag with hers, darting in and out, staking his uncompromising claim to the moist interior of her mouth. He left no corner in its dark warmth unexplored or unaroused. She learned from him, teasing the tip of his tongue with her own before slipping inside to taste him as he had tasted her. Now that the need for restraint was banished, the freedom to respond was itself an excitement.

Her hand rested on his shoulder for a moment, then curved around his neck to press him closer still. In the back of her mind she registered the fact that he'd changed his clothes since the afternoon, and that he looked heartbreakingly handsome in burgundy. She ran the flat of her hand up between their bodies, over the thick alpaca sweater now covering the hard ridge of stomach muscles rippling under her palm. The sweater's V-neck created a craving in her fingers to explore the tantalizing expanse of his neck and chest it left exposed.

At her touch his hand firmly grasped her jaw, the fingers splayed either side of her mouth. The first touches of his lips to hers had been gentle caresses, tender and sweet. Now she wanted more.

He gave it.

His lips took hers in a series of kisses that shocked her with their searing hunger and blatant carnality. His tongue slid out of her mouth, roughly licking her upper lip. He sucked it between his teeth, flicking the underside of his tongue back and forth over it with a lashing strength. He nipped sharply all along the inside of her lower lip until she was ready to cry out and beg him to take it into his mouth as well.

Her lips became wet with the moisture from his as he stabbed his tongue into her mouth again and again. Inarticulate little moans escaped on a sigh as Katie felt a turbulent passion rise and writhe, responding instinctively to the experience and naked wanting of Garth's kiss. Breathing deeply of the special, clean fragrance that was his alone, she let her desire take control, leading her where it would.

She felt the rigid control Garth exercised over his growing passion begin to crack. His body tensed under the hand she pressed over his heart and hers trembled in response. He pulled away from her with a groan.

"Katie...sweetheart, stop it," he pleaded. "I'm about an inch away from losing what little control I have left. Give me a chance to slow down. I want this to be good for us."

"It'll be wonderful once you start kissing me again," she whispered seductively, reaching up to run her fingers through his shining dark hair. It felt soft and thick as it slid between her fingers, like fur. "Can't you tell, Garth? I want you as much as you want me. It feels so wonderful and free to be able to tell you so at last."

"This isn't how I wanted it to be...rushed, without planning or forethought." His tone roughened, the deep huskiness she found so sexy making him sound savage, out of control. "But when I look at you with your hair tumbled around your sweet face, all I want to do is this!"

He plunged his hands into the richly colored tresses, winding them around his wrists and pulling her forward for a bruising kiss that told her how close to the edge he was. "And when I see your eyes beguiling me with the passion I put there, and your mouth rosy and swollen from my kisses, it's damn near impossible not to finish what I started!" His hands restlessly traced the length of her arms, tightening convulsively. "I want the pleasure of seeing you glowing and satisfied from my love-making."

Katie threw off the quilt and held out her arms in mute appeal. She was unprepared for the swiftness of his assault. Garth crushed her against him with a low growl, and a quivering sensation began deep inside her.

"I can't get enough of you...can't get close enough to you," he muttered thickly. "Your mouth...sweet and timid one minute, sassy and bold the next. That's right, sweetheart, kiss me like that again!''

She unleashed her own tongue into his mouth, stroking in unison with his. Her mouth cherished him with kisses, her tongue dipping and curling, doing to him every exciting thing he'd earlier done to her.

"Please, Garth, I can't stand to be without you...inside me, anymore!'' The words came easily to Katie's lips, more easily than she'd dreamed possible. "Please, make love to me!''

"I intend to, sweetheart! Just as soon as I make sure you're ready for me.'' He responded forcefully, running his fingertips along the tender skin of her cheek and down her throat. They trailed hotly between her breasts, stopping to fit the swelling contours that seemed to beg for his touch before continuing down her stomach to tangle in the silky curls covering a fierce, throbbing longing for his possession. He dipped his fingers scarcely inside, giving a grunt of satisfaction at the moisture he discovered there before tenderly stroking the outer portals of her womanhood with a thrumming rhythm that thrilled her.

She pressed her upper body closer to his, rubbing her breasts sensuously against his chest in slow, sinuous movements. They felt heavy, full, aching for a fulfillment she knew instinctively that Garth would supply.

His strong, supple fingers responded to her unspoken request, coming up to cover the swollen mounds. He caressed them gently, almost teasingly at first, then with greater urgency, lifting, massaging, and finally, kissing them with a finesse that left her breathless. "So pretty, so hard,'' he whispered, flicking his tongue over her nipples repeatedly. The gentle rasps made her gasp aloud.

"Oh, Garth...that feels so good," she moaned, arching up to give him greater access.

"That's right, Katie. Let go. This is for you, sweetheart, enjoy it." He stroked her aching nipples to ruby fire and diamond hardness.

She felt as though a golden wire was stretched tautly between them and the deepest recesses of her womb, with Garth vibrating the wire until her entire body resonated with the golden lovesong he played upon it. She no longer recognized the careful, practical person she'd been all her life in the writhing, wanting woman she felt herself to be in Garth's arms. All she cared about was the feelings he aroused in her, and the fact that it was Garth who was arousing them. Garth who was kissing her, fondling her, finding all the sensitive parts of her body, then loving them with a skill and cleverness that astounded her. She arched toward the strumming fingers for more of the wild sensation only he could provide.

"Sweet, sweet woman," he breathed. "I want to please you...make this special for us. What do you like? What feels good for you?" His words were a husky whisper, more felt than heard.

"Everything you're doing!" Hot needles of desire pierced deeply into the heart of her hidden feminine places, little rippling contractions signaling her body's willingness to accept Garth as a lover and presaging a greater pleasure yet to come.

"Tell me," he commanded in a guttural tone. "What do you feel?"

"Wild, hungry...desperate! Make love to me now, Garth," she implored urgently.

"Soon. I want you burning for me, sweet woman!"

"I *am* burning for you!" The low, throaty quality of her own voice surprised her. Spirals of pleasure shimmied up and down her spine in response to the fluttering of his quick, clever fingers. "Make love to me!" Coaxingly, she slipped her hands under the bottom edge of his sweater and stroked across the hard, flat plane of his stomach just above the waistband of his jeans. Her palms slid up his ribcage and back down. She could feel the layers of muscle over bone, encased in warm fragrant flesh and the heartbeats that thumped faster with her every caress.

With something approaching desperation, she plunged her fingers into his jeans, caressing him in a more intimate manner, then reveling in his answering leap of eagerness. He hardened convulsively, and she felt a heady joy as she stroked the proof of her power to arouse him. "I want to see all of you, Garth. Take these off?" she asked, shyly eager as she fingered his waistband.

His answer was to stand quickly and yank his sweater over his head with one smooth gesture. She couldn't tear her eyes away from the hard, almost sculptured beauty of his upper body. His eyes held hers in thrall for a moment, the sweater dangling from his hand forgotten. Katie swallowed. The sweater dropped to the floor soundlessly.

Garth's hands reached up and unsnapped his jeans, then drew the zipper down with agonizing slowness. He stepped out of his jeans and briefs to stand quietly proud before her. The shadows from the dying fire danced over the lean, solid lines of his powerful body making him look like some ancient warrior home from the kill. He was gloriously naked and thrillingly virile, everything about him was unequivocally male. And everything that was female in Katie responded.

Moving slowly back toward the sofa, he enfolded her in his arms, letting his strength and warmth and wanting sweep over her in tangible waves. Then he carried her tenderly to the floor before the fire, placing a couple of thick sofa cushions beneath her before sinking down on her softness.

The caring and tenderness flowing between them created a compelling desire in Katie to please him, to reciprocate with passionate, exciting caresses of her own. She let her mouth, her hands, her entire body tell him what she didn't say in words until he trembled in her arms.

"I can't wait any longer, Katie girl." The words were harsh strangled gasps torn from his throat. His knee swiftly nudged her thighs apart, and with the slight awkwardness that came from eagerness, he positioned himself above the place yearning to be filled by him. "We can get creative later," he growled. "This time the old-fashioned way will have to do...I want you now!"

He entered her with one swift, strong, deep thrust that plunged him as far into her as a man could be. And the act revealed to him that he'd been the first. His eyes widened in shock as his virile strength absorbed her tiny shudders of first-time pain.

He opened his mouth to speak, but she covered his lips with gentle fingers, urging him on with subtle, instinctive movements of her body. He groaned, then quickened the pace of his vigorous thrusting and in a very few moments it was over.

CHAPTER ELEVEN

GARTH SHIFTED HIS WEIGHT SLIGHTLY, bearing the brunt of it on his elbows. He looked down at Katie with an expression that was at once anxious and infinitely tender. Winding a long, damp strand of auburn hair around his finger, he spoke in a curiously sad voice. "Why, Katie girl? Why didn't you tell me you were a virgin?"

"Does it really matter?"

"You said you were familiar with the honeymooner position, and I naturally assumed you understood what I really meant." He sounded disappointed, but she couldn't tell if it was with himself or with her.

"I did, but technical knowledge doesn't necessarily mean practical experience." Her body raced with unsatisfied, but still aroused desire, and her hips rotated against Garth's in an invitation at once innocent and provocative. "I'm not angry if that's what's worrying you."

He dropped his chin to her forehead. "Dammit, you should be! I haven't been like that with a woman since I was twenty-one years old. But at least then I had an excuse." His voice oozed bitter self-recrimination.

Katie spared a glancing curiosity for that long-ago incident, then quickly dismissed it from her mind. There was more than enough in the present to concern her. "Don't go all macho and stupid on me. I'm well over the age of consent." She felt Garth tense in her arms. "I knew exactly what I was doing; I wanted to do it, and I did."

"You should have told me." Garth nuzzled her temple, dropping light kisses across her forehead and at the corners of her eyes. "A woman deserves better her first time out than I just did by you."

"You did fine by me," she praised him shyly, running her hands over his sleekly muscled flanks, reveling in the sensation of being physically joined to a man—this man. Smoothing her palms up and down his arms, she felt the hard sinews tremble beneath his sweat-slick skin. She buried her face in the silky hair of his chest and breathed deeply of the essence that was Garth's alone. His was a clean, rich, musky scent that made her quiver with excitement whenever he was near, intensifying her awareness of him. "If you ask very nicely, maybe I'll give you another go," she whispered, nipping his chin daintily with her teeth.

He laughed, his broad shoulders shaking, filling Katie with a surging joy, as though she'd pleased him with some wonderful gift. His arms tightened around her, and he rolled onto his back, pulling her half on top of him. "I swear that's one of the things I...like best about you, Katie. You have such appetite for everything—food, coaching, even fighting with me!" He cradled her head against his chest, his large hand pressing her cheek over his heart. "And now this."

"Before...this, I wouldn't have thought so," she admitted. She could hear and feel his strong heartbeat, and her own raced to keep time with it. "So are you going to?"

"Going to what?" he teased, cupping her small, firm derriere, filling his hand with it, testing its round fullness.

"Give me another go." She drew herself fully on top of him, straddling his powerful, rock-hard thighs.

He laughed ruefully. "Wouldn't I just love to, but no can do."

Katie colored, glad the darkness hid her embarrassed flush at not realizing sooner the physical impossibility of what she asked. "Need a couple more minutes?"

"No, but you do. It would hurt you."

"Yeah, but it'll hurt so *good*!" She wiggled her hips, using the tensile strength of her own thighs to rock herself back and forth against the burgeoning hardness coming to life once more beneath her. Heat and power blazed where their bodies touched, flooding Katie with more desire than she'd ever imagined it was possible to experience. A burning ember flared briefly in the fireplace, illuminating the room with a shadowy light. Garth's silvery eyes glittered, and she shivered in excited anticipation at the virile promise she found in them.

"I did leave you...hungry, didn't I?" he murmured, crossing his arms over her back and twisting her beneath him in one powerful movement. His legs, all hard muscle and hair-roughened skin, twined with hers. "Don't say I didn't warn you when you get up tomorrow morning walking like a duck, Katie girl!"

"There is no more Katie 'girl,'" she whispered, her voice a seductive purr, testifying to a new knowledge of herself. "From now on, there's only Katie 'woman.'" She wound her slender arms around his neck, pulling him forward for a long, bold kiss. "Your woman if you want me to be."

"I want. Hellfire, do I want!" He pinioned her roving hands above her head with one of his own, his callused fingers a rough-gentle stimulation against the smooth skin of her wrist. "But I want to make sure there are no misunderstandings between us."

An arrowing fear lanced through Katie. "What's to misunderstand?"

"Katie, twenty-eight-year-old virgins are as rare as unicorns. There just aren't any."

"Not anymore," she agreed, wrapping her legs around the lean hips she'd so often admired over the past weeks. She didn't want to hear what he had to say. She dreaded his next words, feared them. "I'd say you pretty much took care of the last one. Most thoroughly, in fact."

"Not thoroughly enough, it appears." He laughed softly against her sweet-smelling skin, fastening his lips on the tender area where her creamy shoulder flowed gracefully into the elegant line of her long neck.

Nibbling, sucking on her flesh, he sent red-hot rivers of fire rushing down her spine and back up again. She arched the most delicate part of herself into contact with the strongest part of Garth, remembering the day they wrestled, relishing the feel of his skin, naked, warm, and wanting against hers, in a way she'd only been able to imagine before.

He tucked his hand into the small of her back, holding her close. "A woman who's waited as long as you have for her first sexual experience is likely to have expectations I can't and won't fulfill. I don't want you to confuse what's happening here with any of your romantic ideals about marriage and family life. They're not for me, Katie. Not ever.''

His voice was stern, his expression serious, intense. "I care for you; I'm probably halfway toward being in love with you. I want a relationship with you in the most mature sense of the word, but I won't marry you, and I won't make love to you if there's the least misunderstanding about that in your mind. However much I want to.'' He lowered his head to kiss the underside of one aching breast, his thumb delicately caressing the hardened nipple crowning it proudly. He raised his head, exhaling swiftly. "And I sure as hell want to!''

Katie's principles stood toe-to-toe with the confused jumble of what she felt for Garth. She'd always thought she'd be married before she gave herself to a man. But then, she'd never met a man like Garth before. There was just something there in her heart, something vital that needed both of them for its fullest expression. She wasn't even sure what to call it. Maybe it was the potential for love. Whatever this new aching was, it stared at principle across a deep chasm that could swallow the person Katie had been for twenty-eight years.

Before she met him, things used to be clear-cut, she mused. There were things she did, and things she didn't do. And she most emphatically did *not* blithely embark upon an affair with a man who didn't believe in marriage. A man who hated families. Her principles yielded first. She made the quantum leap toward the potential that love would grow between them, embedding her soul into it, vowing to hold on for dear life.

"Garth, I understand everything you've said. I'm not expecting to find a ten-carat diamond ring wrapped in a marriage proposal on my pillow tomorrow morning," she said quietly. "I'm willing to take a chance with you, a chance that something special will grow from this attraction between us. Remember?"

"I'm not going to change my mind about this. I don't believe in marriage," he persisted.

"Do you believe in putting your money where your mouth is?"

"What are you saying?"

"That you should shut up and show me some of this great control you claim you haven't lost since you were twenty-one years old."

"And that's called putting my mouth where?"

She wrapped slim arms around his waist. "Anywhere you want, babe, anywhere you want."

A LONG TIME LATER, Katie lay snuggled close to Garth, soaking up his warmth in the now cool room. The fire had gone completely out, but Garth was too spent to get up and rekindle it. Cradled in the crook of his arm, she toyed absently with the fine straight hairs on his wide chest. Twenty-eight years, she marveled. Twenty-eight years old and she hadn't known her own body—not really known it. Not like she'd learned about it in Garth's arms. She stretched languorously. The man did indeed have masterful control. He could also lose it lightning quick, she grinned to herself in the dark. And she'd learned a number of interesting ways to make him do just that in the past few hours.

A nagging concern slipped into her consciousness under cover of the satisfied lethargy their vigorous loving had induced. In spite of the huge step she'd taken by making love with him, she knew that her principles wouldn't let her remain forever in an affair with no hope of a lasting commitment. She wanted marriage and a family. She couldn't deny how important having both were to her. *Would* Garth change his mind? He'd said he was halfway in love with her already. What would happen if he fell in love the rest of the way? She sighed. It was a small, quiet sound that slipped away in the dark.

The large hand holding her waist tightened its grasp, bringing her more firmly against Garth's lean, hard torso. There wasn't much that was soft on him, but he was a comfortable man to sleep with nevertheless. His other hand gently enfolded the one of hers lightly tracing the ridges and indentations of his washboard belly. He inclined his head to brush glancing kisses across her hair. "I love the way your hair smells, sweet and fresh. "It's very...feminine." He inhaled her fragrance deeply.

"I was right," she murmured.

"About what in particular?" asked Garth, his voice sleepy.

"Your voice. It's perfect for whispering endearments in the dark."

"You mean things like this?" he asked huskily, cupping her face in his hands, then bringing it up to his. He kissed her deeply, sweetly, moistly, before nudging her head to one side and whispering a seductive enticement in her ear. "Or was it more this you had in mind?" He demonstrated further.

Katie's breath quickened, her body responding immediately now that Garth had taught her how. "Actually I was thinking of something racier, something more like...this!" She trailed her hand down the length of his body, reaching for him boldly.

"Woman, you are an absolute natural," he breathed roughly, pressing her hand more firmly against his rigid member, his hips thrusting against the small palm that held him in such dainty, yet forceful thrall.

"A woman can build up a powerful thirst in twenty-eight years, Garth." Katie smiled at the spontaneous leap of his hard flesh.

"Are you saying what I think you are?" he asked in wry surprise.

"I'm still kind of shy about all this. It'd be easier if I showed you," she said seriously, planting warm, wet kisses down the length of his long torso and tightly muscled abdomen. Long, auburn curls flowed over his skin like bright silk ribbons as Katie's lips slid down his body. "You just shake your head 'no' if you don't want me to."

"How can you see in the dark..." His body tensed as she found her mark, then she felt his laughter as he realized her sly joke. The rumbling started deep in his stomach until his whole body was shaking with the sound. "Woman, you go ahead and consider you've got all the permission you need!"

And then Garth's body shook with an altogether different sensation, one she, herself, had learned well under the earlier tutelage of *his* hands and mouth.

KATIE'S NOSE TWITCHED. There was a smell of coffee in the air. She sniffed. Something was being cooked in butter. She took a deep breath. Something sharp and citrusy. Juice? No, that wasn't it, she thought groggily, her curiosity forcing her awake. After-shave. That was it. A nice, manly after-shave. *After-shave?* Her eyes shot open.

"Good morning." Garth set the tray he carried on the coffee table, then sank down on the floor, taking her in his arms and kissing her warmly, sending a liquid heat racing along her nerve endings. "I remembered what a sunny disposition you have in the morning," he teased, "and decided to help it along with a little breakfast."

"Coffee," she pleaded, struggling to achieve a sitting position. In spite of the intimacy of the night before she felt shy and dragged the coverlet up under her arms, refusing to meet his gaze.

Garth placed a steaming mug in her hand. She noticed that he'd added cream. Taking a sip, she discovered he'd remembered she didn't use sugar. Her free hand plucked nervously at the moon-and-stars patterned quilt, her hazel eyes blinking rapidly against the brilliant sunshine streaming into the living room. She was sure her head was a Medusa tangle of knotted auburn snakes, but she refused to relinquish her death grip on the coverlet to find out.

"*Is* it a good morning, Katie girl?" asked Garth, tender concern evident from his tone and the anxious way his eyes scanned her face. He smiled. "Or should I say Katie 'woman'?"

She groaned, closing her eyes and trying to scoot down under the quilt until she remembered the coffee mug she still held. "I'll make a deal with you, Garth. You agree to stop teasing me about last night, and I'll agree to die of embarrassment right here, right now. It'll save us both some time."

He laughed. "Last night was wonderful, Katie. You were everything a man could ever want in a lover. I didn't mean to embarrass you." He grinned at her skeptical expression. "That was some loving you inspired."

"Then I'm fine." She grinned sheepishly.

"I'm glad." He paused for a moment, his tone hardening. "There's something else I have to say. I'm afraid I didn't behave very responsibly toward you last night." The tightness she hated was back around his eyes and mouth.

Katie placed her hand over his. "You more than made up for any initially...precipitate behavior. Just forget it, okay?"

"I'm talking about birth control," he said brusquely.

She swallowed, hard, and with difficulty. Until last night, birth control hadn't been something she even needed to consider. Until this minute, the thought had never crossed her mind.

"I was equally irresponsible," she admitted tensely.

"I expect to be informed immediately if there are any untoward consequences of last night, or any that occur as a result of future slipups. Not that I intend there to be any, but it's something I'd insist we take care of right away."

It? Take care of *it*? Katie quickly considered her options. Abortion? She shuddered; that would be unthinkable. Adoption? The idea was slightly more palatable, but still nowhere near desirable. Unwed motherhood? Not a perfect situation, but the best of an unsatisfactory lot. Very well, she thought defiantly. Unwed motherhood it would be if Garth's infamous "it" ever occurred. He was right about one thing. Birth control was something she needed to think about. She vowed to make a doctor's appointment as soon as possible.

"Well?" He quirked his coal-black brows impatiently.

"You'll be informed should the situation ever arise," she said tersely.

Garth relaxed visibly. "Good. Now, how about some breakfast?"

Looking over at the tray from which mouth-watering smells were emanating, Katie decided to relax as well. "What is there?"

"Don't worry. There's plenty." He smiled at her unsuccessful attempt to appear nonchalant while she eagerly surveyed the number of plates the tray carried. "I also remembered you eat like a stevedore." He placed the tray over her knees.

"I most certainly do not!" She reached greedily for a piece of whole-wheat toast, slathered it with marmalade, scooped onto it a forkful of perfectly scrambled eggs from which the unmistakable fragrance of cooked butter wafted, and took an enormous bite.

"What do you call two croissants, four sausages, at least three eggs, and what looked like half a pound of fruit cup?" he asked, ignoring her air of outrage when he picked up another fork and began eating from her plate.

"A good breakfast."

"For a truck driver." He held out his hand for her coffee mug. "Sharing?"

"I thought I had!"

"And very nicely, too. I still remember how hot you got me when you…"

"I meant my food," interrupted Katie quickly, flustered by the blush she could feel rising in her face. "Are you always like this in the morning?"

"Randy? Pretty much. How about you?" There was a wicked gleam in his eyes.

"Right now what I mostly am is starving." And a liar, she thought unrepentantly, as images of the night before unrolled behind her eyes, causing the blushing heat to suffuse her entire body.

"What you mostly are is one hell of a woman." Garth took the tray from her lap. "My woman." His look told her that was as close as he was going to come to discussing his concerns of the previous night. He seemed ready to accept the kind of relationship she had offered. Their tacit understanding was that she wouldn't demand more than he could give. He made a move as though to draw back the quilt. "A long, hot soak will do wonders for you if you're at all sore."

"Not a bit," she denied quickly. Her denial was given too quickly, judging by the knowing gleam in Garth's eyes.

"Not even after spending all night on the floor?" he asked, an arch lilt to his voice.

"Maybe I have a few, small twinges of discomfort," she admitted with a grin. "Um, I know this sounds ridiculous considering everything I said and did last night, but do you have a robe I could borrow?"

"Katie, there's no reason to be shy around me or embarrassed about what goes on between us; you have a beautiful body. I love to look at you." He pulled back the quilt, offering her his hand and a playful smile. "You had better get used to what your beauty does to me. Now, let's see if I was right."

"About what?" she asked, her inherent inquisitiveness overcoming timidity as she put her hand in Garth's and rose from the tangle of moons and stars on the floor.

"About whether or not you're going to walk like a duck today!"

She swatted his rear. "You have absolutely no shame."

He smiled at her tenderly. "And neither will you by the time I'm finished with you."

Katie swallowed the sudden lump that rose in her throat at his offhand remark. He didn't need to have said it. He probably didn't even mean it the awful way it sounded. Nevertheless, she'd remember very well without his reminder that theirs wasn't supposed to be a permanent arrangement. She could still hope, couldn't she? Determinedly, she pushed down all thoughts of the end. Right now was the beginning of their romance, and if Katie O'Connell had anything to say about it, well, there wouldn't be any end.

She sashayed toward what she hoped was the bathroom door in the sexiest walk she could manage. "That walk didn't look much like a duck, did it?" She smiled seductively at him over her left shoulder, her voice a low, husky vibrato in her throat.

"I think I'd better come with you. I'll make sure you find the soap."

"Much as I like that after-shave of yours, I'm sorry you've already showered," she murmured in a sultry tone.

He caught up with her eagerly, wrapping a thickly muscled arm around her slender waist. "The hell with it! The tub's big enough for two."

DAYS SPED BY in a haze of halcyon happiness for Katie. The possibility that her relationship with Garth would last only until the end of the school year was banished to a dark corner of her mind.

Their time fell into a blissful pattern of togetherness. The number of times Garth now missed practice was almost nil. They spent all of their nights wrapped in each other's arms, and their evenings talking and arguing their way through hour's worth of subjects. A fragile trust was growing between them, which even Garth tentatively accepted, and Katie was loath to disrupt it with thoughts of their differences.

Weekends together were the best for her because there was so much time to spend with Garth. They explored the mountains surrounding Granby, filling their lungs with the pungently woodsy air and working up voracious appetites for the favorite foods they cooked for each other. The hot spring between their two houses was the scene of both wild horseplay and gentle romance. And there was all the time in the world for loving. Making love was sometimes sweet, sometimes hot, but always intense, emotional and satisfying.

Garth, decided Katie with pleasure, seemed different lately, more open. Curling her fingers around the thin china teacup, she traced with her nail a tiny blue cornflower painted near the rim. She took a scalding sip of mint tea and leaned her head against the white porcelain edge of the old-fashioned bathtub, letting fragrant mint steam rise around her. It mingled in the air with the even more heady perfume of her favorite bath oil, a rich lily scent released by the heated water to curl in steamy ribbons among the dark green leaves of the plants with which Katie had filled the greenhouse window in her bathroom.

She took another sip of tea before setting her cup aside. Garth had also done an astonishing about-face in regard to her position as wrestling coach. In the beginning her fiercest adversary, he'd lately become her staunchest ally and supporter. A whole lot of cold, clear dictum was coming down at school-board meetings these days, she mused. Not the least result of which was the lifting of the ban on physical contact with the boys in demonstrating moves.

Little by little, she'd been able to prove her abilities as a wrestling coach, winning the community's acceptance in the process. There were still townspeople who didn't like to see a woman in the position, but there were hardly any left who doubted her ability to do the job. And the backlash she'd feared once it became general knowledge around town that she and Garth were an "item" simply never materialized. There were a few raised eyebrows initially, but people reacted out of curiosity. There was nothing like the hue and cry Katie had been expecting. Of course, she and Garth didn't flaunt their relationship, but they hadn't gone out of their way to hide it, either.

Surprisingly, their love affair seemed to have hastened her acceptance in certain quarters. Having a "gentleman friend," as the townspeople gently re-ferred to Garth, seemed to reassure them she wasn't really some strange creature they wouldn't like to know. They were increasingly willing to make a place for her in their community, and Katie valued their acceptance all the more because it hadn't come easily. She treasured each smile and wave, each invitation to "pass the time of day" when she walked through town. She savored the teasing inquiries about the wrestling team along with the homebaked cakes sent by students' mothers. And she cherished the fact that little brothers and sisters hung around the gym after wrestling practice to be introduced to "Coach."

As for the team, she thought with satisfaction, well, it was starting to look like a winner. Greg Jenkins was turning his natural bent for the sport into a clear shot at the state trophy in his weight division, though his old habit of resistance to a woman coach was dying a hard, lingering death. She'd discovered Jim Bradley's lazy air concealed a fiercely competitive spirit that her newly won permission to demonstrate on the boys themselves had honed to a razor-sharp edge. And little Flash Jones had turned out to be well named. The kid was so quick he executed his wrestling moves in a blur of energy that even Katie's educated eye had trouble following.

She raised her right foot out of the water, languidly considering the blood-red polish gracing her toes. Wiggling them vampishly, she couldn't prevent a smug grin from turning up at the corners of her mouth. The color was scandalously provocative. Especially when paired with the "seductive red one, with the strategic cutouts" lingerie she'd found in a plain brown wrapper on her desk at school one morning.

Thank God she'd waited to open the seemingly innocuous package in the teacher's lounge during lunch hour. The only other person there had been Liz, and *her* response had been unequivocal approval, coupled with a jaw-torqueing "I told you so." The old Katie would have burned beet red. Garth's woman smiled softly, knowingly, and with keen anticipation.

"Waiting for somebody, lady?" Garth's husky growl interrupted Katie's reverie.

She looked over at his tall, muscular frame, leaning casually against the doorjamb, arms crossed over his broad chest. "Not just *anybody*."

Her eyes drank in the sight of him. He was all man and all hers. Well...mostly hers, a painfully honest voice, tiny, reed-thin, but still audible to her finely tuned conscience, insisted. Ignoring the voice, she registered the tired, drawn look that was pinching the handsome planes of his face. Exhaustion and worry over his project had added lines she didn't remember being there before, and she wished she could erase them with her love. There was simply no denying the true nature of her feelings any longer. She loved him, loved him, loved him. She felt the knowledge pour through her body in a rush, and she had to clamp down hard on her back teeth to keep from telling him.

"I'm looking for someone tall, with dark hair, silver eyes and a sexy smile," she enumerated in a throaty murmur, squeezing her bath sponge so that the water dribbled over her outstretched arm and across her chest to run in streaming rivulets between her full, creamy breasts.

"Think I'll do?"

"He's also got to have broad shoulders, a tight belly and arms at least this thick." Katie measured a wide circumference with her hands that Garth's arm would just about fit. Her eyes met his, hot promise and blazing need shooting back and forth between gold-flashing hazel and glittering silver gray.

Without taking his eyes from hers, Garth began slowly unfastening his red-plaid shirt, the one he'd had on the first day she'd met him, button by button, revealing his midriff inch by torturous inch. He undid the cuffs, letting it hang open loosely, his broad shoulders and tight belly causing an almost painful tightening in the vicinity of Katie's middle when he hooked his thumbs in the waistband of his jeans.

"Well?"

It was the Conan voice. Not the one he'd used to subdue the school board all those weeks ago, but the pure damn sexy one, perfect for whispering endearments in the dark, and melting the core of Katie's responsive femininity into liquid need.

"I'm not quite sure." Her voice was a confident purr that belied the uncertainty of her words. "Maybe if I could see a little more?"

"My pleasure." He moved into the bathroom, resting his foot on the edge of the claw-footed bathtub to unlace his work boots, then drawing back to peel off his jeans and briefs almost with a male stripper's skill and slowness. At last, he stood before Katie's devouring eyes, clad only in the loose-hanging plaid shirt.

And suddenly, the bathroom was not the only thing that was steaming.

"It all looks very...promising so far," she commented objectively, folding her hands behind her head, causing her breasts to thrust proudly out of the water. She watched in pleasure as his pupils dilated with excitement, and heard with satisfaction the way his breath caught in his throat. "But the man I'm looking for, the only man I'm interested in, has working man's hands. Strong, a little rough...but gentle. Do you have hands like that?"

Garth's answer was to reach into the tub, running strong, callused fingers over her slippery skin. He stroked across her shoulders and over her arms, rubbing his palms up and down her breasts, flicking her nipples tightly erect with a fluttering action of his thumbs. Inhaling deeply, he whispered gruffly, "You smell good."

Nuzzling the side of her neck, his roughly textured tongue licked traces of the sweet, rich oil from her skin, before tracing a path between her breasts and across to one pert nipple, begging for his mouth's attention. "You taste even better," he breathed.

"The tub's big enough for two," she invited.

Heedless of his shirt, Garth plunged his arms into the water, wrapping them tightly around Katie. Then he lifted her easily from her bath. "I have a better idea," he whispered softly, striding with her held high against his chest, out of the bathroom and across the bedroom in the direction of her down-quilted brass bed.

"I think I'm beginning to really like this macho side of you, Garth." Her voice was a soft coo. "I may even consider lowering my consciousness to a more moderate level of liberation if it means I get to be carried around!"

"Think so?" He passed the bed, heading down the hand hewn stairs toward the river-rock fireplace in the living room.

"It's getting better and better," conceded Katie, envisioning a long, sultry evening making love in front of the fire. It was one of the places Garth seemed most inspired.

"I'll try to oblige," he promised with a bold grin. He opened the door, striding into the snow-covered field behind the house. The blast of stinging cold air and the icy snowflakes that melted on her heated skin in quick succession like lighted sparklers gave Katie her first warning that another of his notorious tricks was afoot.

"Garth, you do realize that your shirt—the only item of clothing you happen to be wearing, I might mention—is flapping in the wind like a sail and that I am stark naked, don't you?"

"I do indeed, Katie girl," he replied jauntily without breaking stride.

"Then do you mind telling me what the *hell* we are doing out here in a damn blizzard?"

His laughter echoed across the small, snowy meadow. "A few scattered snowflakes are not considered a blizzard by us hearty mountain types."

"They are by us sane flat-landers," she retorted. "Take me back this minute!"

"Remember the last time I did what you said when you told me to do it in that tone of voice?"

"No."

"That's because I didn't! Ah, here we are," he said gleefully. He dropped her in a snowbank, then paddled a flurry of powdery snow over her arms and breasts, down her belly and over her thighs, before rolling her over to powder more snow over her backside.

"You are a crazy fool, and so help me God, I'm going to murder you!" she shouted, feeling an uncontrollable urge to laugh bubbling up inside her. Humor broke the surface of her outrage and joined Garth's own rowdy chuckles.

"You looked a little overheated in there. I thought I'd cool you off." He lobbed a few more handfuls of snow at her.

"Stop that!" she yelped, numb with cold, but bent on revenge. Scooping up a handful of snow of her own, she flung it in his direction.

"Then you know what happens?" he asked, advancing menacingly toward her.

"I'm afraid to ask," she giggled between shivers.

"Then we soak in the hot spring, and I get to warm you up all over again."

"Just hurry," she pleaded. She could feel a familiar awareness already, an incipient spark beginning to glow.

"Uh-uh," drawled Garth in disagreement. "It's going to take a long, long time!" He picked her up, then put her in the spring and the heated, slightly sulfurous water rose up to cover Katie's body, helping Garth's quick, clever fingers, and warm, loving mouth to turn the spark into a white-hot flame.

CHAPTER TWELVE

"Hey." Katie poked a slim finger in Garth's ribs. "It's your turn to get up and add a log to the fire. This one's down to a lump of charcoal that wouldn't toast a marshmallow." They were lying in front of Katie's stone fireplace, her needlepoint pillows tucked beneath their heads, and Garth's shearling jacket cushioning their naked bodies against the polished hardwood floor. The drapes were open so they could watch the moonlight dancing on the snow through the floor-to-ceiling windows. It was quiet, peaceful and romantic, thought Katie. It was also getting cold, now that the fire had gone down. She poked Garth again. "Come on. It's your turn."

"Nice try, Katie, but I'm not moving." His deep voice was so lazy with relaxation and contentment that Katie was filled with pride. Such a change from the man who'd walked in several hours ago. They'd planned to have dinner together at her house, but he'd been late. In fact, he'd been very late. And his face had worn the strained, tired expression that always told her there was another problem or delay at the construction site.

She'd fed him, cosseted him and loved him. She'd also tried to worm from him the details of whatever event was responsible for his silent, withdrawn air. She'd been unsuccessful. Over dinner and a bottle of their favorite Beringer Cabernet, they'd talked about everything from the wrestling team to the guest artist series at the Bon Fils Theater in Denver. But each time Katie had brought up the Grand Lake project, Garth had deftly changed the subject. He simply wouldn't discuss with her the increasing incidents of vandalism, or his concerns about their ultimate effect on his ability to bring phase one in on time and according to specification.

"It's not even three feet to the fireplace," she wheedled.

"I'm not moving." He turned slightly, pinning her beneath one long, muscled leg. "And neither are you."

"But the fire's out."

"Give me a minute. It'll be blazing," he promised, capturing her lips with his, then kissing her deeply. His hands ranged over the silky limbs trapped by his strong body, inciting, igniting, until the blaze he'd promised was well kindled.

"Better," she murmured. "Much, much better. You could patent this. Maybe we could call it 'instant start,' or something. It would make lighter fluid and wood chips obsolete."

Garth chuckled, the sound husky, deliberate, sexy. "Turn over and let me do the other side, just to make sure the heat is evenly distributed." He gently tucked his hand into the small hollow at the base of her spine, flipping her easily onto her stomach, then kissing the soft, warm skin along her shoulder. Pushing away the heavy weight of her hair, shimmering in the light from the glowing coals, his lips and tongue caressed her spine from the nape of her neck to the rise of her buttocks.

She reached around, grabbing a handful of thick, dark hair, and brought his face up to meet hers for a hard kiss. Garth let her set the pace of the embrace, then stiffened suddenly.

"Did you hear that?" he asked. The muscles previously tensed with sexual tension now hardened even more as though preparing for a fight.

"It was nothing, Garth. Probably the wind rattling something around on the porch. You can hear everything with the drapes drawn, you know," she reassured him calmly. It wasn't like him to be so anxious. The problem at the site must be something big if it had him jumping at the wind rustling through the pines beside the porch.

"No. I heard something. I'm going to check it out."

"Garth, don't be ridiculous. There's nothing out there but the wind. Draw the drapes if it bothers you, but hurry back." She smiled, her face full of a slow, inviting seduction that promised him the world.

He was already on his feet, moving stealthily toward the porch, his spare, silent movements belying his size. Throwing open the door, he strode into the night. Katie could hear a muffled gasp, scuffling, and finally, a loud thud that brought her to her feet in a flash. She reached for the fireplace poker and ran toward the door.

"Stay inside, Katie," ordered Garth harshly before she could step through the door. "And put your clothes on. Fast."

"What? Garth, what's going on out there?"

"Do as I say. Don't argue." His voice snapped, whiplike and in a colder tone than he'd ever used to address her.

She dropped the poker, and hurried back to the fireplace, rapidly donning her carelessly discarded clothing. His tone hurt her, as much as his command.

"Are you dressed yet?" His impatient question whistled in through the open doorway along with the frosty wind and tiny, swirling snowflakes.

"Yes."

"Then do you mind telling me just who the hell *this* is, and what the hell he's doing sniffing around like he has all the right in the world to be here?" The dark lump Garth threw into the room landed in a heap at Katie's bare feet.

"Oh, my God!" She bent down hastily, pushing back a shock of dark auburn hair the same shade and texture as her own from the lump's forehead, then stroking lightly down his cheek. When she drew her hand away, she didn't need to look to know that the sticky warmth sliding over her fingers was blood.

"Well?" Garth's cold query demanded a response.

Katie rose stiffly from her knees, her heart constricting at the low groan emanating from the crumpled figure in front of her. "*This* is my brother. What the hell have you done to him?"

"What I'd do to anyone I found skulking around your house in the middle of the night. I introduced him to my fist, up close and personal." Garth's slicing wit turned malignant, cutting sharply, painfully into Katie as it always did when she detected an intent to hurt.

"You don't believe me, do you?" She didn't bother to disguise her sense of insult. "Take a good look at him. If you can see his face through the blood. This is my twin brother!"

Garth dropped down, gripping a handful of Brian's hair and jerking his head back. Brian moaned.

"Be careful. You're hurting him." Katie knelt by her brother, cradling his head in her arms. "Brian, are you okay? I'm so sorry."

"Be quiet. You have nothing to be sorry for," said Garth sharply.

Katie grunted, somewhat mollified. "Well, at least you're sorry."

"Don't misunderstand me, Katie. *I* don't have anything to be sorry for either." He jerked his thumb at Brian. "*He* sure as hell does, though. Don't you ever knock, buddy-boy?"

"There's never been a reason for me to." Brian rose on unsteady feet to place a thickly muscled arm around Katie for a feeble hug. "I take it this is Conan?"

"Brian, this is Garth D'Anno, the team's benefactor, and a...a friend of mine. Garth, this is my brother, Brian O'Connell." Katie made the introductions hastily. Now that she was sure that Brian wasn't seriously hurt, the compromising circumstances of the situation embarrassed her.

Neither man held out a hand to the other. They just stood, silently sizing each other up, expressions of unmistakable menace glittering on their faces in the room's dim light.

"I said, don't you ever knock?" Garth spoke first, his voice low, controlled but menacing. He stood with his arms hanging loosely at his sides, feet planted slightly apart, not the least disconcerted by his nude state.

"And *I* said, there's never been a need for me to." Brian's face had assumed a taut watchfulness Katie hadn't seen in years—not since he'd first learned how to fight and had drawn a protective limit around himself and Katie that warned the neighborhood bullies the O'Connell twins were no longer fair game. His balls-of-the-feet wrestler's stance told her he was ready to spring at Garth instantly, heedless of the other man's greater size. Unspoken threat and tension filled the room, but Katie didn't know what to say to defuse the heated emotions crackling like live wires between the two men she loved.

"What about your sister's privacy?" queried Garth sarcastically, one arm snaking out to clasp itself deliberately, protectively, possessively around Katie's waist. He pulled her firmly against him.

Brian took a step forward. "I can only assume that you're here at my sister's invitation, given your presence in her house at this hour." He let his eyes travel the length of Garth's body, before locking eyes with him, his message, his question and his warning clear. At least to Katie. He wanted Garth to explain himself.

"Assume what you want," responded Garth carelessly. "My presence here is none of your damn business."

"Katie, it was a long, cold drive from Stapleton Airport in Denver. Think you can scare up a cup of coffee and a sandwich?" asked Brian quietly.

Before Katie had a chance to respond, Garth tightened his grip on her waist. "She's not your servant, O'Connell."

"Why don't we step outside and finish this discussion where we won't disturb my sister?"

"We have nothing to discuss." Garth flicked his steely silver eyes over Brian dismissively. "Sit down and tell us why you were sneaking around outside like a thief.'' He motioned Brian toward the sofa, then steered Katie toward a large overstuffed chair set at right angles to it, pulling her down on his lap.

Brian looked at Garth and Katie for long minutes, then moved reluctantly toward the sofa. Katie exhaled slowly, the sound coming out as a deep sigh of relief. She hadn't realized she'd been holding her breath.

"The Pan-Am team got a surprise weekend off. I decided this would be a good time for that visit we discussed, Katie," explained Brian meaningfully. "I didn't see any lights on, and I hated to wake you. I thought I'd get the key from our usual hiding place and surprise you at breakfast." He grinned suddenly, rubbing his jaw tenderly, before wiping the blood from his nose with his sleeve. "I had no idea you'd acquired such an effective bodyguard lately."

"Let me get some ice for your nose, Brian." Katie rose, glaring at Garth defiantly. "I'll bring you something to eat and drink, too."

"Better get two icepacks, Sis. Your *friend's* jaw was too square to resist!"

Katie regarded the two men warily. Did she dare leave them alone?

"It'll be all right, Katie," assured Garth, reaching for his clothes and unself-consciously stepping into his slacks. Katie couldn't help but admire the sinewy length of his legs as they disappeared into the soft, gray flannel and the wide lateral muscles that flexed attractively as he pulled the shawl collar of his berry-colored sweater over his head. "Your brother and I will get acquainted until you get back."

"That's exactly what I'm worried about," she remarked tartly before spinning on her heel. This was about to be the fastest sandwich and drink she'd *ever* made. Not five minutes later, she hurried back into the living room to discover Brian comfortably ensconced before the fire, which now burned cheerfully. He was alone.

"Where's Garth?" She scanned the room with anxious eyes.

"He went to split more logs. I think he was trying to give us a few minutes alone." Brian regarded Katie intently. "Are you sure this is what you want to do, Katie?" he asked, getting to the heart of his visit.

"There's nothing else I *can* do." She set the tray, heavily laden with roast beef and cheese sandwiches, an extra plate of tomato slices and two cans of beer, on the coffee table, now restored to its original place between the sofa and the fireplace. "I love him. I have no idea where this relationship is going, but...I love him," she repeated quietly.

Brian reached for a sandwich, chewing and swallowing several bites before responding. "He's a lot of man, Katie. And he's been around the block a few times."

"I know." She rubbed her toes against the rough stones of the fireplace.

"I'll be there for you if it doesn't work out." His eyes narrowed. "After I kill him, that is."

"Don't, Brian. This is between Garth and me. No one else. I love you. But my romance is none of your business. Not now, not...if it doesn't work out."

Long minutes passed. "I understand, Boo-Boo." Brian's simple acquiescence acknowledged their new separateness with bittersweet eloquence. "But that doesn't mean I won't still help you when you need me.''

"Thanks. You know I feel the same way.'' She turned her head so Brian wouldn't see the tears threatening to spill over her lashes, gold-tipped in the firelight. So many uncertainties existed in her relationship, so many pitfalls. There was only one absolute truth. She loved Garth. She always would. The reaffirmation brought her peace, along with a new resolution to enjoy the love she felt for him. Their love would be a joyous thing—for however long it lasted.

"Sis?''

Katie faced him with a smile, strong, mature, sure of herself and her feelings. "Hmmm?''

"Did you have to pick such a *big* son-of-a—''

"Gun,'' finished Garth unexpectedly. He dropped an armful of newly split logs on the hearth, then gave Katie a proprietary kiss.

Brian laughed, and Katie joined in. Her once profane mouth was infamous in her family. "She's heard, and said, a lot worse.''

"I still think she's entitled to some respect in her own home,'' warned Garth softly.

Brian looked at him steadily, then nodded his head, the small action acknowledging the other man's place in his sister's life. From now on, until Katie told him otherwise, this was Katie's man. "I think you're right. Want one of these sandwiches?'' He pushed the plate toward Garth. "Sorry all the ones with extra tomatoes are gone,'' he teased.

"They better not be…unless you want to go another couple rounds on the porch?'' He rubbed his knuckles along the side of his jaw. "And please say you'd rather not.''

Katie relaxed completely at Garth's smile. Somehow, her brother and her...man had managed to come to an understanding. It had not happened easily, and not without the peculiar territorial dance men did around women they cared for, but she knew there'd be no more fights.... Her man. She liked the sound of those words. She liked it very much. Her man. Reaching for a sandwich, she passed the food to Garth. But not before taking a huge bite right out of the center. There were certain privileges that went with being his woman, after all. The wide grin she gave him was utterly unrepentant. Then she took another bite for good measure.

THE WEEKEND PASSED too quickly for Katie. In no time at all, she was kissing her brother good bye in her driveway.

"I'm so glad you came up, Brian." She hugged him heartily one more time, unwilling to relinquish his presence. "I only wish you could have stayed longer."

"*I* only wish I could have arrived with a little less ceremony!" Brian rubbed his still-swollen nose. It wasn't broken, but it was bruised a glorious purple blue.

"Try knocking next time." Garth's tone was only half-teasing as he offered Brian his hand. A cautious tolerance had developed between him and her brother over the past two days. They did not quite share a friendship, but theirs was a more comfortable truce than she'd have put money on after their initial meeting on Friday night.

The two men shook hands, then Brian got into his car. "I really enjoyed seeing Granby, Katie. And the hot spring is fantastic! Garth, I wish you all the luck

with your project. Thanks for showing me around."
He waved, then rolled up his window and drove away.

Garth lobbed a handful of snow at Katie. She knew
his playful mood was intended to keep her from feeling sad at her brother's departure, and she loved him
all the more for his thoughtfulness. Scooping a handful of snow out of the drift on her right, she quickly
packed a hard snowball, hit Garth square in his broad
chest and the fight was on.

For over an hour they chased each other through the
snowy meadow behind Katie's cabin, tumbling in the
drifts like children, and pelting each other mercilessly
with balls of hard-packed snow. But by the time they'd
returned to the house, leisurely eaten a quiet dinner
and snuggled together in bed under her thick down
quilt, Katie realized that Garth's lighthearted playful-
ness concealed a deeply troubled mood that not even
their lovemaking could ease.

The light of a million bright stars, pinned to a mid-
night-blue sky, shone down through the skylight,
casting a dim glow on the chiseled planes of Garth's
face. He lay tense and restless, staring into the night.

"Trouble at the project again?"

"It's a long story," he said shortly.

"I've got all night."

"I may be totally off track, but I think someone is
deliberately sabotaging my project."

"Garth, no!" She rose up on one elbow to look him
more squarely in the face, aghast at the potential
threat such a thing might pose to Garth himself.
"What happened this time?"

"You know the major construction is done; we're
doing the finishing work now. Someone poured gas-
oline and turpentine over $125,000 worth of carpet-

ing and drapes stacked in my on-site storage facility, then left a box wrapped in plain paper and addressed to me sitting on top of the pile of empty cans.''

An uneasy feeling twisted its way up Katie's spine. ''What was in the box?''

''Matches. A pretty obvious indication that what happened isn't simple vandalism, wouldn't you say?'' His features bore a sardonic expression turning him into a dark, brooding stranger she almost feared. ''More like a threat. Or a promise.''

''Oh, no.'' She launched herself into his arms, closing her mind to the myriad unwelcome images crowding in. Images of Garth's strong body smothered in flames, the skin that felt like rough silk under her fingertips charred and burning. ''Garth, this has gone far enough. You have to go to the police, report what's been happening, and get some protection. You could be hurt!''

''It won't go that far,'' he said flatly, a chilling menace underscoring his calmly spoken words.

''But who would do such a thing? and why?''

''Unfortunately, I can think of any number of individuals, and they all have what they consider to be excellent reasons!''

''Tell me,'' she demanded.

''Are you sure you want to hear? I promise, you won't like it,'' he warned, turning on his side to face her in the semi-darkness, his eyes gleaming like the night vision of a feral creature.

''Tell me.''

''Willis.''

''The school-board president?'' she asked in disbelief.

"And the president of the bank financing phase one!"

"Why would he want to sabotage your project?" She reached out to trail her fingers over the muscles of his upper arm, her tone confused. "I thought banks made money by lending funds they thought would be *successfully* repaid. It doesn't make sense for Willis to try and force you into default."

"Sure, but if there were arson I wouldn't get my funding for phase two, and I think he hates me enough to make that risk worth his while." Garth sounded bitter, but Katie sensed hurt in his voice as well.

Katie was confused. "That makes even less sense. Wouldn't the bank president be *anxious* to attract new business, new loans to his bank?"

"Not if denying those loans meant he could get me out of Granby. If I defaulted, the bank would simply foreclose on my project, then bring someone else in to finish it, probably arranging some kind of sweetheart financing as an incentive." He thumped his pillows savagely, then leaned against them, stock still, brooding in the dark.

"But why?" She held her breath, wondering what it was about what she was going to hear that she wouldn't like.

"He still blames me for getting his daughter pregnant when we were in high school!"

Katie could only look at him.

"Nothing to say?" he asked aggressively.

"Only that you've got my complete, undivided attention," she replied in an even tone. But her attention was slipping fast. In fact, her mind was tumbling over all the ramifications of the fact he'd just revealed.

A child. Garth had a child. A cold, reason-strangling jealousy enveloped Katie at the thought of another woman bearing Garth's child, of cradling that precious piece of him in her body and later, in her arms. With a great deal of will, she forced her attention back to what Garth was saying.

"Willis sent his daughter away to have the baby, hoping the scandal would be minimized if the good people of Granby weren't daily confronted with the sight of pregnant, unmarried Kelly Willis. She didn't come back until after she'd graduated from college. And she came back alone."

Katie was aghast at his implication. "Alone?" she repeated.

"As *without* child as she'd earlier been *with* one. I learned later she'd married a local man. A few months into the marriage, they 'adopted' a little boy...the exact age her child would have been. I *know* the child they adopted is her natural child, though Willis denies it." He ground his teeth in frustration, the sound grating on Katie's raw nerves. "They live in town now." He paused. "The boy's on your team."

Katie suddenly knew. And the knowledge was absolute. There could be no doubt of the boy's identity. "Greg Jenkins," she whispered softly.

"How did you guess?" Garth sounded surprised.

"I...little things...I just guessed."

Little things—in fact they were all the things she loved about Garth himself. The penetrating gaze, the fiercely protected independence, the self-confidence verging on arrogance, the sometimes biting humor. The shoulders. The shoulders were a dead giveaway. At seventeen Greg's hadn't achieved the width and manlinesss of Garth's, but their bodies were remarkably similar, and the family resemblance was undeniable. Greg stood where she imagined Garth had at the same age; on the threshold of his life, all the bright promise of youth just beginning to burst forth in an even more splendid maturity.

The only difference was in their coloring. Greg had fair skin, a shock of dark red hair, and bright blue eyes. Funny. She'd have imagined Garth would have stamped his child with his more dominant type of coloring. Katie gritted her teeth against another jolt of painful jealousy.

No wonder Garth didn't want a family, or marriage. If he couldn't marry the woman he wanted, claim the child that was his, he didn't want any substitutes. No wonder he was so bitter. The woman he'd loved had married someone else and deprived him of his own child by claiming that Greg was adopted. Katie castigated Kelly Willis in her mind, silently calling the woman by every excoriating epithet her vivid vocabulary would conjure. There were plenty.

"That's why you've made such an effort to get to know Greg," she stated flatly. "Why you donated all that money to the wrestling team."

He tensed. "Partly. Wrestling is something we have in common. Not that it's done me much good. Willis has done a thorough job of poisoning the boy against me. Greg has apparently heard all the old stories about me and blames me, the same way Willis does, for hurting his 'adoptive' mother. You've seen Greg in action. No matter how hard I try, he won't let me near him."

Even Garth's frustrated rage, hammering hard with no place to go but inward, reminded Katie of Greg. And now the empathy she'd felt once for the boy flowed out toward the father. She thought of all the times Garth had tried to engage Greg in conversation, or offer pointers on wrestling, only to be thwarted by the boy's surly, uncooperative attitude. She must have been blind; all this time, she'd thought it was just Greg's generally rebellious way of relating to adults. She'd had no idea the reason behind it was something so personal.

"And you think Willis still harbors enough resentment, enough anger, to try and hurt you through your project?"

"Yes. I think he's afraid of me."

"Why would he be afraid of you?"

"He thinks I've come back to Granby to prove the truth about Greg. He's afraid if I do, I'll take the boy away from Kelly and Jenkins. He's desperate to get me out of town. In spite of my personal feelings for Willis, he loves Greg." Garth laughed bitterly. "And why shouldn't he? He's the boy's grandfather."

"*Is* Greg the reason you came back to Granby?"

"Part of the reason."

"Would you really take him away if you could prove he was your son?"

"Katie, I'll *never* be able to prove Greg is my son!"

"I don't understand."

His large, rough hand scraped through the thick texture of his dark hair. "It's so complicated I hardly know where to begin."

"The beginning of a story has always struck me as a likely place."

"I know for a fact that I can't possibly be Greg's father," he stated baldly.

"But you said…"

Garth opened his arms. "Come here. I need to hold you."

Katie slid into his waiting arms, relishing the comfort of having them tighten around her. She pressed her face over Garth's heart, and he stroked her hair, his big hands gentle. "I've wanted to tell you about my past for a long time, Katie girl."

"Why haven't you?" Relief lightened her mood considerably. Greg might be Mr. Willis's natural grandson, but Garth wasn't his father. However this confusing tale turned out, she could handle it now.

"I wasn't sure how you'd accept my past. It's not easy for me to open up. I haven't had much practice." He rested his chin on her head. "But tonight, I don't know how to explain, except to say that I had such a sense of communion with you after we'd made love, I couldn't seem to keep my worries inside anymore. I needed to tell you about...everything."

"Garth, even if you *were* Greg's father, it wouldn't change what I feel for you. I'm not saying there wouldn't be a whole lot of ambivalent feelings chasing each other around inside my head, but I...care enough about you, about *us*, to work them out." She nestled more closely against him, scattering soft kisses across the broad chest under her cheek and blowing gently on the fine black hairs growing there in such tantalizing profusion. "Now tell me why you're so sure Willis is behind the sabotage at your project."

"Willis blames me for getting Kelly pregnant. I didn't. I never even slept with the girl. Hell, I hadn't slept with any girl." He gave a short, dry laugh. "I was probably the only sixteen-year-old male virgin left in Granby!"

"Then how can he blame you?"

"Kelly was my girlfriend when I was in high school. She was bright, pretty, a spritely scamp with the whole town at her feet. She even had long, auburn hair."

"Wouldn't she just!" remarked Katie with wry emphasis.

Garth hugged Katie close, plunging one of his hands wrist deep into her thick tresses, tangling them around his fingers. "But her hair wasn't as rich looking as yours, and it wasn't as soft, or as sweet smelling. And she never wore it in a braid."

Katie considered his words. "If you tell me she got ugly, wrinkled, fat and gray, all is forgiven."

Garth chuckled, the sound low and intimate in the velvet semidarkness where the only illumination was from starlight, gleaming down through the skylight above them. "No, I can't tell you *that*, Katie girl. What I *can* say is that she no longer interests me romantically and she hasn't for a long time. She's happily married, and I'm happily involved. Kelly's just a kind of bittersweet souvenir of my youth."

"Tell me everything," she ordered, settling herself comfortably against him. "Like I said, I have all night."

CHAPTER THIRTEEN

"I DIDN'T HAVE A FAMILY or a childhood like yours, Katie," he began tentatively. "My father didn't embody upscale stability the way a college professor does, and my mother didn't sing him sweet little songs about 'working man's hands.' My old man was a mean, conniving braggart who couldn't keep a job. We moved constantly because someone else, the boss or a fellow worker, always 'had it in for' him. He'd get laid off or fired, come home and take his rage out on us for a while. Then we'd pack up what little we had and move on."

"Us?"

"My father, my mother, my brother and me."

"Couldn't your mother do anything to help the situation?"

Garth snorted in disgust. "My mother couldn't help herself out of a paper bag. My old man would beat her down and beat her down until he'd goaded her into a screaming rage as bad as any of his. Then he'd beat her down some more. My 'home' was a war zone. That's why I'm so dead set against marriage and family life. I'll *never* live like that again!" The muscles in his shoulders tightened convulsively, as if mentally warding off blows. "The really funny part of it was that my parents had convinced themselves they were staying together for the sake of us kids."

Katie smoothed her hands up and down the arms holding her, trying to relax him.

"My brother and I were pawns—each of us was just another weapon the two of them used against each other."

"At least you had each other," she consoled.

"Not hardly. My brother was five years older, and he hated me. I used to try and stick up for my mother. My father called me a 'mama's boy,' and tried to beat the 'softness' out of me. He encouraged my brother to do the same thing. The two of them made my life hell."

Katie could scarcely believe it. Such a domestic situation was entirely outside her frame of reference.

"I remember once when I was seven, a third grader gave me a bloody nose because I wouldn't give him the cookies my mother had put in my lunch bag. I started screaming for Pete, thinking my big brother would help me. Instead, he shook that boy's hand. He told the boy to go ahead and punch me in the nose anytime he wanted because I was such a sissy, that I deserved it! And I kept coming back for more. I tried everything, sure if I was a better little brother, Pete would love me. We'd be friends. We'd play army men together. We'd be on the same side in a fight on the playground. But our parents' fight made *us* enemies, too."

"I'm sorry, Garth," said Katie quietly.

"Don't be. Things got better for me when Pete went away to college. We were living in Granby by then. I was having a fair amount of success on the wrestling team, my teachers were encouraging me to go on to college, Kelly Willis was my girlfriend, and my brother was out of the house. Except for the constant battles between my parents, I was happy. Happier than I'd ever been before.''

Katie could imagine what the teenage years must have been like for Garth. She envisioned him developing a sense of self-worth, gaining confidence and maturity daily, and emerging from the cloud of a miserable childhood into the light of a happy, young adulthood.

''Then my brother came home from college.'' Bitterness and long-festering hurt darkened his tone. ''I was sixteen that summer. My brother saw what was happening with me, and it drove him crazy. Pete had always been the golden boy of Granby. He didn't like it that I was doing well at school, on the wrestling team, and that the townspeople had started to speak well of me. He didn't like it at all that the prettiest girl in school was my girlfriend. It's his nature, like it is my father's, to be mean and brutish. He's a spoiler.''

Katie could see it all. Pete must have been wild to put Garth back into what he considered ''his place.'' Suddenly she knew, without hearing Garth say it, exactly what had happened that summer. ''He made a play for Kelly Willis, didn't he?''

Garth tightened his hold on Katie. ''He must have pulled out all the stops. Kelly's father told her we were seeing too much of each other. She agreed to play the field, but she wouldn't tell me who else she was dating. Halfway through the summer, I knew she'd started sleeping with this other guy. She said she couldn't see me anymore; she was in 'love' with *him*. He'd promised to marry her when she graduated from high school.'' Flinging himself out of bed, Garth paced the floor in agitation. ''Pete convinced that girl he was in love with her, slept with her to prove he could, and all to get at *me*."

Katie heard the smack of what she knew was Garth's fist hitting his palm. "So Greg is really your brother's child?"

"I'm sure of it. The family resemblance is too strong; it was enough to make even you think Greg was my son. He's the right age, and he has Kelly's hair and eyes. I don't care what Willis says, Greg is my nephew! Somehow I'm going to prove it."

"But why does Willis blame *you*? Why are you so sure he's behind the sabotage at your project? I would think he'd be after your brother's blood if he was after anyone's."

"My brother moved to Denver that fall to start his career. The first I learned of Kelly's pregnancy was when her father came screaming over to my parents' house threatening me with statutory rape. It seems my brother had convinced Kelly to name me as the father of her child, because since I was only sixteen, I'd probably get probation, while Pete, being twenty-one, could have been prosecuted and sent to prison. Kelly believed that Pete was trying to protect their future, so she went along with him."

"I thought you said she was bright?" asked Katie caustically.

"Pete could be a real charmer. He had her snowed but good."

"Why didn't anyone believe you when you told them you weren't the one responsible for Kelly's pregnancy?"

"Because I didn't deny it when she named me as the father. I wanted my parents to know, without having to be told, that I hadn't gotten that girl pregnant. I wanted them to trust me and believe me because they loved me, not because I'd proved anything." Quiet dignity and an old hurt danced together in somber reunion over the surface of Garth's handsome features.

"I still believed in family loyalty at the time. I loved my brother, in spite of what he'd done, and I couldn't believe he'd let anything *really* bad happen to me. I expected my mother, at least, to stand by me. So I kept silent, refusing to defend myself. When I finally realized what could happen to me if I didn't speak up, it was too late. No one believed me. Not even my mother."

"Didn't *anyone* question Kelly's story?"

"Of course not, she was Granby's sweetheart," he answered bitterly. "And there *was* some evidence to support her story."

"What kind of evidence?"

"There'd been a big wrestling meet in Denver. Kelly and some of the other cheerleaders rode there on the team bus. I couldn't find her after the meet. It was late at night, and we were in a rough part of the city. I spent all night combing the streets for her and I missed the bus home. When I got on the Continental Trailways bus for Granby the next morning, there she was. She'd spent the night in some motel room with Pete, but when we got off the bus together, everyone believed she'd been with me. When Willis claimed I was responsible for his daughter's pregnancy, my parents completely dissociated themselves from me, leaving me to face his wrath alone. I heard later mom and dad had moved, but after that I never much cared where."

"What did Willis do?"

"He got me committed to the State Boys' Home until I was twenty-one years old. Kelly was under the statutory age, there was circumstantial evidence to support her charge that I'd had carnal knowledge of her, and it looked like I was lying when I finally spoke up after keeping silent for so many weeks. Since the female's consent isn't permitted to be at issue in a case of *statutory* rape, it was an open and shut case.''

"Oh, no.''

"Off I went, green as grass. If it hadn't been for wrestling, I'm not sure I'd have survived. My athletic ability gave me an edge. The others knew I could fight, so they left me more or less alone.'' His tone conveyed a great deal Katie preferred not to hear.

She could well imagine the brutality of a place like reform school. The idea of Garth trapped there, unjustly, for five years raised a pool of bile in her throat that was both bitter and burning. She swallowed hard. "What did you do when you got out?''

He laughed. The sound was a cold, unpleasant rasp that hung in the air like frost. "I found myself a woman and lost the control I've since learned to maintain. Not that there weren't plenty of desperate older boys at the home who would have been glad to hang my sexual initiation from their belt, but they'd have had to kill me to do it.'' He stood looking out over the snowy meadow behind her house, the room's shadowy dimness making his powerful body a dark silhouette against the diamond-paned windows. "I found a job working construction in Denver. There was always someone looking for a strong back. For a while, all I wanted to do was work hard, enjoy my freedom and get laid.''

Katie cringed at the harshly told story.

"In time, I put myself through night school, and eventually started my own construction company. This project will make or break me. I'm not about to let Willis ruin my life a second time. As for my brother, well...I've got a few things planned for him, too."

Katie recoiled from the naked hatred in Garth's voice when he spoke of his brother. She could understand why he felt as he did, but the intensity of his animosity frightened her. This wasn't a Garth she knew. Not the friendly adversary, or the roguish charmer, and certainly not the seductive lover who'd taught her night after night to find only pleasure in his arms. The man with his back to her was someone entirely different, a cold, hard stranger hell-bent on revenge.

"Have you confronted Mr. Willis with your suspicions about him?" she asked cautiously.

"To what end? He'd only deny it. When he learned that Phoenix Construction was *my* company, he called me into his office and warned me in no uncertain terms to stay away from Kelly and Greg, or I could kiss phase two good bye, no matter how timely or conformingly I completed phase one."

Phoenix Construction. Katie frowned, remembering the legendary bird, the phoenix, which consumes itself by fire once every five hundred years, then rises from its own ashes.

"That's why I've got to prove my suspicions that Greg is my brother's son."

"What do you intend to do with the information, if you *can* prove it? The effect on Greg could be disastrous if this all comes out."

"I don't know." The figure by the window raked his hand through his hair, beginning to pace once more. "One of the main reasons I came back to Granby, chose it as the sight for my project, is because I was

happy here once. Even if only for a while and in spite
of how things turned out.''

"You plan on staying here when the project is completed?''

"Yes. I want a future here." Garth's tone was unequivocal. "But people have long memories when it
comes to old scandals. I hoped to set the record
straight. Especially when I learned that Willis put the
story around town that I'd 'forced' Kelly. After meeting Greg, I'm not so sure I can ever set the record
straight in town, but I want Willis to know that I
wasn't the one who got his daughter pregnant, and I
want Greg to know that I didn't do what everyone's
been blaming me for the past eighteen years. Any future I hope to have here depends on it.''

"What about your brother? Would you tell
him?''

"Hell no! He'd only find some way to spoil things
all over again. Greg is a fine boy; my brother doesn't
deserve to claim him after all this time. He forfeited
that right when he walked out on Kelly. Besides, it
gives me a great deal of pleasure to know he'll never
know his own son!''

"And what about Greg?" Katie's soft question
crept across the room, gentling the rigid stance of the
man who heard it.

"If I can prove that he's my nephew, I want the
right to be a kind of benign, if unofficial, presence in
his life. I don't need to have him acknowledge me as
his uncle, but I want to be there for him.''

"Like a loving big brother," said Katie with sudden insight.

"Yes.''

Katie judged the distance between herself and Garth. It was ten feet. Only ten feet, but so filled with old miseries and heartache she wasn't sure she could bridge the space. She understood now the framework that had warped Garth's ability to see marriage and family as a natural outgrowth of love. In his case, marriage and family had been a perversion of love. His experiences had taught him to be disdainful of marriage. They'd left him disillusioned and distrustful of the concept of family and filled with festering hurts and resentments. He was susceptible to love; she sensed that. He just couldn't seem to trust love when he found it.

All she could do was pour out so much of her own love on him that he'd eventually come to realize his early experiences weren't the yardstick by which to measure love. She hoped her devotion would be what he needed to take their relationship one step further, into a permanent commitment. Her principles wouldn't let the status quo continue forever. She would be patient for a long time, yes. But not forever. And her love for Garth wouldn't let her think of a life without him.

"Come back to bed, Garth." She held out her hand to him.

He twisted his head from side to side with quick little shakes. "I'm too restless, too keyed up to sleep right now, Katie."

"It wasn't sleep I was offering you," she whispered lovingly.

"Thanks, but I think I'll go downstairs and polish off that bottle of Remy Martin we opened after dinner."

"Then I'll come with you." She glided out of bed, pulling on the delicate, lace-trimmed robe Garth especially liked, belting it loosely around her waist. The pale lavender silk was bleached colorless in the shadowy, starlit bedroom, but the robe's long folds swished seductively as Katie crossed the room. She put her arms around Garth from behind, laying her cheek against the warm skin of his broad back. Inhaling the faintly musky scent of healthy male flesh deep into her lungs, she played her hands up and down the rockhard ridges of his belly. He turned, clasping her in his arms with an almost ferocious intensity.

"Put the past out of your mind for now, Garth." She oozed a soothing tone into her voice. "Except for proving to Willis that you're not Greg's father, it's over. All of it. The past is finished; it can't hurt you anymore unless *you* let it."

"Not quite finished, Katie." His tone became hard, implacable, his thirst for revenge clearly, defiantly, unshakable. "Not until I settle the score with my brother."

A cold hand closed itself around Katie's heart and began to squeeze. "You said you wouldn't tell him about Greg," she protested. In spite of Greg's rebelliousness, his carefully cultivated facade to keep adults at bay, she'd developed a special fondness for him. Her concern for his well-being raised a strongly protective instinct that revolted at the thought of Garth using the boy as the medium of his revenge. She could hardly believe that the man she loved would even consider such a thing.

"I don't intend to tell him about Greg. I have something better in mind. My plan has been in the works for weeks, and in a very short time it will be

over; the slate will finally be wiped completely clean.''
His knuckles grazed Katie's cheek gently. "Thanks, in
large part, to you," he said gratefully.

The cold hand squeezed harder, painfully. "Me?"
she asked unsteadily, moving out of his arms and
stepping back a few paces. "How could I do anything
to help you? I despise the notion of revenge. At best
it's destructive; at worst it's dangerous. And between
family members the idea is unthinkable, abhorrent to
me." Her face paled at the thought of what he was
asking her to do. Not even for Garth, no matter how
much she loved him, could she compromise her principles to such an extent. "I could *never* be a part of
anything like that, or condone it, regardless of what
reasons seem to justify it."

Garth appeared so wrapped up in his determination to avenge himself, it seemed as if he hadn't heard
her. "My brother coaches at Cherry Creek High
School."

Katie knew the posh suburb of Denver well. Its high
school occupied the same position of league power-
house in the large school, AAA Division that Granby
held in the small school, A Division.

"He's being considered for the position of head
coach at a large midwestern university. He's been told
the competition is between himself and one other
man." His intense tone hinted at a satisfaction nearly
accomplished.

*Cherry Creek. They always had a strong wrestling
team. Their coach the past few years was a flamboy-
ant figure whom everyone called by his first name.
Rumor had it he might be making a move soon to
Ohio State as head wrestling coach.* A sinking, sick

feeling slid down Katie's throat, settling in the pit of her stomach where it churned itself into nausea.

"Your brother is the wrestling coach, isn't he?" she challenged. "Coach Pete is Pete D'Anno!"

"Yes." Garth began again the rhythmic slapping of his right fist against his left palm, but this time it wasn't in frustrated anger. This time his whole demeanor spoke eloquently of anticipation, of a blow that *would* be landed with punishing force. "Making a clean sweep in all weight classes at the state wrestling tournament would clinch this job for him. It would be the break Pete's been waiting for all his life. Straight to the big leagues. I don't want him to get that job. I want him to *know* I'm the one who prevented it from happening."

Katie shook her head energetically, almost violently. "No, Garth. I don't want anything to do with this! I know how you feel, how much Pete might deserve it, but I can't, I *won't* be a part of your revenge on your brother. Your plan is against everything I believe in."

"You already are part of my plan. Don't you understand? I donated that money to improve the wrestling program with three purposes in mind: to get close to a boy I strongly suspected was my nephew, to show the people of Granby that I'd be a valuable addition to their community, and to finally settle an old score with my brother."

"No!" Katie's softly whispered denial was pleading.

"I read in the sports section of the Denver Post this summer that this might be Pete's last year at Cherry Creek, that he might be going to Ohio State. It seemed like the perfect opportunity. All I needed to do was underwrite the cost of finding the best coach available, someone at least as good as Pete, add a few extra bucks for the wrestling program itself and let the natural talent and enthusiasm of the kids take over.''

''You thought you could buy yourself a winning team.''

Garth smiled such a slick, knowing smile that Katie was hurt to see it on the face of the man she thought she knew. ''Buying a team is done all the time in professional sports. Initially I was opposed to hiring you because, apart from my general belief that a woman had no business coaching a boy's wrestling team, I simply couldn't believe that any woman had the skills and experience necessary to defeat Pete. But after observing you at practice, I began to believe my investment would pay off in spades! Both the Denver Post and the Rocky Mountain News are billing our upcoming meet against Cherry Creek as foreshadowing the ultimate contenders in the tournament for the state trophy. If you keep on the way you are, Granby will take the state trophy in at least a few of the weight classes. No clean sweep for Pete, and no head coaching job!''

Realization slowly dawned on Katie like a cold, rainy morning after the first day of sweet, bright spring. ''You set me up,'' she said quietly in stunned disbelief. Her faith in the love she'd hoped was growing between them was dying a quick and excruciating death.

''No, I didn't. You wanted this job; you got it. My motivations for funding the job, or agreeing that you should have it were none of your business. What happened afterward between us was fortuitous. For both of us. But I wanted to tell you about my brother, all of it, because of what I've come to feel for you. I thought you'd be happy to know you were helping me. I thought I'd have your support.''

"Oh, Garth, not now!" Hazel-green eyes, bereft of any warmth and flashing with the pain of betrayal, searched the face that suddenly belonged to a stranger. "It's bad enough that you lied to me, that I fell for your charm the way Kelly fell for Pete's, but don't try to brazen out this charade!''

"I don't understand what you're talking about. I *never* lied to you! There's nothing in this situation remotely analogous to the one between Kelly and Pete."

"You concealed material facts that could have, no, *would* have made a difference to me had I known them.''

"Where were all these fine, shining principles when your *brother* was off thumbing his nose at his contractual obligations to Granby?" he sneered.

"That's different," she protested hotly.

"Why? Because he's your brother?''

"Because no one was hurt by his actions.''

"That's still a matter of opinion." His silvery eyes glittered coldly in the moonlit room. "Doesn't a lover rate the same loyalty and commitment as your brother does from you?''

"A *lover*, yes." Katie swallowed hard, the words wouldn't come easily. "A *user*, no. Why didn't you tell me all of this sooner, when I would have had a chance to make a free choice about whether or not I wanted to be involved in your scheme? Was this supposed to be my eleventh hour 'chalk talk'? The thing that would spur me on absolutely to victory?''

"Just what are you accusing me of, Katie?''

"Let me lay it out for you. You *used* me!" she spit out furiously. "You never cared for me *personally*. I was just a way to get back at your brother. That I was a hot little number who fell into your hands like a ripe plum was probably icing on the cake, but you even found a way to use that to your advantage, didn't you? I would have gone through fire for you, Garth, and you just kept stoking the attraction so I'd be spurred on to do better, to prove myself ever more worthy of your love, of your support with the school board. Right? *Right?*"

"Now that you have all the *material* facts, what do *you* think?" he countered tersely, his body tense, his mirror bright gaze intent.

"I think that once you found out how much I really knew about wrestling, when I'd proved I was a good enough coach to give those kids a shot at the state trophy, you realized what a *convenient* medium of revenge I'd be!"

"In what way convenient?"

"You not only got revenge on your brother, you got a playmate after practice. *And* you got to twist the knife in him a little, too. Using a woman as the instrument of his defeat would be more than fitting vengeance; you loved the idea of his chauvinist jock guts twisting because a *woman* beat him, didn't you?"

"You're damn right I did! You might be a woman, but you turned out to be one hell of a coach. I loved the idea of you beating Pete. But that hasn't got anything to do with *us!*"

"It has *everything* to do with us. I never had a chance to change your mind about love and all the rest of it, because to you I was merely a way to even an old score and a warm body at night." Her body shook with anger and hurt and tears she wouldn't permit herself to shed.

"Katie, I told you—"

"That's right, you *told* me, no permanent commitments for you, not ever. So I can just take my lumps, is that it?"

Garth stood perfectly still, clenching and unclenching his fists at his sides. He didn't say one word, and it infuriated Katie all the more that he wouldn't even rouse himself to deny her charge...because more than anything, she wanted him to tell her she was wrong.

"Come on, Garth, convince me. I'm willing...no, I'm *dying* to be convinced that your sick compulsion to avenge yourself wasn't the reason you changed your mind about me, the reason you embarked on an *affair* with me."

Garth opened his mouth to speak, then clamped it shut, the tick in his jaw working viciously.

"I've had to prove and prove to you my ability as a coach. Now *you* prove that your *caring* is based on something other than my ability to give you your revenge!" She swallowed several times, trying to fight down the tears and the dinner that threatened to appear simultaneously. "Call Pete. Explain all this; tell him you've changed your mind and want to be a family with him instead. Then maybe I'll believe you."

"To satisfy your puerile notion of how brothers should behave toward one another? The *hell* I will!" he exploded. "Don't do this, Katie. I don't have to prove anything," he said in a low tone. "You either love and trust me, or..." He fell silent.

"Or what? You won't love me anymore? You never loved me anyway!"

"I don't have anything to prove," he repeated stubbornly. "I didn't eighteen years ago, and I won't now."

"That's right, you don't *have* to do anything. And neither do I. I don't have to follow in Kelly Willis's footsteps. I don't have to be a pawn in the D'Anno brothers' internecine conflict. And most especially, no matter how much I thought I loved him, I *don't* have to stay in a dead-end relationship with a man who doesn't know the first thing about love!" She let her tears fall unchecked.

"If you can believe I never truly cared for you, there's no point in trying to convince you of anything." She thought she heard sadness in his voice, but Katie no longer trusted her ears where Garth was concerned.

He dressed silently. And when he left, she let him go with an equally eloquent silence of her own.

CHAPTER FOURTEEN

"HEY, COACH, listen to this." Flash Jones breezed into the weight room ten minutes early, waving a newspaper in his hand.

Katie continued the leg exercise she was doing. "I'm all ears, Flash. Read on."

" 'Tiny, but determined mountain David to take on metropolitan Goliath three deep in each weight class.' It's a front-page article in the Denver Post Sports Section about *us*! They say we're supposed to 'make a run at Cherry Creek's until-now undisputed dominance in the field of high-school wrestling.' They mention me, Greg and Jim by name. We're famous!"

Youth. Exuberance. How blissful, Katie thought. *And how short-lived.* "That's great, Flash." She stopped, took a few deep breaths, then stepped over to the treadmill, beginning a quick, aggressive pace she hoped would work the edge off her aggravation. It galled her to know that against every principle, she was committed to a course of action that would abet Garth's vendetta against his brother. She had no choice. An even stronger principle demanded she continue to give her team her best efforts. College scholarships for some of the boys were riding on the victories she could coach them to achieve.

Not that Pete D'Anno didn't richly deserve a lot worse punishment than Garth had in mind, but to be forced into helping one brother flay a strip off the other's hide went completely against every belief that made Katie who she was. She grimaced, only partly from the strain of her exercise. If there was anything she hated more than moral dilemma, she didn't know what it was. Unless it was Garth D'Anno. He'd used her, tricked her and made her fall in love with him. Then he'd placed her in a situation she had no hope of resolving.

Garth. The thought of him brought a searing pain no less intense now than it had been at any time during the past two weeks. She gritted her teeth, and her pace became punishing. She might as well admit the truth to herself. She didn't hate him at all. No matter what he'd done to her. No matter that *he* didn't love *her*. Katie O'Connell loved Garth D'Anno. Loved him, loved him, *loved* him.

Garth. Memories of him made her heart do a funny little dance. She'd find something of his, left casually in some corner of her house, and she'd be a basket case for the rest of the day. She couldn't—even for a moment—manage to forget him.

Finding the red-plaid shirt he'd worn that night he'd rolled her naked in the snow was one example. The shirt had been forgotten, left in a wringing heap on the back porch. She'd gone out to get more wood for the fire, and the red-plaid had jumped out at her with all the hurting power of a megaton bomb. Remembering the sexy striptease he'd done in her bathroom, a wave of intense longing for him overwhelmed her. Washing the shirt, pressing it and banishing it to the bottom of her drawer had done nothing to exorcise its power to hurt her with the memories it evoked. She'd finally hauled it out in a fit of pique one night, fully intending to burn it with suitable ritual. Now she slept in it. Every night.

The past two weeks had introduced her to a whole new world of hurt. She was solitary and celibate and she loathed being so. Now that she knew what she was missing, she craved intimacy. But not in a general way. Hers was a very specific kind of longing that could only be satisfied by Garth. She missed the warmth of sharing things with him just as much as the love-making. Everyday things like the news, jokes, the triumphs of her team reaching their potential, the long talks, the impassioned arguments, she missed it all. She missed him.

Principle was turning out to be a cold bedmate to snuggle up to, both physically and emotionally. A woman couldn't put her arms around its tight, muscled belly and squeeze. She couldn't pour her heart out to principle and receive a measure of emotional comfort. About the only thing she could do was suffer. And in the end the principles that were satisfied by the termination of her relationship with Garth wouldn't change the end result. If she won, as it was her moral obligation to her team to try and do, Garth would still have his revenge on his brother.

And she still wouldn't have Garth.

"There's even a picture of you, Coach. Look." Flash shoved the newspaper under Katie's nose.

"Just put it over there." Katie indicated the general direction of her gym bag with a vague wave of her hand. "I'll get one of the cheerleaders to cut the article out for the scrapbook."

"I can ask Jenny to do it," he suggested hopefully.

Katie noticed the way his bright eyes twinkled at the thought of an excuse to talk to the husky girl he'd developed a mad crush on. She outweighed him by at least twenty-five pounds, was two inches taller, a year older and as shy and taciturn as Flash was outgoing and loquacious. Theirs was a match made in heaven such as existed only between adolescents.

"Good thought," answered Katie seriously. Then she shot him a quick grin that said she'd seen right through him.

"Be back for practice, Coach."

"Don't be late, kiddo." Three more minutes; that ought to be enough aerobics for this session, she promised herself, vowing to slog through to the goal she'd set herself for today.

"What did you do to your hair?"

Garth. Who else could sneak up on her with such utter disregard for whatever activity she happened to be pursuing when *he* decided he wanted her immediate attention? Since they'd split up he'd continued to show up at practice and to attend wrestling meets. A very uneasy cease-fire existed between them. She couldn't call a truce, and neither one of them would call for peace.

"I cut it." Katie swung her head, making the pony tail, which held her now shoulder-length hair, dance from side to side. "I wanted something different," she said defiantly, remembering all the times Garth had tangled his hands in her hair, smelling its sweetness, complimenting her on its length and thickness. "I love it this way."

"I liked the braid better. And I liked it loose best." Garth's husky tone sounded regretful.

"How you like my hair is a matter of complete and utter insignificance to me." Katie kept running, trying not to remember how the only times Garth had ever seen her hair loose had been in bed.

"It was pretty. Feminine."

Katie thought so, too, but she'd rather fry in hell than admit it. She'd been in a particularly blue funk last Saturday, wanting to swim in the hot spring, but afraid of running into Garth. Unable to keep thoughts of him from invading her peace of mind and the freedom of her afternoon, she'd recalled a psychology lecture she'd heard in college. The professor had gone on at great lengths about symbols of independence. For a woman, an especially powerful symbol was her hair. Cutting it was one of the strongest things she could do to declare her independence.

Katie had hunted down a pair of sewing shears and cut eight inches from her mane, hoping to be flooded with a new feeling of power and freedom. She'd looked at the auburn swaths lying on her bathroom floor and cried for hours instead. She seemed to be doing a lot of crying lately. Tearfulness was one more gripe she had with the broad-shouldered, lean-hipped man leaning against the wall watching her run. He seemed to have stimulated her tear ducts along with her libido.

"At least it will grow back," he added, silvery eyes watching her in hawklike fashion.

"Nope. I'm keeping it this length."

"On the other hand, I think this way your hair might be even prettier. *More* feminine."

The team trooped in, and Katie hopped off the treadmill, refusing to look at Garth. Tension hung in the air between them, impossible to ignore.

SEVERAL DAYS LATER Katie returned to the gym well after practice had ended. One of her barrettes had slipped from her hair during the vigorous workout, and she wanted it back. Pushing open the door, she saw Garth and Greg in a vicious clinch. She'd been afraid the situation would eventually escalate into such an encounter. Greg's antipathy toward Garth was too strong, Garth's patience was too small and both of them were too stubborn and too physical to talk out a problem as big as the one festering between them. *Damn their D'Anno blood anyway!*

Katie ran over to the two male figures grappling on the gym floor, aghast at the furious way they were going at each other and anxious to stop them before either was hurt. Her voice rang out shrilly. "Greg, get up this minute! Garth, you should be ashamed of yourself; he's seventeen years old, but you should know better!" Their grunting efforts told Katie they hadn't heard a word. "Stop it, I said!" She bent down, pummeling Garth's wide, bare shoulders. He was seated astride Greg, who was on his back on the floor.

"Hey, no sweat, Coach. Garth...I mean Mr. D'Anno was teaching me one of his best riding-time positions," explained Greg. He blushed, color bathing his face and neck. "It's called the Honeymooner."

Garth looked at Katie over his shoulder, then rose easily on his haunches, offering a hand to Greg. The boy rose, and they dusted themselves off, grinning at each other and at Katie. When had the two of them become such good buddies, she mused.

"I see." Oh, yes, could she see. Garth's shoulders, his prominent pectorals, the hard-muscled belly, the narrow hips that drew a woman's eyes toward...well, they drew a woman's eyes.

"Ever hear of the position, Coach?" quizzed Garth, his voice honey-sweet.

"I'm familiar with it. More than I'd like to be," responded Katie tartly. She turned on her heel and fled from the gym, consigning her lost barrette to a deep, black pit for bringing her back to witness the sight of Garth's well-toned body doing the second best thing he knew how. Damn, he looked good in jeans. She grinned to herself, hurrying to the Blazer, then she grimaced. His jeans were no longer any of her concern. She turned the ignition on the Blazer and roared back to her house.

"STILL PRACTICING the Russian Series with them?" As usual, Garth had come in quietly.

"You're at practice almost every day. What does it look like we're doing, to you?" she asked, without turning her face from the intent study she was making of the boys wrestling several feet away.

"You notice me, then," he replied smoothly.

Katie suppressed a sigh. He didn't miss a trick. And his quick mind, challenging her to think and be her sharpest, her best, was one of the things she missed most. "Jim, when that whistle blows, stand up immediately, then whirl around to face your opponent." She addressed her comment to the boy in the *par terre* position, his sparring partner above him, hands clasped loosely around his waist. "Don't think, don't do anything but shoot up, then whirl around. Put everything you have into that move. Trust me. It works."

"I don't come to practice strictly to watch the team, Katie," continued Garth, the smoothness in his voice melting like caramelizing sugar, the sound oozing down her spine. "I like to watch the coach in action, too. Her moves are pretty impressive." He moved closer, dropping his voice a notch. "You'll *have* to forgive me if my attention is diverted periodically so that I'm not totally up on everything the boys are doing!"

Katie inhaled swiftly in satisfaction. Here was an opening for a good one. At last. "I don't *have* to do anything, Garth," she said sweetly. The tightness she'd learned to hate crept across his face, etching tiny wrinkles into the skin around his eyes and mouth. Without a word, he turned on his heel and left the gym.

Suddenly, the place seemed empty.

IT WAS SEVERAL MORE DAYS before Garth came back to practice. Katie was in the middle of a question-and-answer period. "Okay. You men know the drill. Pair off by weight, and let's see you put some of the things we've discussed into practice." She stepped over to the edge of the mats to watch.

"I'm impressed, Katie. I wasn't sure you'd be able to pull this off."

"Coaching a boys' wrestling team?" she teased, before remembering that she and Garth no longer had the kind of easy relationship that made teasing permissible between them.

"The Russian Series. Teaching the moves was quite an undertaking. Most high-school coaches wouldn't have been able to teach it." There was respect in his silvery gray eyes, and something else, barely glimmering, as if he didn't want her to see it.

"The moves do look good," she agreed. "So far, they've given us the edge I was looking for in competition." Katie fixed her attention on the team, refusing to meet those magnetic eyes. "Some of these boys need wrestling scholarships if they're going on to college. I thought the Russian Series would impress the college recruiters."

"You really ought to call this the 'Rushing Series,'" he praised, after watching a few of the boys shoot their moves.

"It's incredible, isn't it? They're really good!"

"Especially Flash. That kid shoots so fast he makes me dizzy. Look at that!" Garth placed his big hand on Katie's arm to get her attention. The warmth of his touch seeped immediately through the thin T-shirt she wore under her singlet, and his gentleness shot its own move on her heart, closing around it to tug on the threads of memory still interwoven there.

"And Greg is so natural, so strong. He's like an ox; he battens on his opponents until he gets them down," enthused Katie. "Then there's Jim Bradley. He's easily the most competitive kid on the team, but not in an obnoxious sort of way. They've all got a special something that makes their styles unique, but effective."

"It's not just them who are special, Katie. It's you. You've done quite a job with them. I envy them your attention, your concern," he said softly.

Katie yanked away from him, watching his fingers stretch toward her arm for a moment, then fall heavily to his side. "What do you want from me, Garth? You can see for yourself that I haven't slacked off my coaching any, if that's what you were worried about. There's no need to continue with the 'suave and charming' routine. It's not going to make me work any harder.''

"Can't you guess what I want?" he asked enigmatically. There was something sorrowful about him. He seemed lonely. "I almost want to tell you." He jammed his hands in his pockets and smiled at her. An apparently honest, entirely appealing smile. Before she could stop herself, a tiny smile of her own was shining back at him. Then she remembered everything that had happened between them, and it became a frown.

"If this is a sample of the famous D'Anno charm Pete turned on Kelly, that poor girl never stood a chance." Her tone was grim, unremitting. "I, on the other hand, have been immunized most effectively against the D'Anno charm. So save it. I'm not interested."

Garth looked at her for a long moment, then he shrugged and took up a position on the bleachers.

THE WEEKEND OF THE MEET with Cherry Creek, Katie found herself in the uncomfortable position of having to ask Garth for a favor. It took some serious chewing and swallowing before she was able to get all of her pride down her throat and approach him. "Garth, do you have a minute? I need...I'd *like* to speak with you."

"Would you like to share a cup of coffee? I'll buy this time."

"No, I don't really have the time. I need a favor," she began self-consciously. "For the team."

His face fell. "Sure. Anything for the *team*."

"I need another adult to drive tomorrow, someone with a four-wheel drive. You know how slippery the mountain roads between Granby and Denver will be if the forecast snowstorm hits before Saturday. I was wondering if you'd planned on attending the meet...it's with Cherry Creek."

"I know." Garth's eyes narrowed, his fists clenching once, tightly. It was the first time they'd spoken of his brother since the night he'd told her about his plan for revenge. "Nothing could keep me away. I can't wait to see Pete's face when he gets a look at this team shooting the Russian Series on his boys. It will be a pleasure to drive for...*the team*."

"Thanks."

KATIE SHEPHERDED HER TEAM anxiously through the parking lot. They were so keyed up, she was afraid their tense excitement would assert itself in some less-than-desirable social behavior. The team had picked up on the undercurrents of personal emotion about this particular meet she'd tried so hard to hide from them. The media had turned the event into a sort of grudge match between two teams which could only meet in exhibition before the state tournament due to the way the leagues were structured. The boys had embraced the grudge match theory with the fervor of new converts. Now they were looking for an excuse to release the pent-up emotions they'd been saving and feeding all week in preparation for the event.

"Take it *all* the way to 'em," vowed Jim Bradley.

"Right. No mercy. Make 'em hurt!" agreed Greg. "Maybe give them a little taste of what's in store beforehand, in the locker room."

"Wrong," said Katie quietly.

"Aw, Coach. You know what they've been saying in the papers. This is a *grudge* match." Greg's face bore a truculent expression that boded ill for Cherry Creek's heavyweight.

"You will behave like gentlemen in the locker room." Hers was the flat voice of command. "The place to show your stuff is on the mat. That's the only place it counts." Katie held the door to the gym open and let her team file past her. "It can be a very scary thing for an opponent when you don't say one word. No matter what he says to you, not one word. Just look him straight in the eye."

"Like Mr. D'Anno does sometimes," said Greg ingenuously, the light of understanding clicking on in his eyes.

The strings binding Katie's heart tightened. "Exactly." The boys straightened their backs, practiced what she knew would come to be called "the look," and walked off proudly. She thought she could recognize a bit of her own stance in their arched backs, and she smiled indulgently. *They were so damned impressionable.*

Walking onto the gym floor, Katie was amazed by the number of people crowding the bleachers. It seemed as though half of Denver was in attendance, and a fair portion of Granby, as well. She waved to Liz, seated high in the bleachers, then made her way to the section of seats reserved for her team and checked the footlocker she always brought. Not that she could do anything about it now if there wasn't enough, but counting the juice containers and pieces of fruit inside was a small ritual she permitted herself before each meet. It helped calm the attack of nerves that started without fail ten minutes before the first match and continued until the referee's whistle started the action.

"Can you spare one of those juices?" asked a low, husky voice.

It was Garth. She'd wondered where he'd disappeared to after dropping off his load of wrestlers in the parking lot. Katie whirled around, so glad to hear a familiar voice in such hostile territory, she didn't care that a brilliant smile lit her face for the man who'd hurt her so deeply.

But it was not Garth. It was *Pete*. The brilliant smile died, replaced by a small cold one that hid the dislike rising in her gorge. The voice was similar, and there was a slight family resemblance, but apart from those superficial points of likeness, the man in front of her was nothing like Garth. Instinctive reaction—the likes of which Katie hadn't experienced since she was a child watching Brian take an unprovoked beating she'd been powerless to prevent—roared to life, pounding, pulsing, seeking release.

For a long minute, looking into the rough, crudely handsome, blatantly sexual leer of Garth's brother, Katie wanted revenge. The strength of what she felt appalled her. She searched the crowd for Garth, for the reassurance of his presence. He was there, several rows back, but as yet unnoticed by his brother. That he had seen Pete was evident from the watchful, intent expression he focused on Katie. His face was a secretive mask.

"Sorry, I have just enough for the team." She forced her tone to be coolly pleasant, neutral.

"I've been waiting all season to meet you, Coach O'Connell."

Pete didn't hold out his hand to Katie. He simply reached over and grabbed her hand in his. The presumptuous action annoyed her. A lot. The unconcealed come-on she read in his face did nothing to tamp down the anger beating in her veins.

"When I heard a coach by the name of O'Connell had taken over the wrestling team in Granby, I don't mind saying I had a few fears for my career. Your brother has some reputation. I can't tell you how relieved I was to discover that it wasn't *Brian* O'Connell, but his *sister* who'd taken the position."

Fury took a stranglehold on Katie's vocal cords. There was nothing she could say. She simply didn't dare. Judging from the singles-bar smile plastered across the man's face he actually thought he was making points with her. Remembering her earlier advice to her team, she forced herself to look Pete D'Anno straight in the eye, and she didn't say one word. It took every ounce of steely will she possessed. And it didn't faze the man in the least.

"Shall we say dinner and drinks at the Sportspage after the meet, regardless of who wins?" he asked suavely, as though the outcome was a foregone conclusion.

"I couldn't possibly," she managed to choke out.

"Another time then." He gave her hand a squeeze, before walking off. "And may the best man win!"

Indeed. And may the winner be Greg, and Jim, and Flash, and as many other Granby wrestlers as could manage such a feat.

The meet started, the lowest weights wrestling first. Flash stepped into the red circle drawn on the gray mat, shook his opponent's hand and when the whistle blew, shot a move from the Russian Series with his customary speed.

And Katie's dream of victory died of shock.

His opponent not only recognized the move, he knew several variations of it. Time after time Flash shot, only to have his moves—in fact everything he tried to do—met and repulsed by perfectly executed, equally quick, defenses and countermoves. When the match was over, Flash had lost.

"I'm sorry, Coach. That guy was too much for me."

Katie gave him a fierce hug. "No problem, Flash. You showed some great stuff out there. Your man just beat you. Next time, okay?"

"Sure." The boy shuffled over to take his seat on the bench.

For the next two hours Katie watched her team wrestle valiantly, only to be crushed under the punishing skill of Pete D'Anno's wrestlers, all of whom knew not only the Russian Series and its defenses and countermoves, but a stunning array of other things as well. She knelt at the edge of the gray mat, shouting encouragement, suggestions and exhortations to every single boy. When it was over, she was hoarse and upset. It was her worst defeat to date.

Only Greg had won his match. The irony of his victory was more than Katie could bear. She'd been in an agony of worry for the boy, afraid that Pete would recognize him for who he was. That blood would somehow call to blood. But her fears proved groundless. Pete barely gave Greg a glance since the meet had been decided by the time the heavyweights wrestled. Greg's win was a formality.

"Good job, Greg. I'm proud of you." She clapped him on the back.

"What's to be proud of? That guy didn't know his stupid, fat head from a hole in the ground. The only thing you can say about him is that he was huge, and no offense, Coach, but *you're* stronger than he was!" Greg shook his head disgustedly, then joined the rest of the team, making their way dejectedly toward the locker room to change for the ride home.

Katie looked up to see a furious Garth bearing down on her, his silvery eyes blazing white-hot with anger.

"Well, I hope you're good and satisfied, *Coach O'Connell*. Talk about being set up!" he raged.

"Back off!" she shot back, tight-lipped at being dressed down in public, and still reeling from the ignominious defeat she'd just suffered. "I did my very best out there. We were simply outwrestled. It happens sometimes."

"Not like that, it doesn't. At least, not without a little help."

"What do you mean? My performance was nothing to be ashamed of. I'm not going to hop into sackcloth and ashes because I lost a match merely to satisfy your need for a whipping boy!"

"Spare me your self-righteous explanations about acting on principle, *Coach*. So help me, it makes me want to be violent after seeing the faces on your team, still trusting, eating themselves up with remorse because they think *they* let *you* down. If they only knew!"

Katie looked at him, confused and beginning to think they were talking at cross purposes.

"And save that innocent look. I don't believe it for a minute. We both know how Pete knew to teach his team the defenses and counterstrategies to the Russian Series. You told him you intended to use it. That's how you satisfied your narrow-minded moral dilemma, isn't it? Well, take a good look at the faces of your wrestlers when they come back upstairs. They paid the price of your principles.'' He whirled on his heel and strode from the gym without giving Katie a chance to explain.

GARTH ALL BUT THREW the last equipment bag out of his four-wheel drive, slammed the door shut behind his last teenage passenger and roared out of the high school parking lot, banging his fist on the steering wheel. *Damn her! Damn that stubborn, stiff-necked, prideful woman! And damn her convenient principles, too.* He spun a sharp curve, sliding on a patch of black ice before bringing the vehicle back under control. *Get home first, D'Anno, then lose control,* he told himself bitterly.

Thirty minutes later he was seated in the hot spring, a half-full wine bottle embedded in the snow beside him. Garth took another swig, draining his glass. He didn't especially want it, but it would do the job. Get him drunk. Make him forget. He reached for the bottle, intending to refill his glass, then changed his mind, sticking the glass upside down in the snow instead. Raising the bottle to his lips, he tilted his head back and poured a healthy slug down his throat, swallowing without tasting. *Damn her!*

He'd been shocked to see Pete's team repulsing the Russian Series with ease. A hurting rage rose in him at the memory of just how easily his brother had defeated Katie. With a little help from her, of course. All under the guise of principle, of course. Garth swallowed another mouthful of wine, leaning his head back against a smooth rock. There were a million stars tonight. There always were after a snow. Everything was clear and cold. Like his life.

This afternoon he'd fully intended to have it out with Pete once and for all. He'd wanted to beat his fists into that smug face. He'd wanted to make Pete hurt for all the times he, himself, had hurt, both as a child and later, stuck in that stinking reformatory. When Pete exited the gym, he'd started across the parking lot, ready to confront him. Then he'd seen Katie, her wrestlers clustered quietly around her. He'd recognized the comfort and consolation in the fierce hugs with which she gentled each boy in turn. He'd seen something else, too. A protectiveness toward them. A sense of responsibility. A nurturing. And a deep regret that told him how hard it must have been for her to stick by her principles and give his brother a fair chance to beat her, when she obviously cared so deeply for each boy on her team.

He'd looked back at Pete, swaggering toward a new Mercedes station wagon, all blustering bravado and cocky self-congratulation, but he just couldn't confront him. The desire to hurt Pete had drained away. The heart had gone out of his fight with his brother in the face of what he'd suddenly realized he'd lost by pursuing his vendetta at the expense of his relationship with Katie. It didn't matter that she'd told Pete she was teaching her team the Russian Series.

He loved her. Probably always would. Part of what he loved was the way she stood by what she believed in, lived by it, acted on it. How could he really fault her for something that was as much a part of her as that glorious auburn hair, or her great legs, or her sassy, damn mouth? Sure, it hurt that he'd opened up to her, cared for her more than any other woman he'd ever known. He'd shared his secrets and she'd betrayed his confidences. But it didn't change the one simple fact he was still trying to drown in a bottle of Beringer's best Cabernet.

He loved her. It was that simple. And that painful, because he'd lost her by not choosing her over his vendetta. He'd been stubborn and prideful, too. Instead of taking the opportunity she'd given him to prove what she meant to him, he'd walked away. Another realization hit him with punishing force. *He'd* created her dilemma with his need for revenge. He'd been selfish and unfair. He'd hurt her. And that hurt him. Pete was never going to change. He'd always be a selfish, brutish spoiler. They were never going to have the kind of relationship Katie had with Brian. He'd never have a brother.

Garth stuck the empty wine bottle in the snow forcefully. So what? Pete had *never* treated him like a brother. He said it to himself again. *He'd never have a brother*. The corners of his mouth turned up in a smile. A surprised smile, full of honesty. The truth didn't hurt as much as he'd expected it to.

Okay. It was okay. He'd never have a brother. But he *could* have other relationships—more important ones. The possibilities bombarded his mind faster than he could absorb them. He could have—a gulp of biting cold air was swallowed rapidly—he could have a wife. *If* he could persuade Katie to give him another chance. Katie. She was a woman who'd learned how to sing over a man's hurts and take his pain away with her love. An honest woman. A loving woman. *His woman*.

Garth's excitement grew. And once he had Katie, he knew, he could have other things. Things he had never let himself think of having. A family. Children. He didn't have to live his life the way his parents had. He could do it differently. Better. Happy. He *could* have a family. And a brother-in-law who was a wrestler. And a mother-in-law who baked prize-winning pies. And a father-in-law who knew as much about construction as he did about English literature.

The possibilities were endless. Garth reeled from them. It couldn't be too late. He wouldn't let it be. Each new thought of a relationship he could have transformed the bitterness and sorrow over the one he couldn't into a fierce determination to win Katie back. Once he got out of the spring. And got sober. And gave her a few days to cool off. She'd been pretty hot over the way he'd chewed her out in public. He laughed aloud. A deep, husky laugh that grew with each booming peal.

He was going to get that woman back.

CHAPTER FIFTEEN

KATIE SPENT THE WEEK after the Cherry Creek meet trying to help her team see their loss to "Coach Pete" as a positive thing. She reminded them the defeat had occurred early enough in the season to permit them to learn from it, and that having lost to Coach Pete at this point didn't necessarily mean the same result would occur in the state tournament, over two months away. It was an uphill battle to overcome the sense of failure the boys seemed unable to shake but she kept at it, encouraging them, pushing and working with them to improve their skills.

Being the boys' coach was a lot like being a mother, she mused after practice one day, while checking the locker room after the boys had gone. She picked up a few practice singlets tossed in the corner, tucked someone's English book under her arm, frowned at the pack of cigarettes wedged behind the bench and vowed to wrap the entire team in cold, wet towels if they didn't start getting them into the hamper. The job never seemed to end, and it took a lot out of a woman. She left practice exhausted recently, and little things like wet towels on the floor had started to assume the proportions of capital offenses.

Or maybe it was just the stubborn sense of loss making her feel so cranky and tearful lately since Garth had started staying away from practice. His tall, muscular frame lounging carelessly against the bleachers had been conspicuously absent all week. She'd thought about calling him several times to protest her innocence since he'd stormed off the day of the Cherry Creek meet, but she was still angry at being called on the carpet in front of hundreds of fans. He could think what he wanted about her. It no longer mattered.

The thought of never seeing him again intruded on her thoughts, filling her with a sense of lonely melancholy. *Blast the man!* Much more of this and she'd be writing bad poetry or maudlin songs. Their personal relationship had ended. She grimaced. What relationship? A one-sided affair was a more accurate description of what had occurred between them. If Garth chose to think she'd abused the team's trust, willfully abandoned her responsibility to them by tipping off his brother to the fact she was teaching them the Russian Series, then she just couldn't care...more.

Katie let the things she held in her hand drop to the floor in a careless heap. She spun around, charged out of the boys' locker room and into the girls', determined. There would be no more mooning around. No more moping. She was going to let her love beat her principles into submission on the balance beam until principle agreed to a compromise. There had to be one. And when she was through, she was going to hunt down Garth D'Anno and give him a piece of her mind.

And any other piece of her anatomy he cared to claim.

The stress of the past few weeks had been building until she could scream. She'd been out of sorts and ridiculously oversensitive; even Liz, a paragon of patience, had remarked on her temperament. And as was prone to happen to Katie when under stress, her bodily processes had been affected. Though it offended her no end to admit hormones could be at fault, the fact of being several weeks late with her period had to be taking *its* toll as well. A good workout was just what she needed.

Twenty minutes later, Katie would have settled for a good, stiff shot of Irish, uncaring that St. Patrick's Day was nowhere in sight. She'd thought to warm-up with a routine she'd done hundreds of times. Instead of breezing through the routine she generally used as a warm-up for more difficult ones, she was plodding through it with all the grace of a horse on roller skates.

Picking herself up off the mat, where she'd fallen for the eighth time in as many tries, she remounted, trying to understand what was wrong. She couldn't get her balance; her center of gravity seemed to have changed. It was odd for she hadn't gained any weight recently. If anything, she was a few pounds underweight. She'd give the routine one more try before strapping herself into the safety belt secured to the gym ceiling by a long, sturdy cable. In fifteen years of practicing gymnastics, she'd never been careless. She didn't intend to start now. If she was having a bad day on the beam, she'd take the necessary safety precautions to avoid serious injury. Katie launched herself into the air.

"Looks scary from here!" called out a husky, male voice.

She landed in a crumpled heap on the mat beside the balance beam. "Hellfire, Garth, when are you going to learn not to..." Katie's angry voice trailed off as she caught herself using one of Garth's pet expressions.

The look he gave her told her he recognized the term's genesis in her vocabulary.

"Sneak up on people?" he finished for her, trying not to laugh. "Are you okay? Where does it hurt?" He held out a hand to help her up.

"Haven't we had this conversation before?" asked Katie snappishly. She waved his hand away, preferring to nurse her misery in a lump on the floor.

"As I recall, my 'procreative abilities' were in jeopardy then. Are they still?"

"No. It's my own fault. I can't seem to find my center of gravity," she said in a disgusted tone of voice.

"Want to do the 'crane'?" he teased, a warm smile lighting his face.

"No thanks. I might as well hang it up for today." She took a deep breath and made the quantum leap toward love once more. The sight of Garth, strong, handsome, smiling...approachable, made the leap easier than she'd expected.

"Garth..."

"Katie girl..."

They spoke simultaneously. Shocked silvery eyes met equally surprised hazel-green ones. It had been a long time since he'd called her 'Katie girl.' The familiarity of the endearment, the tender way he said it, made Katie's eyes flash gold and bright with happiness.

"Want to wrestle me to see who goes first?"

"As *I* recall you were a ringer the last time that happened." She rose to her feet, groaning at the revolt brewing in her muscles, her lower back especially. "I feel it's only fair to warn you that I've made great strides in my technique since last time." Circling warily, she faced him on the mat.

"Cheating on me?" he growled.

"Daily."

"Liar." Garth shot one arm out to grab her. "My woman doesn't need to cheat. I give her everything she needs. Or I will if she'll come back to me."

She couldn't believe she'd heard him correctly. It *couldn't* be this easy. Not after all the tortured angst of the past few weeks. "What exactly are you saying?" she asked him quietly, weaving to avoid his hand.

"In plain English the translation reads 'I am a stupid jackass, and as soon as you stand still long enough for me to catch you, I'm never going to let you go'!" He lunged at Katie.

One look at Garth's face—honest, vulnerable, and wanting—convinced her that it could indeed be that easy. She saw the love shining out of him, a shimmering aura she could almost touch. True love. The one-man-to-one-woman, forever-after, committed kind of love. The knowledge took wing and flew from her heart to Garth's, carrying with it the message of her own love for him.

There'd be a lot to talk out before all was said and done, but for now she had a small score to settle with this man. The notion became a twinkle in her eye as the plan fleshed itself out in her mind. Oh, she'd give in to him all right, but not before she'd led him a merry chase for at least two weeks. She side-stepped, turning to avoid his lunge.

"Don't even think it," warned Garth.

"What?" she asked innocently. Had he added mind reading to his other talents recently?

"I've been watching a very interesting display of emotions and ideas chase each other across your face for the past few seconds. Not one bodes very well for me."

"I don't know what you're talking about." She tossed her ponytail over her shoulder, looking for an opening. Did she dare try a takedown from the Russian Series? Garth lunged again, and she stepped lightly, delicately away, ignoring the tight feeling gripping the muscles of her lower back. She drove her right leg forward, trying to hook her heel behind Garth's, and cringed as a spasm of pain shot through her lower abdomen.

She finally had the chance to talk to the man she loved, settle things between them, and her body decided to remind her it was female. She couldn't resist the grin tugging upward on her lips. But then being a woman seemed a natural course of events whenever Garth was around. Her body just did what it was supposed to do. If she could last a couple more minutes, she'd make a quick escape to the girls' locker room and salvage her dignity in plenty of time.

"I'm talking about the bad word I think you might be planning to use on me. Revenge. The one word that doesn't belong in the lives of people who love each other. The one that will never be spoken between *us*, or in *our* family. The destructive, dangerous word that's become abhorrent to me since I met a woman who taught me about love."

Katie could feel tears welling up behind her thick coppery lashes. She could hear the sincerity behind the words he was using to woo her. He was using her own convictions to prove to her—the way she'd asked him to once before—that he loved her and wanted her. To prove it in the right way. For the right reasons.

"I don't want us to walk away from the feelings we have for each other, Katie. No vendetta with Pete is worth losing you. Trying to make him pay for what he did to me was simply a waste of energy. Ultimately, my plan was costing me something I wanted more than my revenge...you. Pete's never going to change, but I can. Loving you, you loving me has made that possible. I'm going to forget about Pete. Permanently. I came in here looking for you to tell you just that."

Katie swallowed the lump that had risen in her throat. "Garth, I've been in here, trying to work up the courage to go looking for you to tell you that I don't care *what* your original motivations were. You cared for me. I should have trusted that. It should have been enough."

"We're going to work this out, aren't we, Katie girl? Shall we take another chance, a better chance this time, on love?"

"Yes, Garth. It's what I want most of all." A sharp twinge of pain reminded her of her predicament. "Garth, there's so much we need to say, but..."

"Later, Katie. We'll sort the whole mess out and talk as much as you want, but right now I want to hold you." He held out his arms, abandoning all pretense of wrestling. "Please?"

Katie felt a downward pull and the warmth that told her humiliation was imminent. "Garth, I am about to be more embarrassed in front of a man than I have ever been in my life. I want more than anything in the world to throw myself into your arms and never let go. But can I have five minutes...oh!" The sharp twinges became painful, gut-wrenching cramps, as if tearing away huge pieces of her insides.

"Katie, what's wrong?"

Suddenly, she realized that what was happening wasn't at all normal. She doubled over in pain, taking little shallow breaths. A sense of wonderment dawned as pure instinct told her what was wrong. What had been wrong for weeks.

"Oh, Garth, help me. I need to go to the hospital." Another series of painful, hurting cramps knotted her lower abdomen. She turned tear-filled eyes to him. "I think...I may be having a...miscarriage!"

Garth picked her up in his strong arms. She could feel their steely power tensing beneath the gentleness that cradled her.

"I'm sorry, Garth...there's so much I want to tell you, but I...hurt."

"Ssh now, sweetheart. Let me get you to the hospital first."

The need to talk to him was as strong as the pain. "No, Garth. There's so much we have to settle, so much we have to say to each other."

His smooth careful stride didn't break once as he continued to move toward the door. "Look at me, Katie. Really look at me." His low voice vibrated with a husky intensity she could only obey. "I love you, Katie. And I know you love me. That's all that matters. That's the only thing we've ever *really* had to say to each other, we were just too proud, too stubborn and too rigid to do it. Everything else we'll take care of as we go along. Right now, I'm taking you to the hospital. So please, just shut your sweet mouth, and let me get you there."

She sighed, biting her lip against another series of ravaging cramps. "I love you, Garth, love you, love you, *love* you." The words were a soft whisper breathed as she rested her head on the shoulder that was more than broad enough, and at last, loving enough to absorb her tears.

"AH, MRS. D'ANNO. You're awake." The doctor gave her a scolding smile. "I was just telling your husband to keep you off the balance beam for the next few months. Walking and swimming are better exercises for pregnant ladies."

Katie's tongue felt thick, furry. "Mrs. D'Anno?"

"It's okay, Katie girl. I had to tell the doctor we'd been married for a while, but had planned to keep it a secret until the wrestling season ended." Devilry and merriment shone silver bright in his eyes. "Now, of course we'll have to tell everyone!"

"Of course," she managed to say dryly. Wicked. The man had wicked eyes. She loved them. She loved him.

"We'll keep you here with us a few days to rest. You took quite a fall from what your husband says, but that's a tenacious little D'Anno you have there." The doctor smiled warmly at Katie and Garth, then left.

"Mrs. D'Anno?" asked Katie, arching her eyebrows quizzically.

Garth's smile was utterly unrepentant. "I had to say that, Katie. You know what Granby's like. We don't want people to whisper about *our* child, do we? And you being Mrs. D'Anno will be a fact soon enough. Won't it?"

Love rained out of him, and Katie drank it in, absorbing it with every pore. "Do I have any choice?"

she asked wryly. Seeing his stricken expression, she hastened to reassure him. "Shall we sneak off to Denver and find a little church somewhere? It doesn't have to be a big wedding, but I'd like my family to be there." This was touchy ground, but it had to be covered.

"They're going to be important in our lives, Katie; important to *our* family. I want them to be there."

Untrammeled joy raced along the path from her head, which registered his words, to her heart, which knew them to be true. "I'm so happy right now, I could dance!"

"Forget it. Move and you don't get the big, fat, gaudy rock I plan to make you wear. I want to make sure everyone knows you're married!"

Katie appeared to consider his words. "Define big and gaudy."

"I think you mentioned ten carats once..."

"Don't you dare! I'd have to hire somebody to help me wear it!"

"Wait and see." He grinned. "Am I going to catch hell from your dad and Brian for getting you 'in trouble'?"

"I don't know, think you can take them *both* in a fight?"

"I hope I don't have to find out." He bent down and gently kissed her, tracing the soft lines of her face with his fingers. "You really had me worried, Katie. All I could think of was that I'd waited too long to tell you how sorry I was for the mistakes I'd made along the way of our relationship."

Katie smoothed her hands up and down the length of his powerful forearms. "You weren't the only one, Garth. I should have been more compromising, more willing to look at things from your perspective instead of insisting that my way, my opinions and my beliefs were the only right ones. It wasn't easy for me to learn that love and principle aren't mutually exclusive." She let her love shine out at him, warming him with it, letting it soften all his rough edges. "Even worse, I acted just like everyone did eighteen years ago. I expected you to defend and prove yourself, taking it as a sign of guilt when you wouldn't. I should have simply trusted you, trusted what I felt from you and for you."

"I didn't give you much reason to trust me. I was so damn closed off, I pushed away your love when it was the thing I wanted most." He kissed her again, a sweet, lingering kiss that kindled a warm glow she could feel in the deepest part of herself. "I wanted you to love me and trust me, but without any risk to myself. I expected you to take everything I dished out. That was wrong, selfish, and I won't ever be that way again." He caressed her lips with his thumb. "I never even told you how much I love you. I have from the first minute you opened this sassy mouth."

"Does this mean we finally get to have some peace and harmony between us?"

"Are you going to do everything my way?"

"Never!"

He sighed. "Then I guess this isn't going to be a very peaceable and harmonious marriage." He grinned. "But damn, will it be exciting!"

"I don't doubt that at all." Katie's voice carried a rueful tinge.

Garth laughed, easing himself onto the hospital bed and carefully cradling her against his chest. He rested his chin on her head, inhaling deeply. "Your hair smells so sweet. Are you really going to keep it this length?''

"Probably not. I'm a sucker for your 'pathetic' voice. Garth,'' she began nervously. "I have something to tell you.''

"Something else?'' he quizzed playfully.

"I don't know how to prove it to you, but I really didn't tell Pete I was teaching my team the Russian Series. I have no idea how he came to—''

"Stop right there, Katie. You don't have to prove anything to me. From now on that's the way it's going to be with us. We're going to trust each other, okay?''

"Then you believe me?''

"Absolutely. Pete's a good coach even if he is an...well, anyway, I believe you.''

Katie laughed. One of these days, *after* they were married, she was going to give him a complete demonstration of her entire vocabulary. "Answer me something, Garth? Something that's been driving my curiosity crazy for weeks?''

"Name it, Katie girl.''

"When did you and Greg get to be such good buddies?''

"When his mother told him I wasn't the guy who got her in trouble in high school. That she'd broken up with me long before she got pregnant, and that we'd never slept together anyway.''

"Kelly told him about Pete?'' The woman couldn't do this to her, thought Katie morosely. She wouldn't dare do something so right, so nice, so decent after all these years of deception. Now Katie would have to like her. Just when she'd planned to carry a steaming, lifelong jealousy for the fact that Kelly had been Garth's first girlfriend.

"Not exactly. Kelly and her husband came to see me. She apologized for what she'd done, and said she wouldn't deny it if I told Greg I was his uncle. But I can't do that to the boy. I love him. He's part of a real family. Kelly and Jenkins, and his two little brothers—there's a lot of love between those people. It wouldn't be right to risk Pete spoiling it. Better that Greg just think of me as a friend."

"Does he know Kelly is his real mother?"

"Yes. She was afraid Greg would want to know all about his real father, but he said Jenkins is the only father he's ever known or wants to know. He's a good son. Loyal." Garth's tone carried a strong note of pride.

"I'm sorry he'll never know you're his uncle, but that doesn't mean you can't have a good relationship with him anyway," consoled Katie.

"I think I'm well on my way, Katie girl. And not just with Greg. Mr. Willis actually came out to the construction site and gave me his *personal* check as restitution for the full value of all the vandalism. He was all set to resign from the bank, and turn himself in once Kelly admitted that I wasn't Greg's father." Garth chuckled softly. "I told him I'd consider the slate wiped clean if he granted me the phase two loan at prime once I brought phase one in on time and according to spec."

"Think you can do it?" she teased, knowing full well that he could.

"Now that I'll have a wife and child to support, I damn well better! And get as many more construction projects as I can besides. I understand from her brother that the woman I'm about to wed can wreak hell and destruction with a charge card!"

"That traitor!" she complained, secretly pleased that Garth seemed ready to develop an independent friendship with her brother. They'd be good for each other.

"You know," mused Garth, a mischievous tone creeping into his voice. "I never expected you to be this way. And I sure never expected to like it this much if you were."

Katie knew she shouldn't ask. It would probably be something purely, typically, outrageously Garth, but there was something in his voice. Something that promised love, commitment and a lifetime of caring that begged her to. And the hint of beckoning merriment was irresistible. "What way?"

"Barefoot..."

Katie knew what came next. Knew it, and incredibly, didn't mind. Laughter bubbled up in her like champagne, mingling with the laughter shaking his muscular frame.

"And pregnant!"

They burst out laughing in unison. Hearty laughter. Healing laughter that would wash away all the old hurts at last and help meld their differences into a partnership that was stronger, brighter, better than either of them could ever be alone.

EPILOGUE

"Oh, Garth, do you really think they have a chance?" an obviously pregnant Katie asked her new husband several months later. She looked anxiously in the direction of the boys' locker room at Colorado State University's Moby Gym, so called because it looked like the legendary whale. Her wrestling team had disappeared into its bowels some half an hour earlier to change for the third day of competition at the state wrestling tournament.

"Well, I think Greg has a good shot, and Jim Bradley is another possibility." Her husband gazed at her indulgently. She'd worked hard for this event. Her team had managed to qualify, then advance to the semifinals in all weight categories, but with two days of stiff competition behind them, the boys were exhausted, and so was Katie.

"What about Flash?" The tiny, 105 pound sophomore had captured a special place in Katie's heart, as had Garth's nephew, Greg Jenkins...and every other boy on her team.

"Unless I miss my guess, Flash is a shoo in. The competition can't touch him for takedowns, and he just keeps coming at them."

"I hope you're...oh, my god!" She caught her breath sharply.

"Katie, what's wrong? The baby?" Garth's eyes were full of tender concern. Since her tumble from the balance beam several months ago, he'd been in a state of anxiety that the fall he caused her to take would injure the baby they both wanted so much.

"No...it's okay now, but they moved. The little devils are arguing about whether they're going to be wrestlers or gymnasts. They've been fighting about it all morning. Whoever wins gets to be the boss when they're finally born." Katie gave Garth a fond smile, then grabbed his hand and placed it over her stomach so he could feel the activity.

"That's a relief, I was afraid...*they*...did you say *they*, as in more than one?"

"Mmm-hmm. Didn't I tell you? Guess I forgot. I've been so anxious about this tournament—"

"Baloney," interrupted her husband with a snort. "You were just waiting to get me in a public place so I couldn't wring your little neck when you dropped this bombshell!"

"I finally went for that ultrasound you've been pestering me to take. It's definitely twins. Isn't it exciting, Garth?" She linked her arm through his, warm hazel eyes flashing gold into brightly gleaming silver ones.

"Twins...I feel sick. Oh, hell, Katie, you're so damn small. Can't you ever do anything the normal way? Do you *always* have to be unconventional?" He turned a pale-green color. He'd been turning that shade of green a lot lately since Katie had developed morning sickness. It tickled her silly.

She helped him to a bleacher seat on Moby's enormous gym floor. "Here, Garth. Sit here for a minute." Katie forced his head between his legs. "Breathe deeply, honey. That always helps." The grin she flashed him was full of devilry. "There's more. You know those cute little pandas you bought? One pink, one blue so that regardless of whether we had a girl or a boy the baby would have a perfect toy?''

He looked at her warily. "Yes."

"You're going to take one back...we'll need two pink ones."

"Girls...*two* girls?" His head plunged between his knees once more. "That does it. Tomorrow I buy the padlocks."

"Do I dare ask what for?"

"The *girls'* room of course. You didn't think they were leaving the house before age twenty-one, did you?" He managed a weak smile, but his face was still pale. "If they're anything like my beautiful wife, I'll have my work cut out for me from day one beating the boys back!"

"Just teach them all your best wrestling moves, Garth. Then they can take care of themselves."

"I sort of had my heart set on attending ten or fifteen years' worth of gymnastics meets if the baby was a girl, Katie. Especially now that you've accepted the position as head coach of the girls' gymnastics team starting next fall."

"Don't be smug," she teased. "You know I always intended to go back to coaching gymnastics after this year. I'm a gymnastics coach, after all. The only reason I coached the wrestling team was to help my brother." She studiously avoided mentioning her dream house out near The Broadmoor. Garth still felt guilty about the fact that she'd had to give it up when they'd decided to make Granby their home. The town was growing, and they wanted to be part of it. Phoenix Construction had landed some nice contracts that would keep Garth busy and close to home for the next few years. A whole new life spread out before them, a life so full, so happy, so loving, that gingerbread trim paled in comparison. Katie hoped to make Garth believe it eventually.

She suppressed a tiny smile. *Eventually*. But not before he'd completed a few small additions on the house that used to be his and now was theirs. The lacy gazebo was coming along nicely. It was very "gingerbready." The interior wainscoting in the upstairs bedrooms added a Victorian flavor she found charming, and he was going to start her sun room with the huge greenhouse windows next month.

"Then you won't deprive me of the thrill of seeing my wife coach my daughter...daughters to gymnastic glory?"

Katie recognized his tone. He was teasing her with his male chauvinism, the one thing he knew she couldn't resist. A resigned sigh escaped her lips. "Okay, we'll encourage them to be gymnasts. But that's no guarantee they'll do it," she warned.

"Yeah, I know. Chances are, they'll do whatever they damn well please. Like their mother."

She chuckled indulgently at the sight of his rugged face pinched from sympathetic nausea. "I thought being sick was my job? You're supposed to be strong, and supportive, and tell me how well I'm doing!"

"You think this is all hysterically funny, don't you? I'm dying of nausea, and you're *laughing* yourself silly!"

Katie assumed a solemn expression. "No, Garth, I wouldn't dream of it. This is a matter of the utmost seriousness. I mean, how will you be able to support us all? There'll be twice the dentist bills if they're each going to have thirty-two teeth like you. Twice the sporting goods bills. Twice the music lessons, twice the food bills, twice the allowance—"

"I thought you said financial responsibility was to be shared? Losing your liberated sensibilities?" He grinned, the color returning to his cheeks.

"Don't you remember our agreement, Garth? You earn the money, I spend it," she explained patiently. "It was in the marriage contract."

"That's right, I do remember. Right after the clause where you agreed to obey me. Good thing phase two is completed. I'll definitely need the healthy profits we'll soon be seeing!" He reached for her, capturing the hands that were attempting to pull handfuls of his thick, dark hair, and jerked her gently onto his lap. "Come here," he said laughingly. "I want to hold my wife…and my daughters."

"I'll break both your legs." Katie had become increasingly conscious of the weight she'd gained, in spite of Garth's fulsome compliments on her new, even more "womanly" figure.

"Never. I've been taking advantage of my position as team benefactor to work out with the weights at the high school." He tapped himself proudly on the chest. "This is one expectant father who isn't going to do any of those goofy, stereotypical things when his wife goes into labor." His silvery gray eyes glowed with love and commitment and respect. "When you give me the word, I'm going to be able to pick *all* of you up and carry you out in very dignified fashion to the car, which will already contain your prepacked hospital bag."

"You mean you're not going to drive off without me?" she teased.

"Nope," he said, shaking his head emphatically. "I'm going to drive you, at very safe speed, to the hospital, where you will have been preregistered, and deposit you in Dr. Hillyer's more than capable care. Then I am going to meet Brian and your father, both of whom will have been notified to get their tails to Granby at your first twinge of labor pains, and the three of us are going to stay blind, roaring drunk the entire time so you and your mother can attend to women's work in peace.''

"Shi…"

"Careful, I understand laps around the football field could be tough going for someone in your condition!"

"One step forward and eight steps back with you, Garth." She turned a pathetic expression of her own on him. "You won't leave me, will you? I really need you to be there."

"Oh, Katie girl, of course I'm kidding. I wouldn't miss these births for the world. You're my wife. The other half of myself. No way you're doing this without me." He cupped her face in his hands and kissed her, warmly, lingeringly, and in total disregard of the hooting whistles coming from the bleachers around them.

"Good," she said, a contented glow settling over her delicate features, softer now because of the man holding her and the maternity he'd blessed her with. "I always knew you were the kind of man a woman could depend on. Will you do me a favor and go check on the team while I introduce myself to today's referees?"

"Sure, sweetheart."

"If that was *my* wife, pregnant like that, *I* sure wouldn't let her come to a thing like this, even if I *was* one of the coaches!" A loud-voiced man in the front row boomed his comment unfortunately close to Garth's pathway.

He turned a furious face on the man. "You stupid ass!" He pointed at Katie. "She *is* the coach, and a damn good one, too. You keep a civil tongue in your head, or so help me, I'll wrap you in it and mail you somewhere you wouldn't like to go!''

"Sorry, lady.'' The man drew back, panic written all over his face.

"Come on, Garth. It's okay. Just check the boys, hmmm?'' She still wasn't quite used to having someone besides Brian jump in to help fight her battles, but she liked it fine. A naughty grin lit her face. He might be a consummate chauvinst about many things, but when his wife decided she wanted something, nothing had better stand in the way of Garth's helping her get it. Her grin dissolved in a frown when she caught sight of a long-legged college girl giving Garth a come-hither look. Katie nudged him. "You know that girl?'' she asked silkily.

"Huh? What girl?'' Garth looked around, perplexed.

"The piranha with all the sharp, white teeth,'' she said caustically. "And the tight jeans.''

"Sorry,'' he said, a loving tone warming his husky voice. "The only woman I notice in tight jeans is my wife. She's got the cutest little tummy lately.''

"Yeah, right,'' said Katie dryly. When they passed the girl, Katie snuggled even closer to Garth, tightening her grip on his hand. "You have such a nice smile,'' she said in a friendly, conversational tone.

The girl smiled back. "Thank you.'' She ranged her eyes over Garth's tall, muscular frame appreciatively.

"And such beautiful teeth,'' continued Katie.

"Huh?'' The girl intensified her examination of Garth.

"I wonder how they'd look on a necklace,'' mused Katie with a speculative air, tapping her index finger against her chin. Garth began to chuckle.

"Why?" queried the girl, trying to maintain eye contact with Garth in the face of the proud, loving look he bestowed on his wife.

"Because this is *my* man." Katie ran her hand up his chest possessively. "I've got the babies to prove it." She patted her stomach emphatically. "And you're going to be wearing those chompers around your neck if you don't get, and keep, your beady little blue eyes off my husband!" Then she sailed off in the direction of the locker room as only a five foot three gymnast, fully pregnant and fully enraged could do.

By the middle of the afternoon, three of Katie's wrestlers had made it to the finals. Greg, Jim Bradley and Flash were now only one match away from a state trophy in their weight classes. It promised to be a long evening at the finals with Flash going first in the 105 pound match and Greg wrestling last in the heavyweight category.

"I'm warning you guys," said Katie ominously. "If you don't settle down and quit bouncing around you're going to burn yourselves out before your finals." She could feel the nervous energy and highstrung excitement emanating from them in almost tangible waves. The anticipation was driving her nuts. Her own nervous energy and highstrung excitement was more than she could handle.

"A little example would go a long way about now, dear wife," murmured Garth.

"Right." Katie took several deep, calming breaths. "Come with me." She led them back to the seats reserved for the Granby team. Friends and relatives smiled and waved, but no one dared intrude on the finalists this close to their match. Even the other team members sat quietly, thumping pats on the back communicating their good wishes.

"Coach, did you get a look at my man?" asked Greg nervously. "He looks like a defrosted Neanderthal!"

Katie opened her mouth to reassure him, but a rough male voice from the seat behind her beat her to it. "You just remember what she taught you that day in the weight room when she picked *me* clean off the ground, boy, and you won't have any problem. Technique. And legs. The most important part of the match goes on under your head gear. None of Coach Pete's boys can combat that." Greg nodded his head.

"Thanks, Coach Luter." Katie smiled at the man. It was all she could do. Surprise on top of anxiety had completely stilled her tongue.

"Another thing we do in Granby is stick together," he said gruffly. "Like all those wrestlers screaming for the football team at *our* state final." He pointed to a row of grinning males three seats away. "Just wait till your three go to the mat. The noise is going to rip this place apart."

Katie swallowed hard, blinking fast to forestall the moisture gathering in the corners of her eyes from falling. "Thanks. I mean it. Thanks."

Coach Luter grunted, nodded and sat back. Garth leaned over and brushed a light kiss across Katie's cheek. "You've turned into such a softie, wife. Just remember that you two will be fighting over the weight room again in about eight months. He may have given in for the boys' wrestling team, but I can't wait to see his face when he learns his football players are going to have to share with the girls' gymnastics team!" he whispered in a gentle undertone.

Katie laughed. "You're right." She turned to the three anxious faces around her. "Okay. Let's go over it one last time. What are you going to do?"

"Think. Think ahead. Act." They recited in low unison.

"Good. Think offensive move and alternatives. Always be thinking of your *next* move. That's how you control the match. Now, what do you make *him* do?"

"React to me." The response came quickly and firmly, like a litany.

"Right. Every action creates a reaction. If he's reacting to you, he won't be thinking takedown. You'll have him immediately on the defensive, and that's exactly where you want him." She grabbed Greg's hands without warning, squeezing tightly, refusing to relinquish her hold. "Where do you control the hands?"

Greg looked up sheepishly, and the three boys responded together, laughing, the tension eased. "Everywhere we are. Hand control. Hand control. Match control!"

"Way to be," she praised softly, refusing to look at Garth. He razzed her unmercifully about her application of sports psychology.

"Flash, don't let your man tie you up. Your biggest asset is your speed. The more moves you shoot, the greater will be your percentage of takedowns. I've been watching this guy. He's bulked for 105, and he's scared of your speed. He's going to try and neutralize your asset. Don't let him."

"Will do, Coach," he said earnestly.

"Jim, keep your head. Don't get mad when he's on top, just stand up and whirl. Put everything you have into it, like at practice. And remember two things. First, he knows *you* know the Russian Series. He'll be looking for one of the three setups. Once you commit, do it *fast*, and be thinking of the move you'll make *after* he reacts. Two, he knows the series, too, so be watching for one of the three setups, then turn whichever one he chooses against him with the counter.''

"Okay, Coach." Jim clenched and unclenched his hands, fluttering his fingers rapidly to keep them loose.

"Greg, your man is an ox. Make sure *you're* the man who drives him. Size is nothing to be scared of. He'll be expecting you to tie up like most heavyweights do, not shoot a lot of moves like the lighter guys, so rack up some points fast. Once he figures it out, and he should pretty quickly, he'll be looking to tie *you* up. Don't be shy about the judo trip. It's basic, but it works. Remember, step, push into him, and use his momentum when he pushes back to jerk him to the side where his other foot is blocked by yours. He'll fall like a tree. A very large tree!''

"Think the bear hug is too risky?" asked Greg uncertainly.

"The bear hug is always risky, Greg. You have to grab him low and make sure you lift his feet completely off the ground. If not, he'll drag his toes, and you won't be able to twist him under you," she warned.

"Right," he acknowledged gloomily. "Then I end up pinned, instead of him."

"Feel him out a little. If you think you can lift him, you might try it if you're behind, close to the end of the match. I'll let you know when time is running out. After that you decide. But if you go for it, remember—''

"I know, I know. It's all in the legs." Greg shot her a smile so like Garth's, Katie spared a momentary prayer for Marie. The poor girl wouldn't know what hit her when Greg asked her to the Valentine's Dance next week.

She glanced at the clock. "Okay, start warming up. It's almost time for the finals to start." As the boys moved over to the warm-up corner, Katie slipped her hand in Garth's. "Everything okay with you?"

"You mean because Pete didn't come rushing over to say hello when he saw us walk in together?" Garth's lip curled upward, his expression wry. "Not a twinge. I mean what I said all those weeks ago, Katie girl. I don't need Pete. I have you, our babies and all the other happy relationships that came with you."

She squeezed his fingers, liking the warm, callused strength she held in her hands. "I love you, Garth. Wish me luck?"

"You don't need it. You have something better, and you gave it to your team."

"What's that?"

"Skill. Speed. Agility. Strength. And most importantly, brains." He patted her rear. "Now go get us a couple of three-state wrestling trophies."

And she did.

"I'M SORRY you didn't win the team trophy, Katie," said Garth a long time later, nuzzling her hair with his chin. He held her cradled against his chest.

"Me, too," she replied sleepily. "But at least Greg, Jim and Flash won. And Brian was able to get his recruiter pals there, so I think a couple of the boys will get offers of scholarships. Greg especially."

"That's great." He reached down to rub her tummy with his large, gentle hand. "Hey, Katie girl," he called in a whisper.

"Hmmm?"

"You're sure we have twins? Girls? No chance the doctor could have made a mistake?" There was an anxious, wistful note in his voice that tugged at her heart.

"Disappointed they're both girls?"

"Hell, no. I love the idea. All those cute little dresses, dolls, long red curls, tea parties, giggles and high-pitched voices calling me 'daddy.' It's going to be great."

Katie shook her head, a silent laugh welling up inside her. The poor man had a lot to learn about little girls. Especially theirs.

"It's just that I had this great idea for a dollhouse. I want to get started on it right away, but if there's a chance I'll have to turn it into a fort, I'll wait."

"I'm really sure, Garth. We are definitely having girls." He'd probably still have to turn it into a fort at some point, but Katie O'Connell D'Anno *never* broke her word to her husband. Twin girls it would be. She'd have a word with Sister Mary Simon first thing in the morning. All her "old girls" knew she had a direct pipeline to the powers that be. Not that she didn't trust the marvels of modern medicine, but for the really important things she wanted the absolute assurance of an appeal to the highest power.

"Have I told you today how much I love you?"

"Not nearly enough, Garth, not nearly enough." She rested her hand against the side of his cheek, stroking softly.

"I love you, Katie girl. I love you, love you, love you."

"I love you too, Garth. Let's be married a long, long time."

"A lifetime, my love."

He cradled her closer, and they drifted off to sleep.

Take 4 novels and a surprise gift FREE

Six exciting series for you every month... from Harlequin

Harlequin Romance®
The series that started it all

Tender, captivating and heartwarming...
love stories that sweep you off to faraway places
and delight you with the magic of love.

◆

Harlequin Presents·
Powerful contemporary love stories...as individual as the women who read them

The No. 1 romance series...
exciting love stories for you, the woman of today...
a rare blend of passion and dramatic realism.

◆

Harlequin Superromance®
It's more than romance...
it's Harlequin Superromance

A sophisticated, contemporary romance-fiction
series, providing you with a longer,
more involving read...a richer mix of complex plots,
realism and adventure.

Harlequin
American Romance™
Harlequin celebrates the American woman…

…by offering you romance stories written about American women, by American women for American women. This series offers you contemporary romances uniquely North American in flavor and appeal.

◆

Harlequin Temptation™
Passionate stories for today's woman

An exciting series of sensual, mature stories of love…dilemmas, choices, resolutions… all contemporary issues dealt with in a true-to-life fashion by some of your favorite authors.

◆

Harlequin Intrigue™
Because romance can be quite an adventure

Harlequin Intrigue, an innovative series that blends the romance you expect… with the unexpected. Each story has an added element of intrigue that provides a new twist to the Harlequin tradition of romance excellence.

Harlequin Books·

PROD-A-2